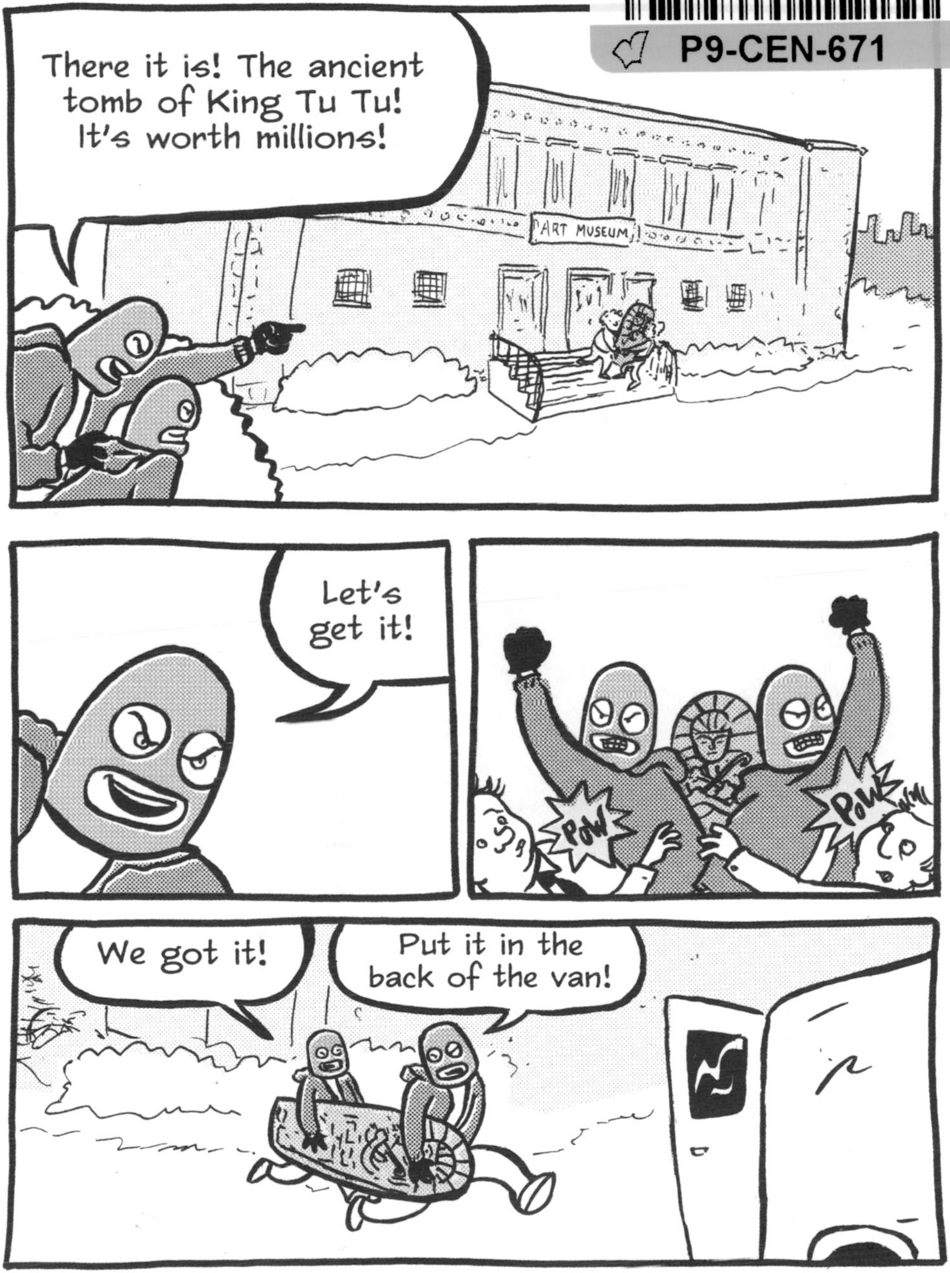
There it is! The ancient tomb of King Tu Tu! It's worth millions!
ART MUSEUM
Let's get it!
POW
POW
We got it!
Put it in the back of the van!

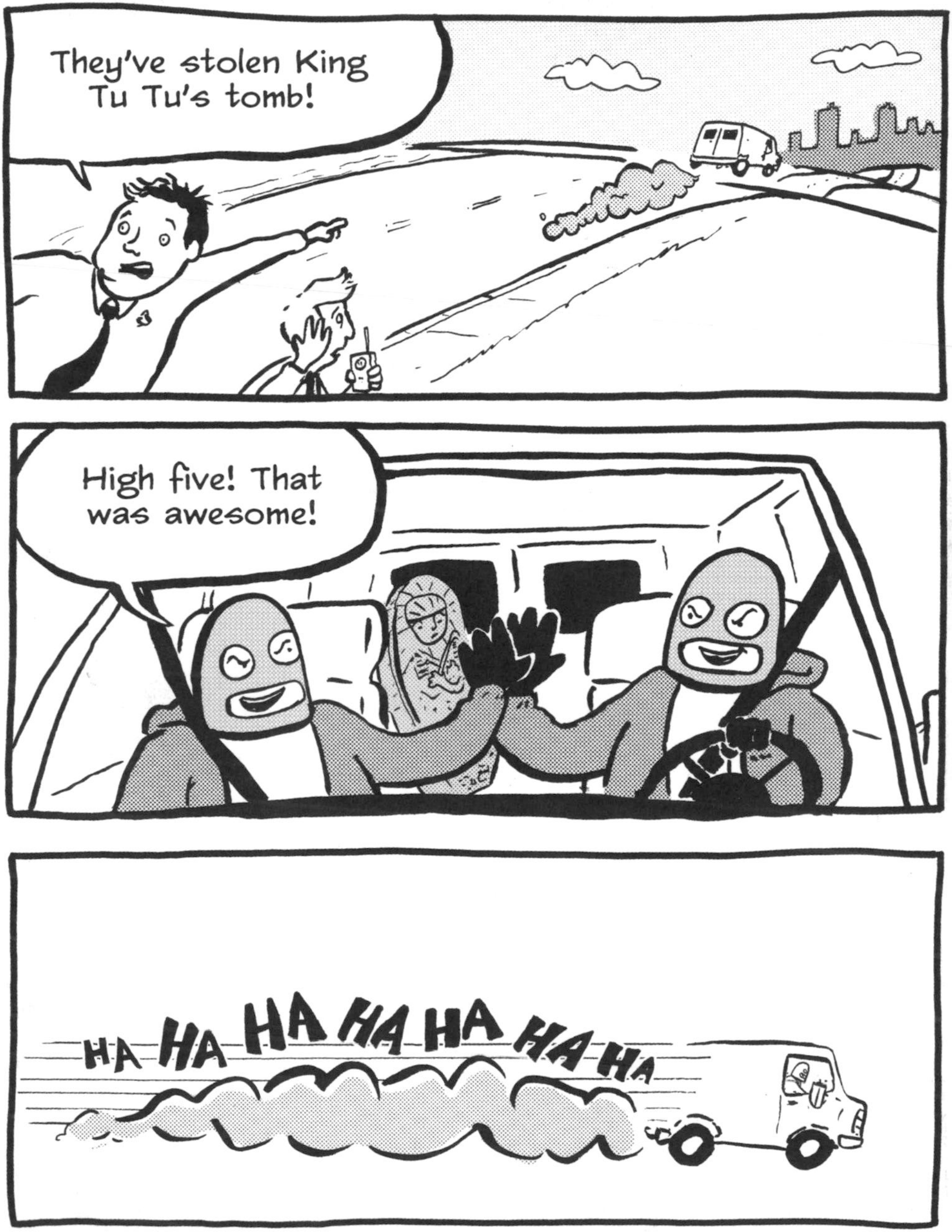
They've stolen King Tu Tu's tomb!
High five! That was awesome!
HA HA HA HA HA HA HA

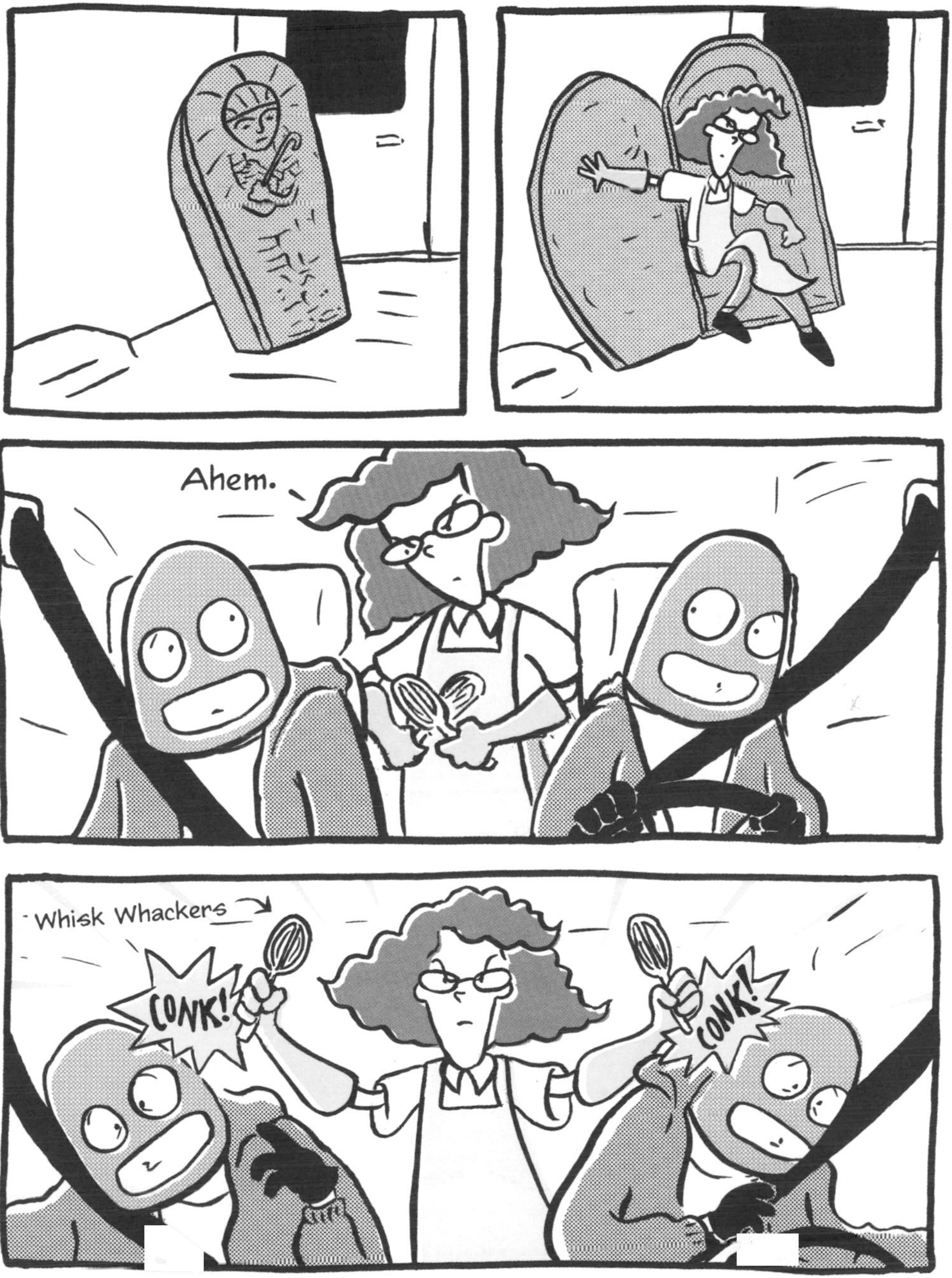
Ahem.
Whisk Whackers
CONK!
CONK!

LUNCH

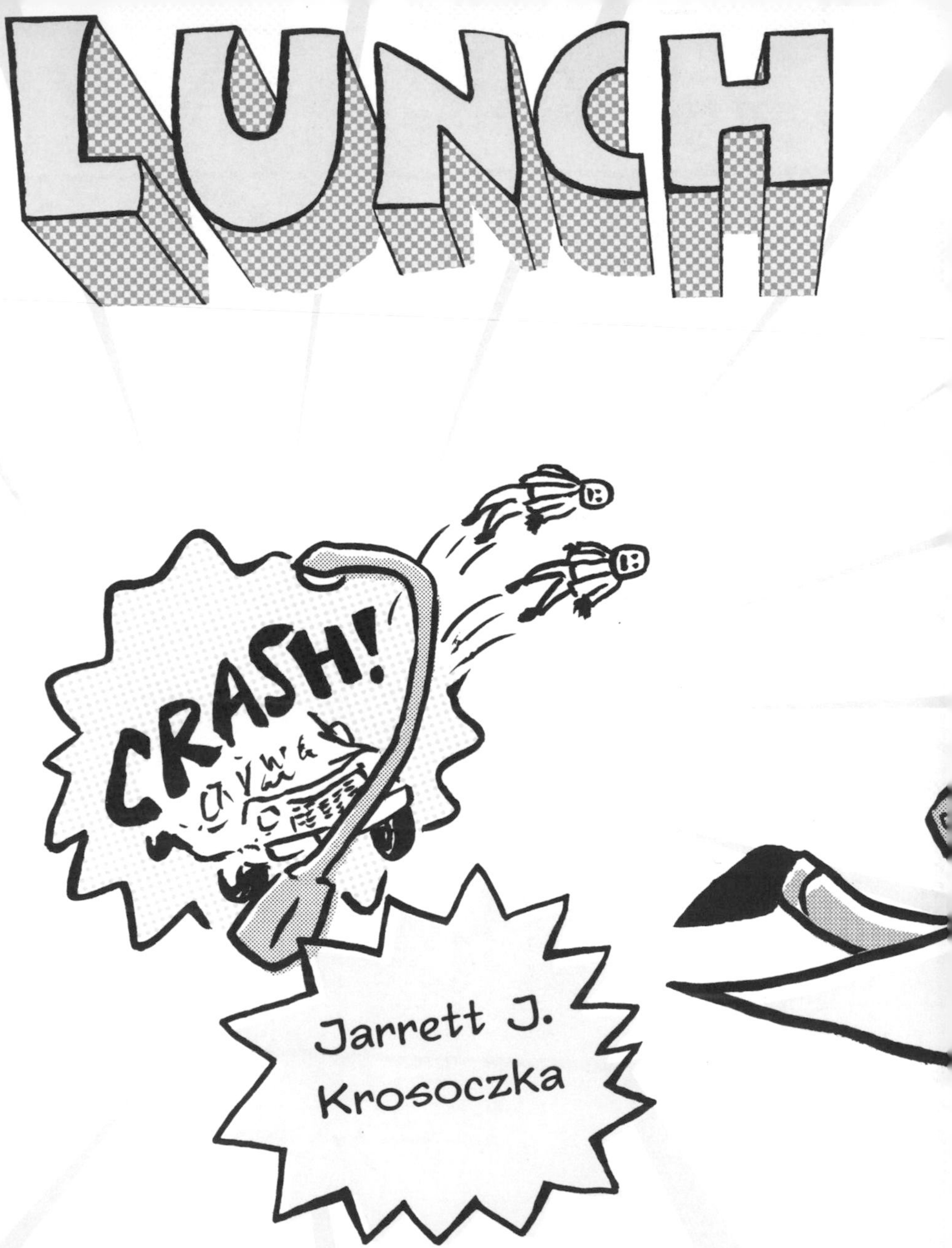
CRASH!

Jarrett J. Krosoczka

LADY

and the Author Visit Vendetta

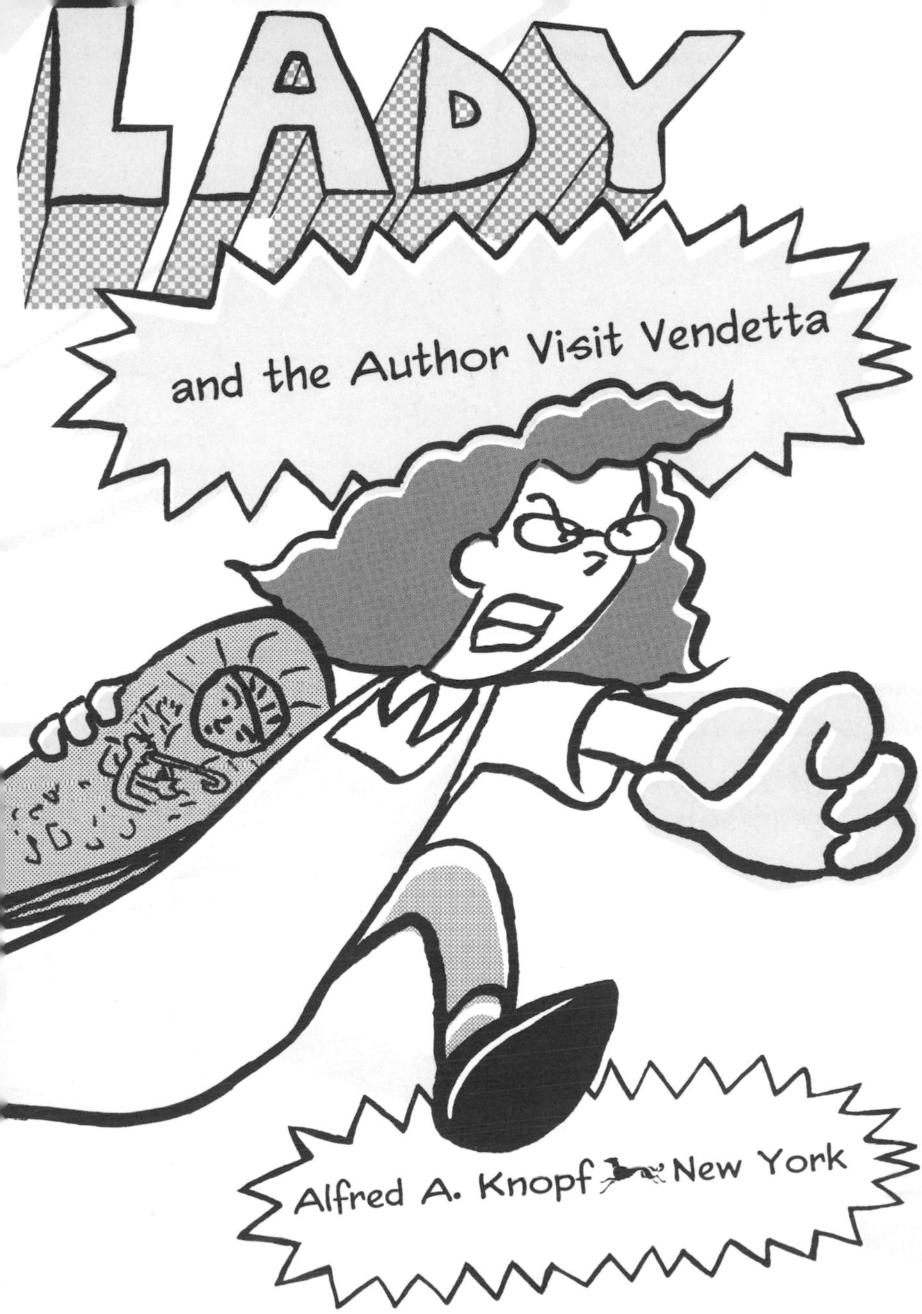

Alfred A. Knopf New York

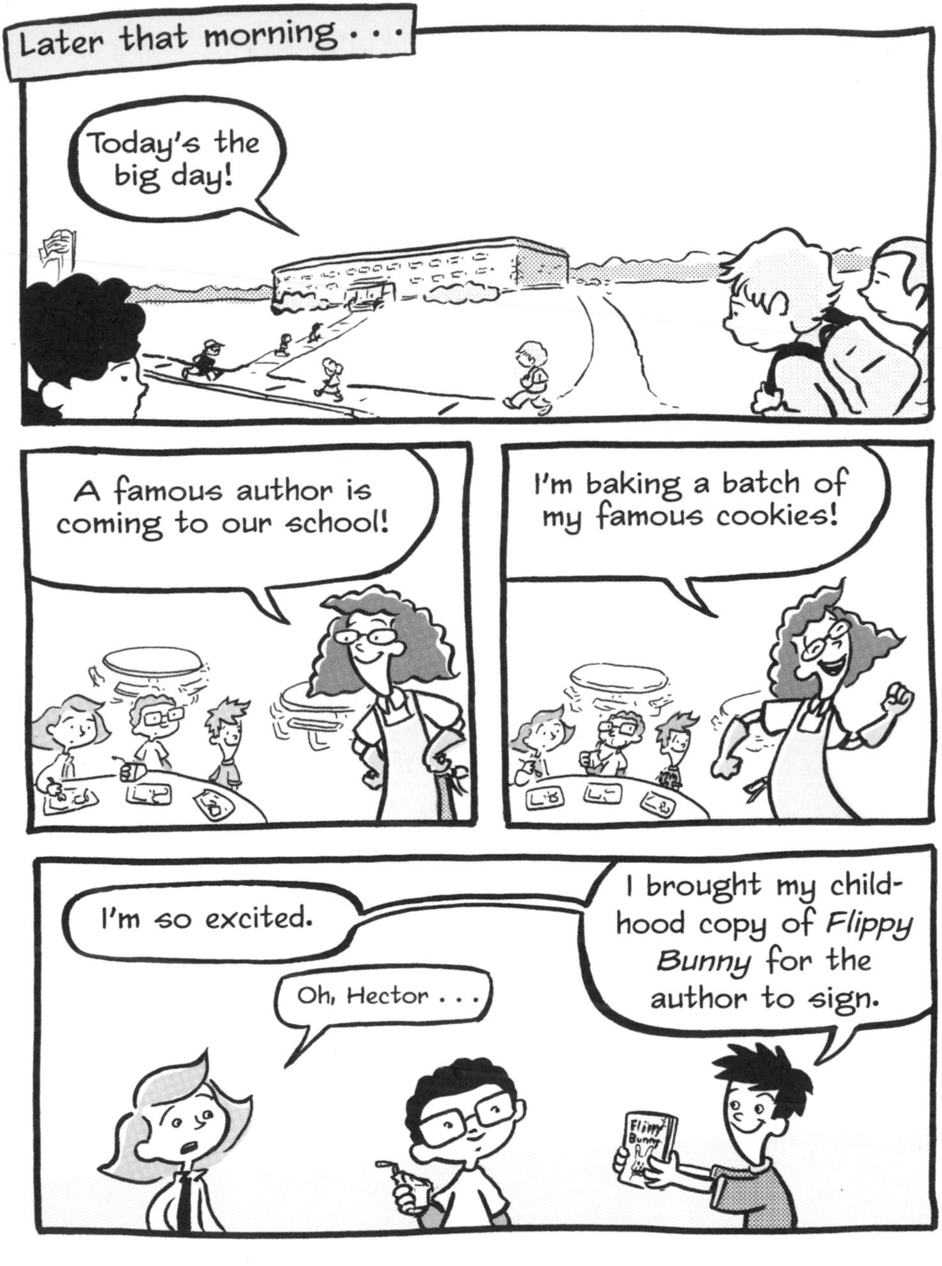
Later that morning . . .
Today's the big day!
A famous author is coming to our school!
I'm baking a batch of my famous cookies!
I'm so excited.
I brought my child-hood copy of *Flippy Bunny* for the author to sign.
Oh, Hector . . .

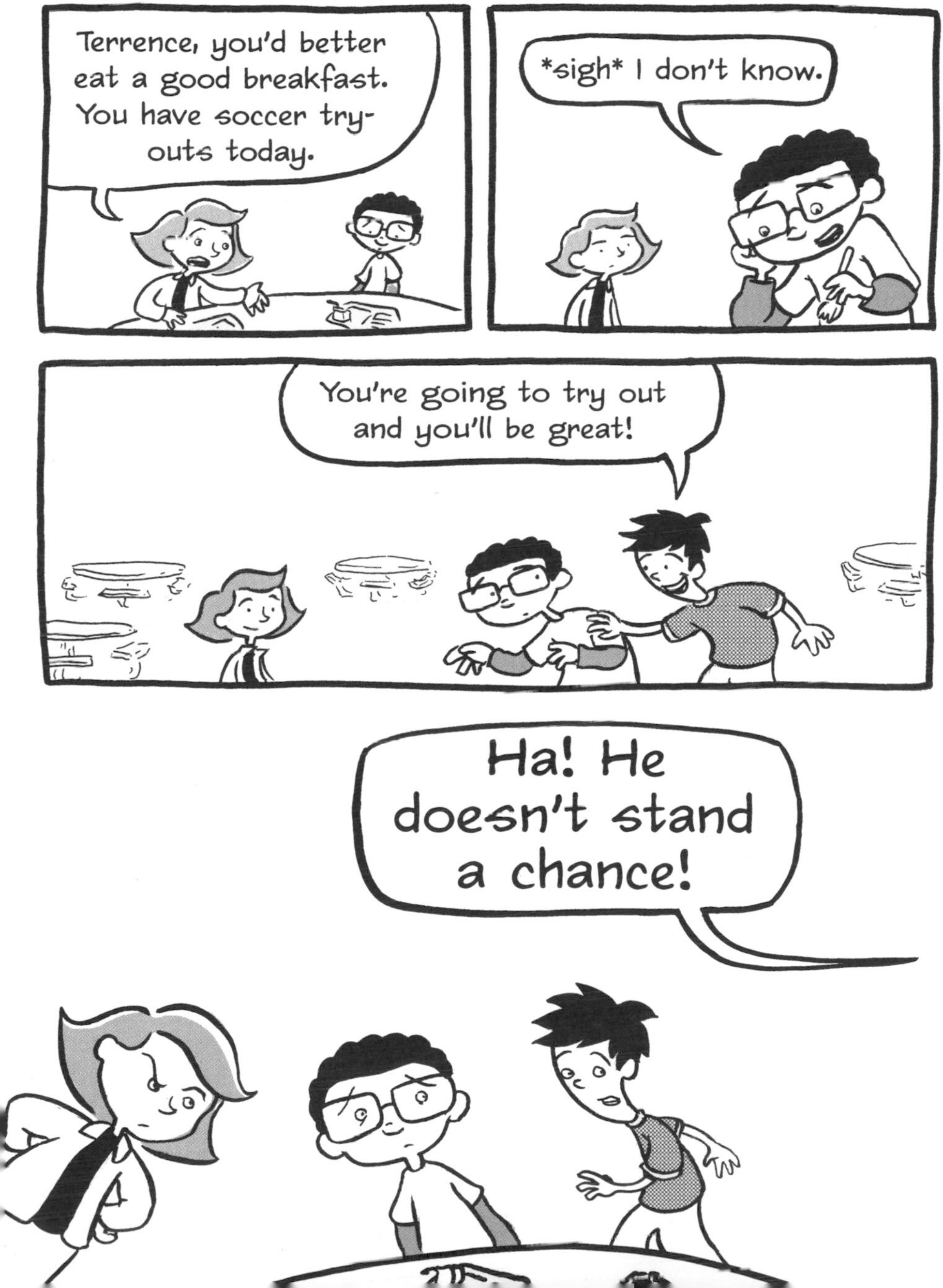
Terrence, you'd better eat a good breakfast. You have soccer try-outs today.
sigh I don't know.
You're going to try out and you'll be great!
Ha! He doesn't stand a chance!

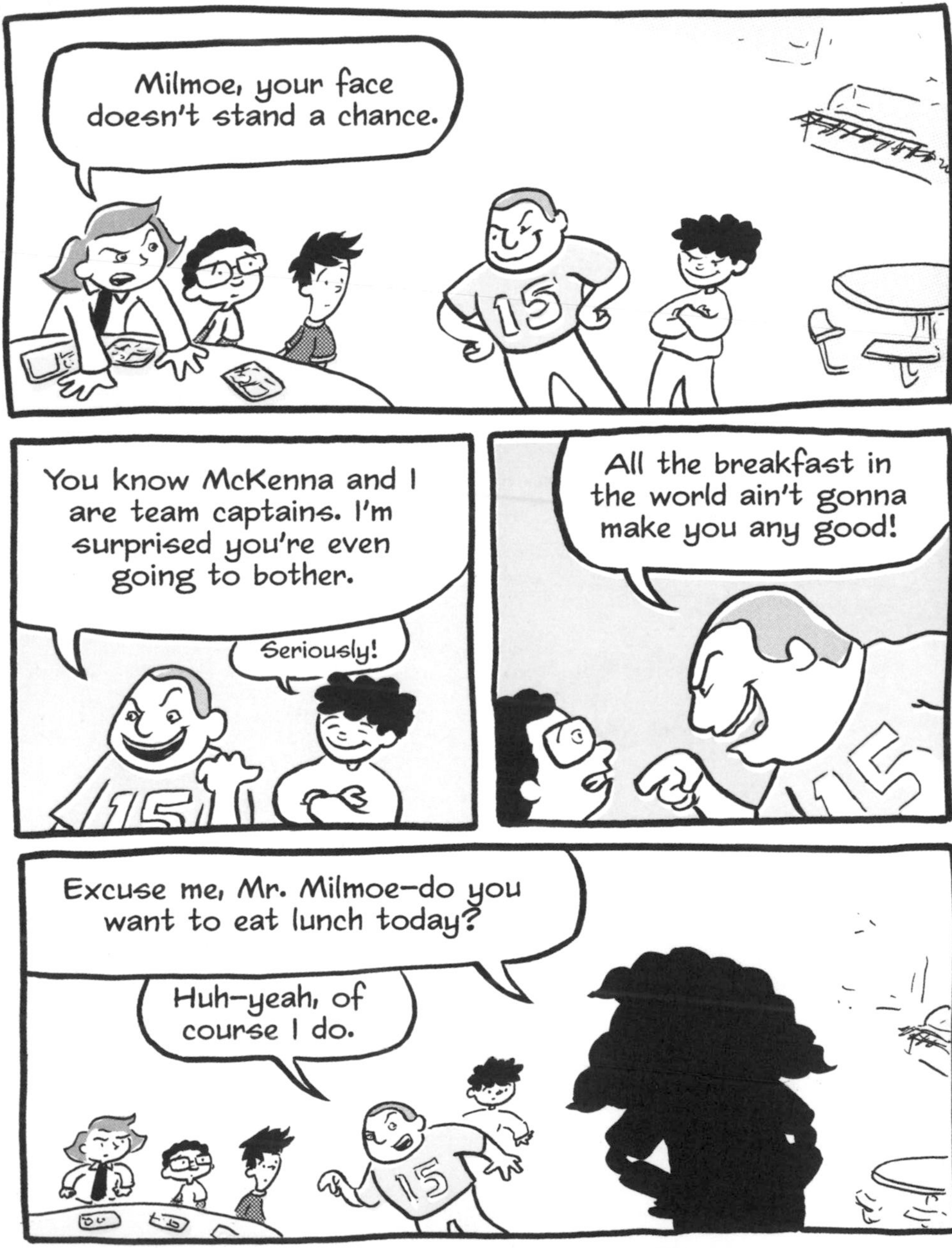
Milmoe, your face doesn't stand a chance.
You know McKenna and I are team captains. I'm surprised you're even going to bother.
Seriously!
All the breakfast in the world ain't gonna make you any good!
Excuse me, Mr. Milmoe—do you want to eat lunch today?
Huh—yeah, of course I do.

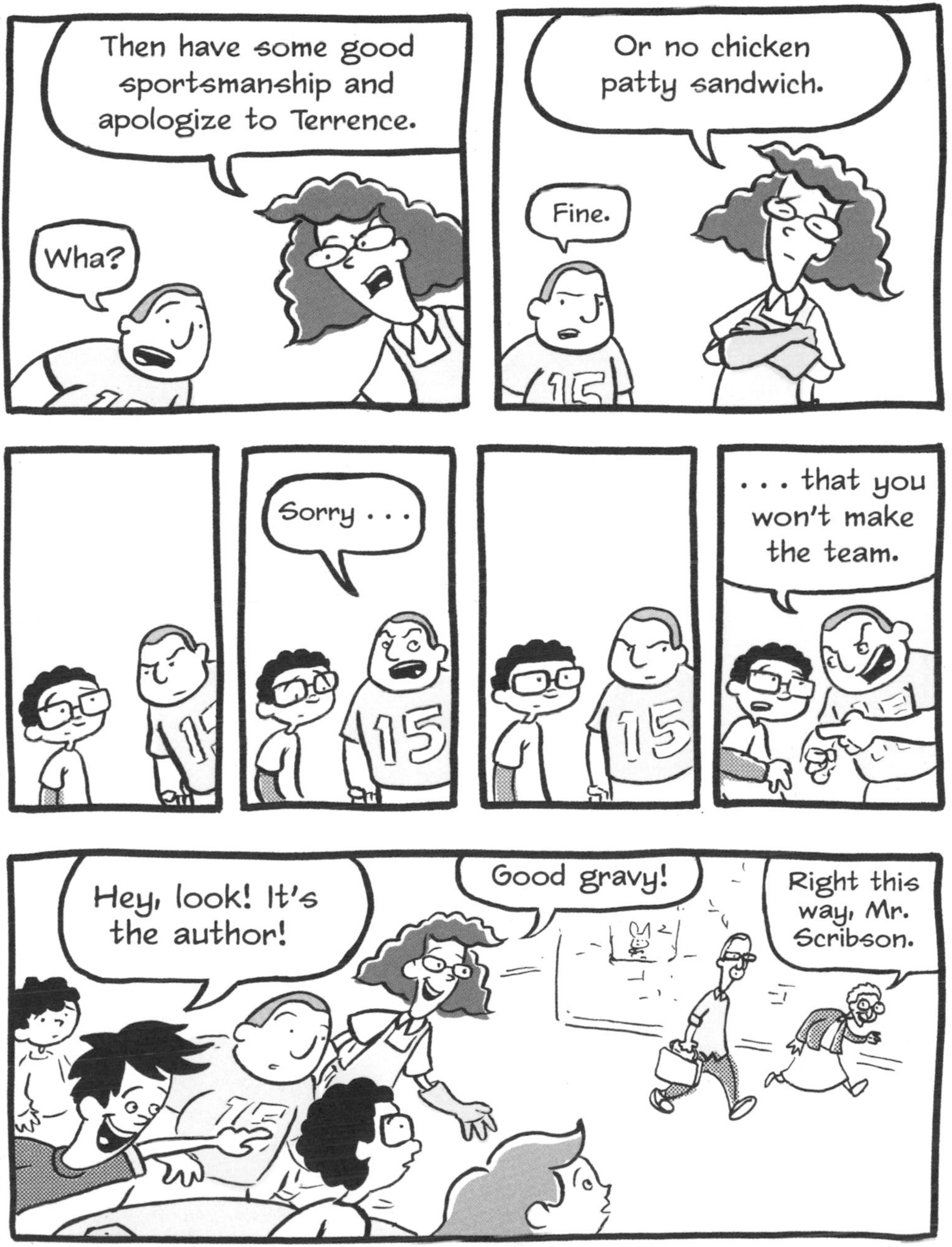
Then have some good sportsmanship and apologize to Terrence.
Wha?
Or no chicken patty sandwich.
Fine.
Sorry . . .
. . . that you won't make the team.
Hey, look! It's the author!
Good gravy!
Right this way, Mr. Scribson.

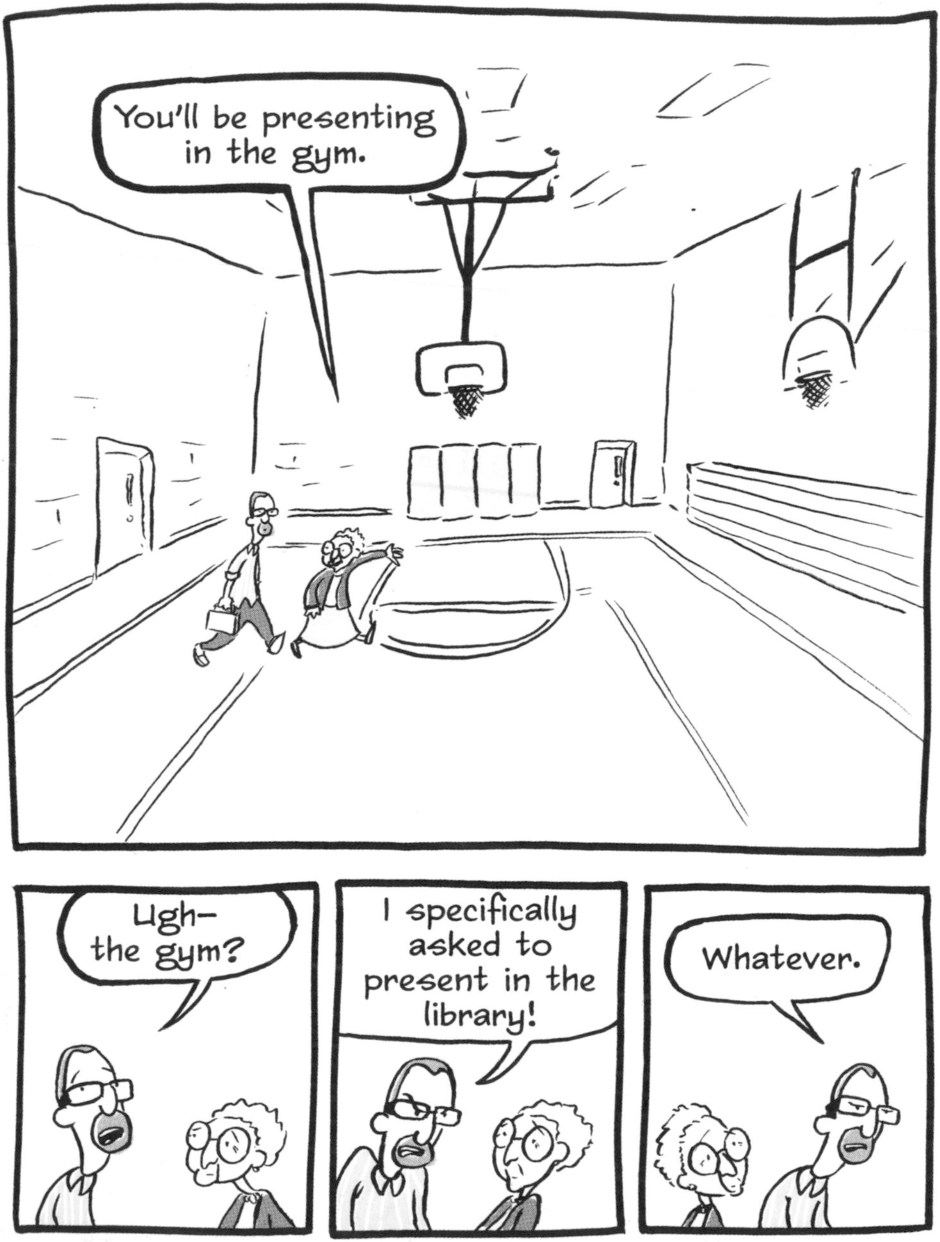
You'll be presenting in the gym.
Ugh— the gym?
I specifically asked to present in the library!
Whatever.

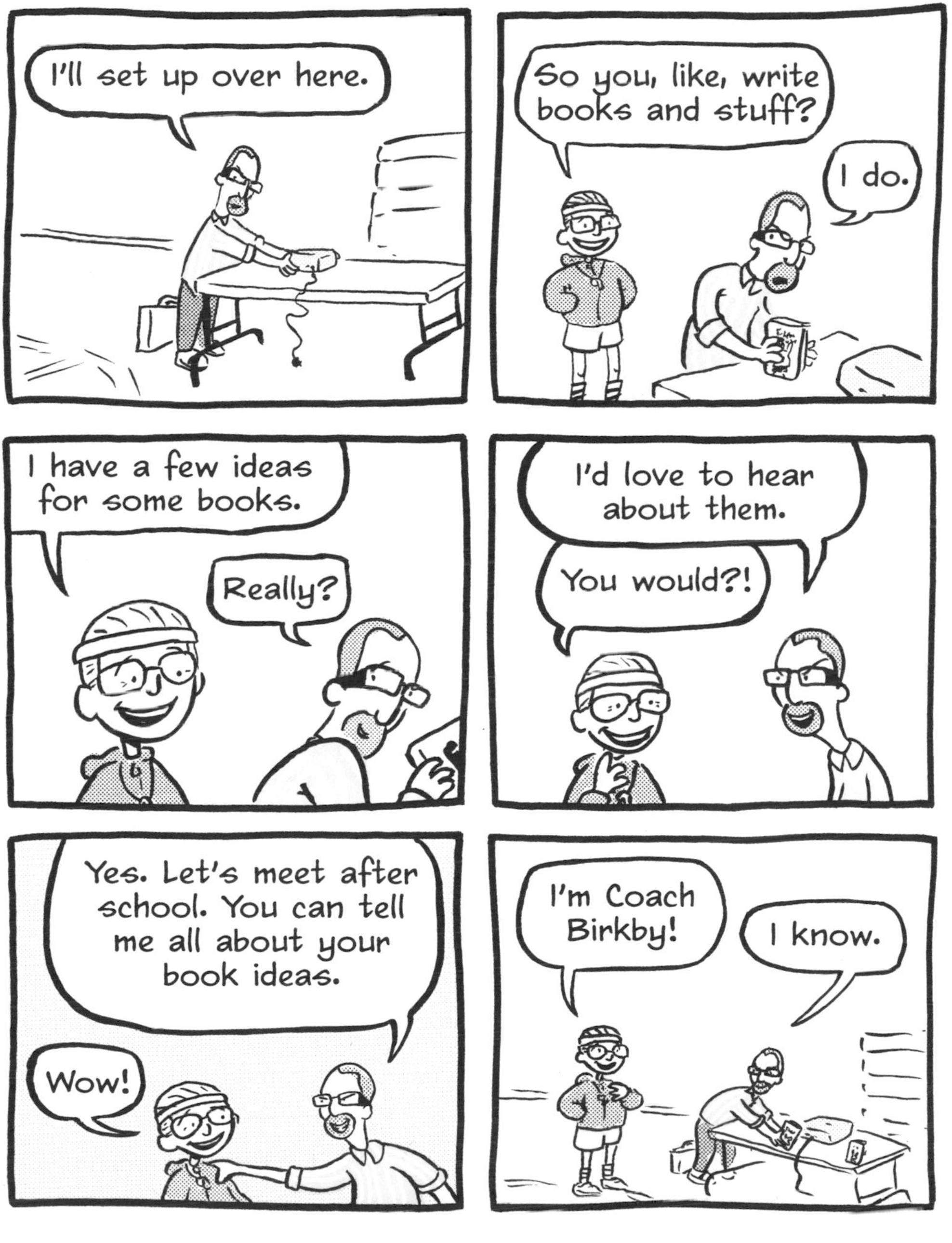
I'll set up over here.
So you, like, write books and stuff?
I do.
I have a few ideas for some books.
Really?
I'd love to hear about them.
You would?!
Yes. Let's meet after school. You can tell me all about your book ideas.
Wow!
I'm Coach Birkby!
I know.

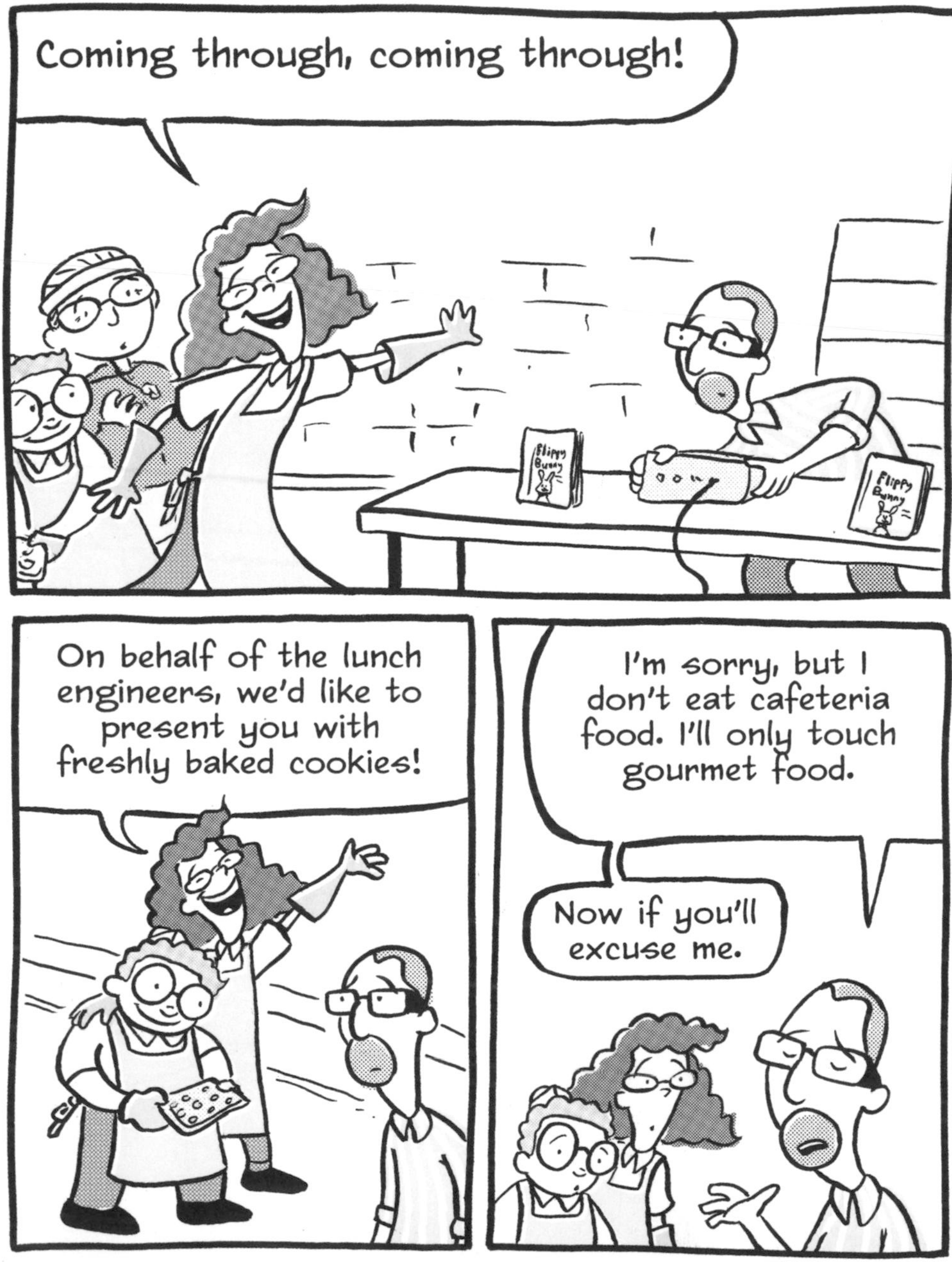
Coming through, coming through!
Flippy Bunny
Flippy Bunny
On behalf of the lunch engineers, we'd like to present you with freshly baked cookies!
I'm sorry, but I don't eat cafeteria food. I'll only touch gourmet food.
Now if you'll excuse me.

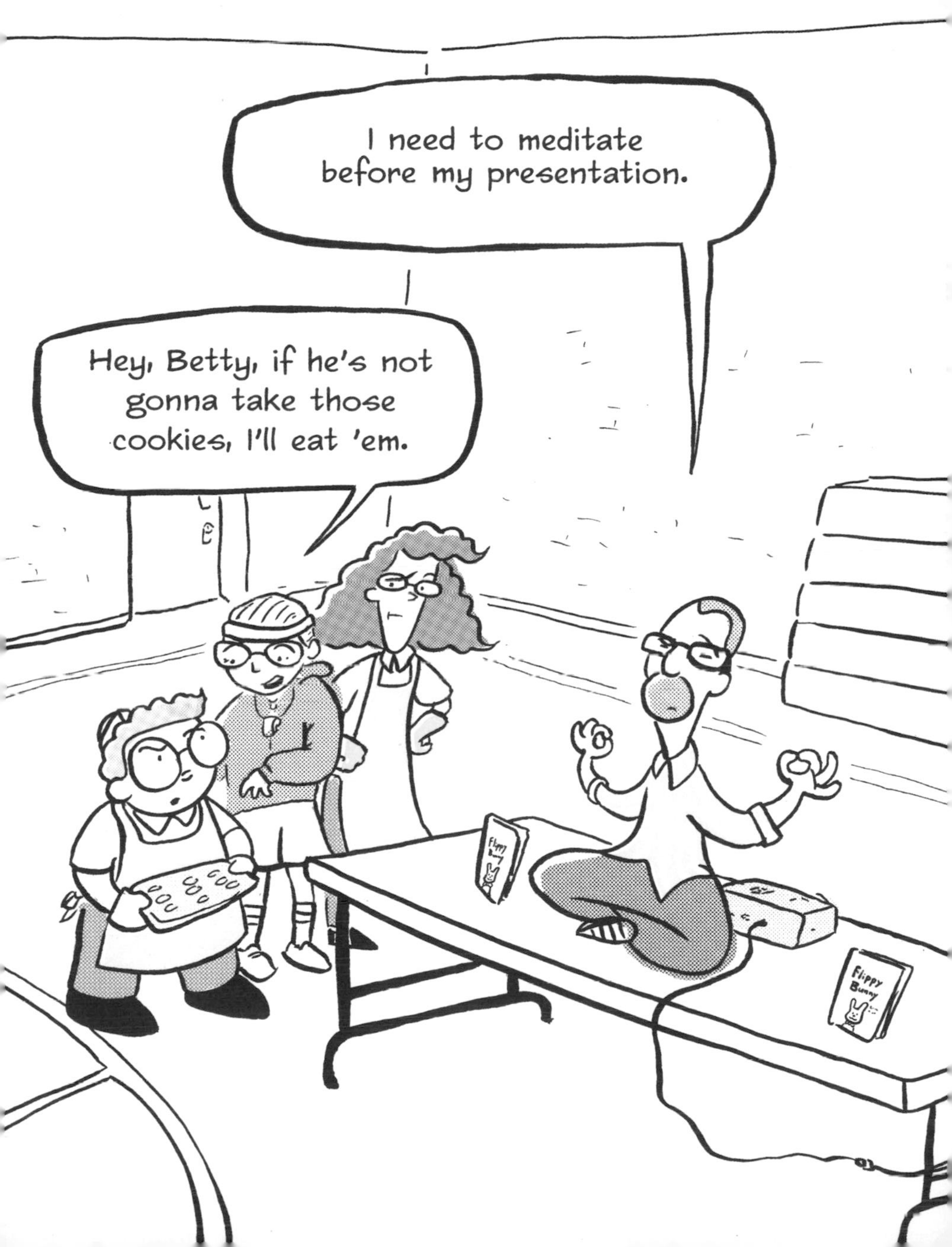
Hey, Betty, if he's not gonna take those cookies, I'll eat 'em.
I need to meditate before my presentation.
Flippy Bunny
Flippy Bunny

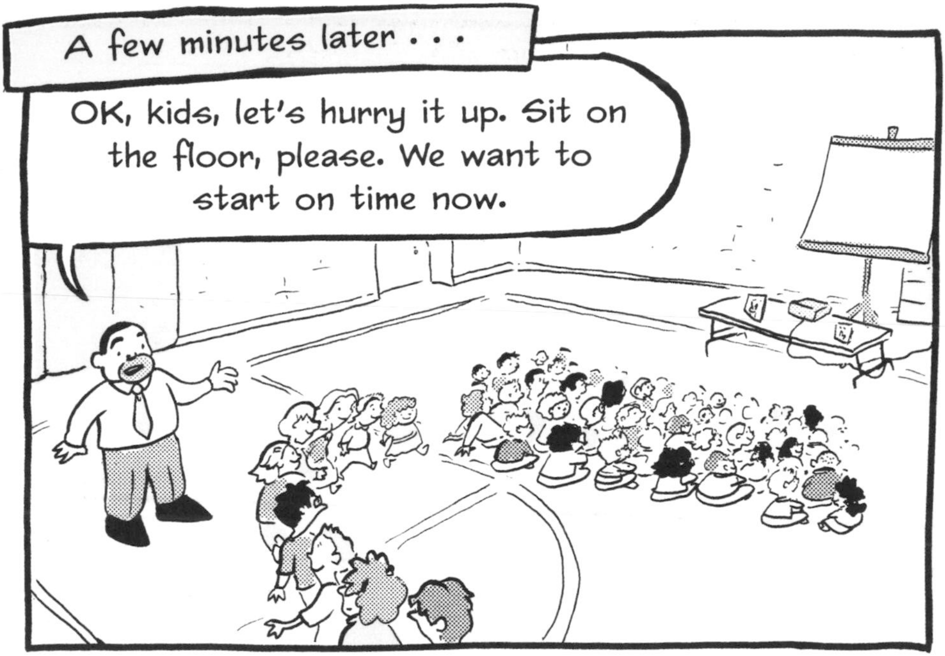
A few minutes later . . .
OK, kids, let's hurry it up. Sit on the floor, please. We want to start on time now.

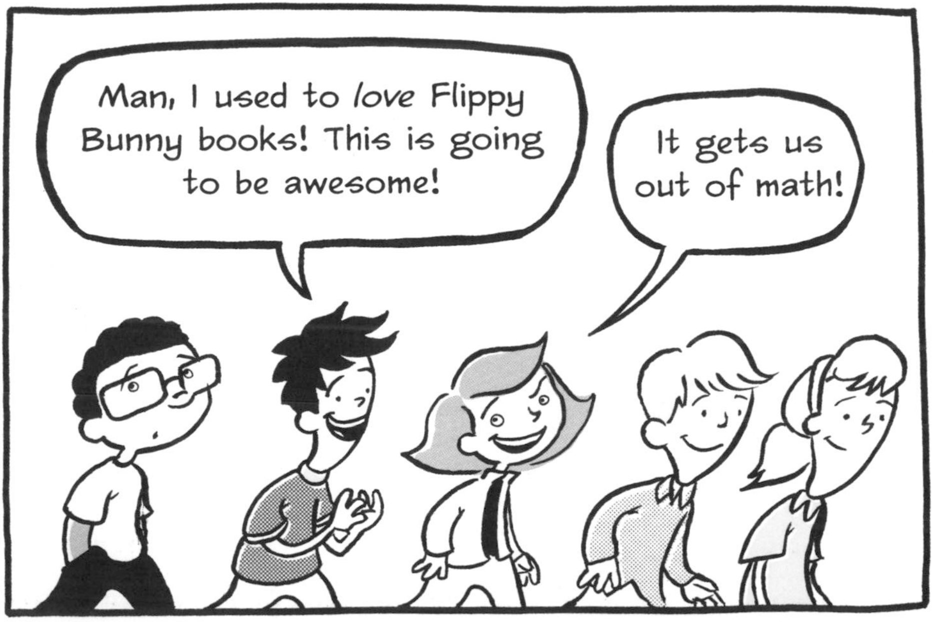
Man, I used to *love* Flippy Bunny books! This is going to be awesome!
It gets us out of math!

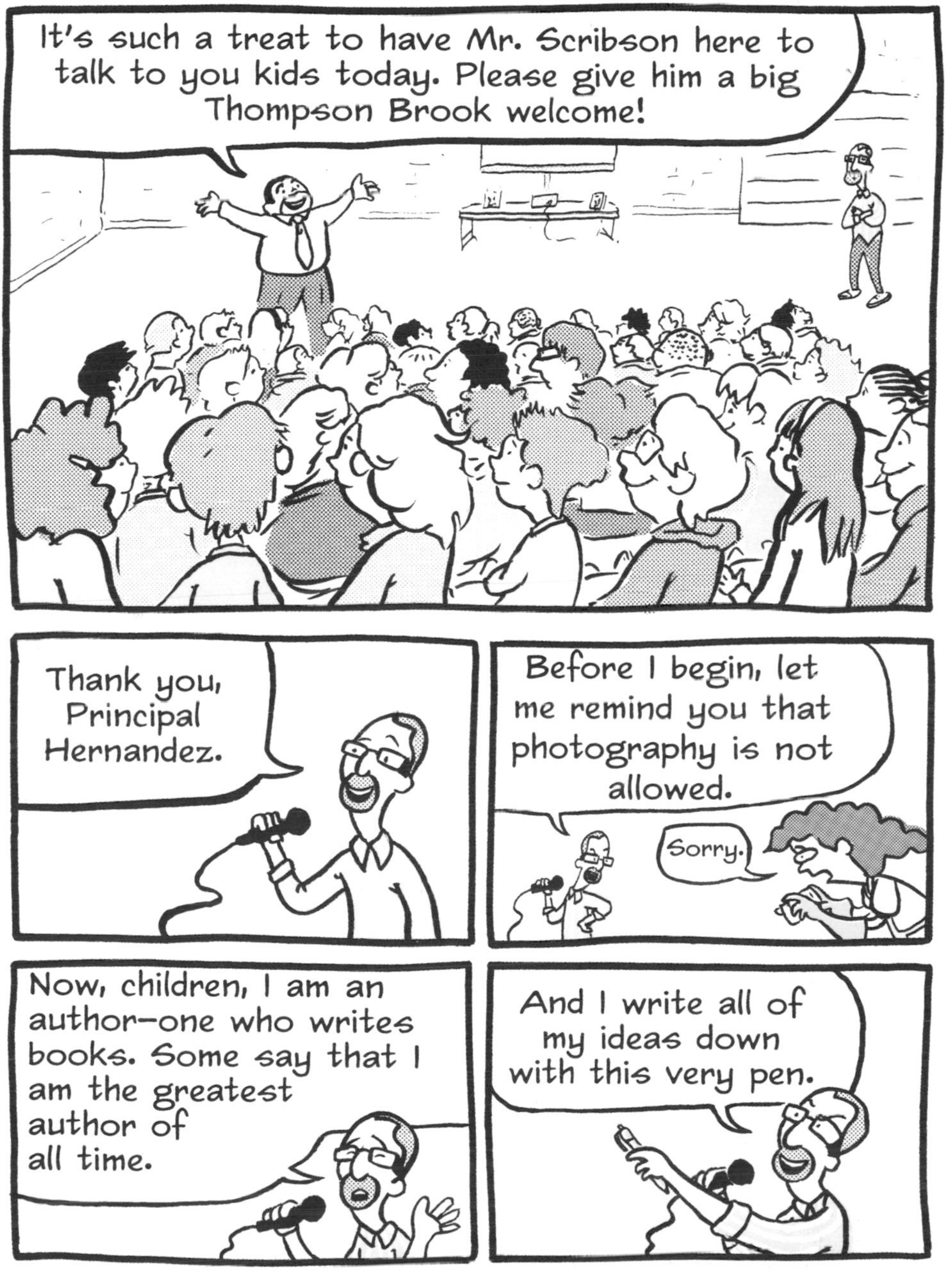
It's such a treat to have Mr. Scribson here to talk to you kids today. Please give him a big Thompson Brook welcome!
Thank you, Principal Hernandez.
Before I begin, let me remind you that photography is not allowed.
Sorry.
Now, children, I am an author—one who writes books. Some say that I am the greatest author of all time.
And I write all of my ideas down with this very pen.

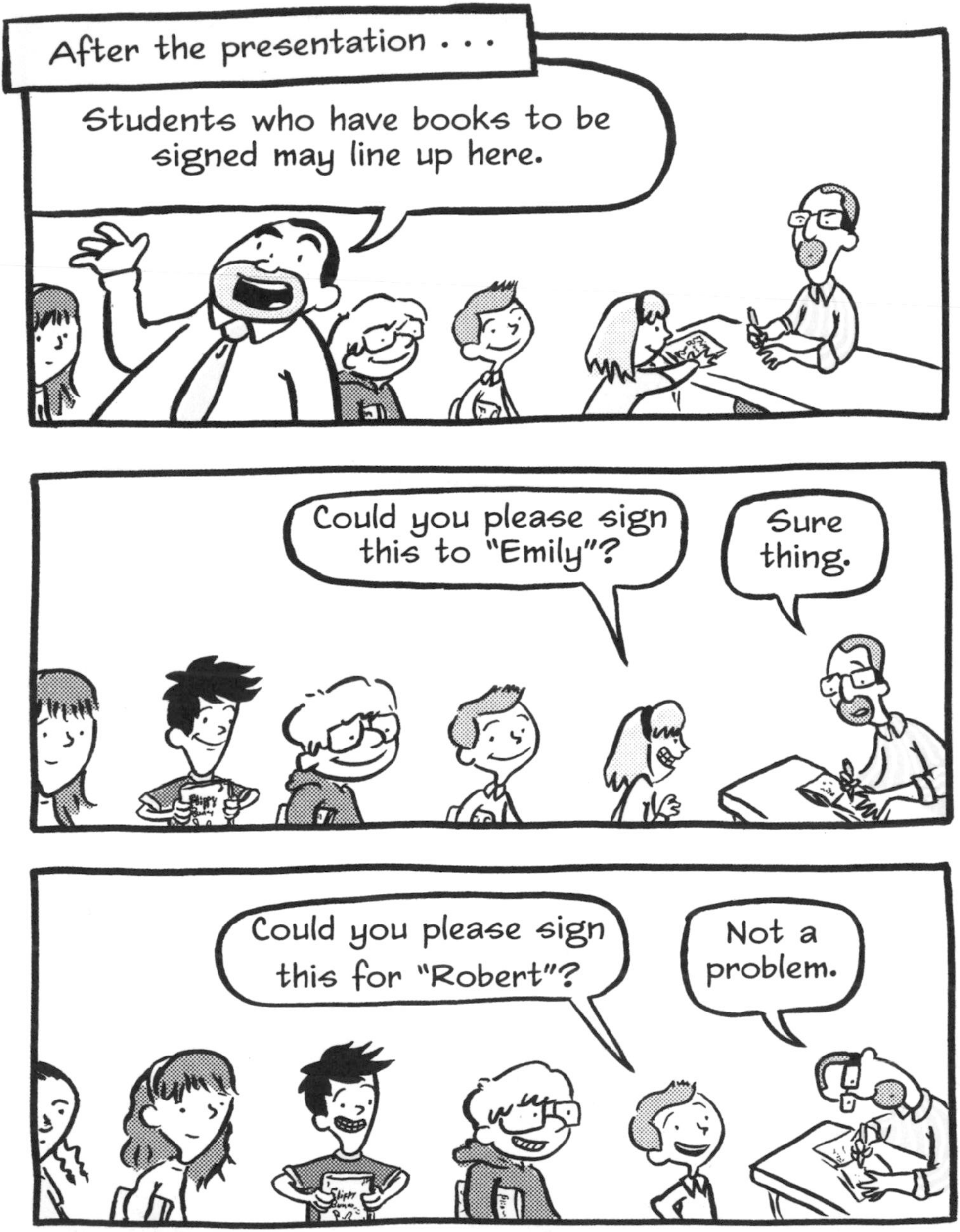
After the presentation . . .
Students who have books to be signed may line up here.
Could you please sign this to "Emily"?
Sure thing.
Could you please sign this for "Robert"?
Not a problem.

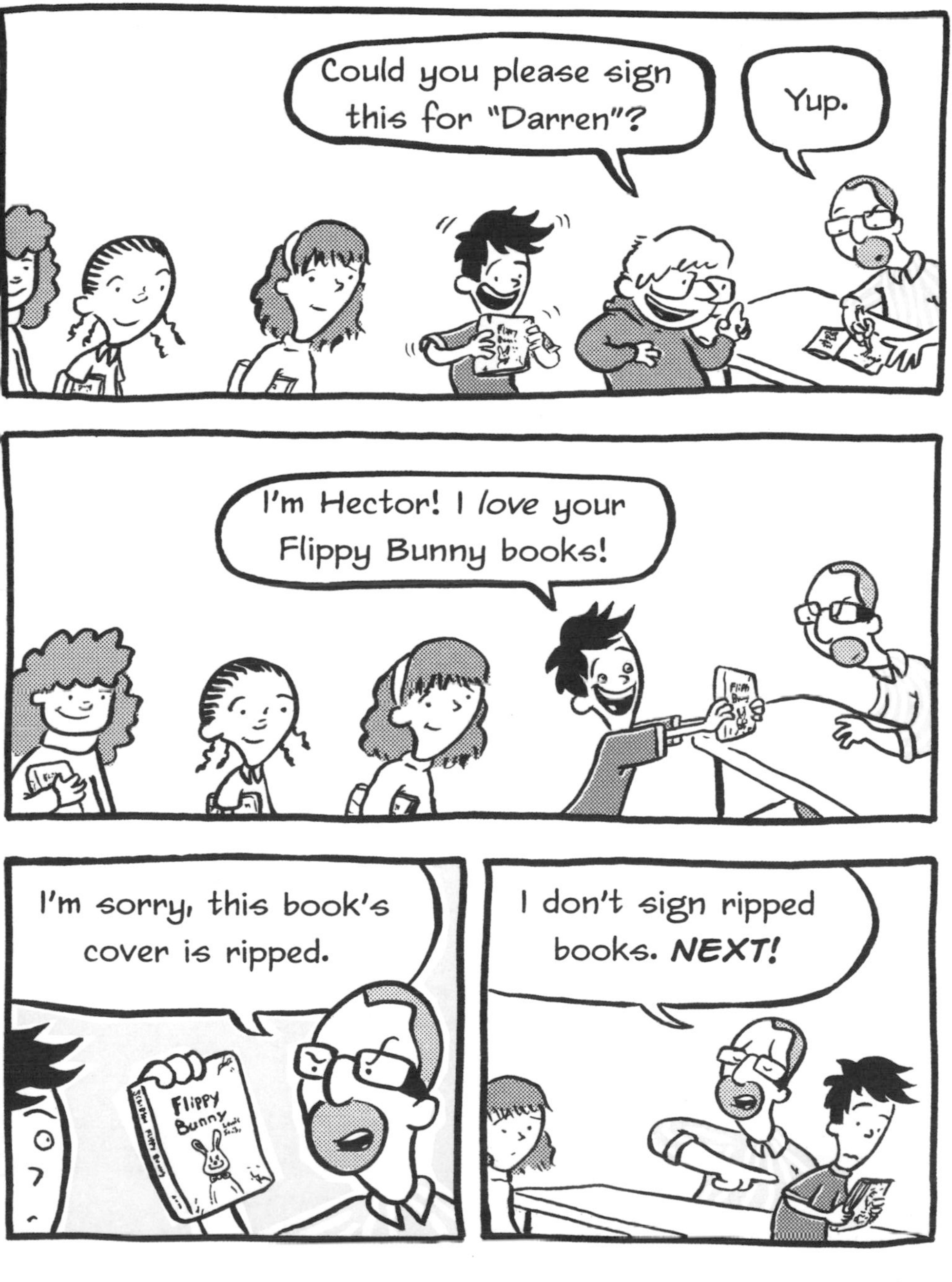
Could you please sign this for "Darren"?
Yup.
Flippy Bunny
I'm Hector! I *love* your Flippy Bunny books!
I'm sorry, this book's cover is ripped.
Flippy Bunny
I don't sign ripped books. ***NEXT!***

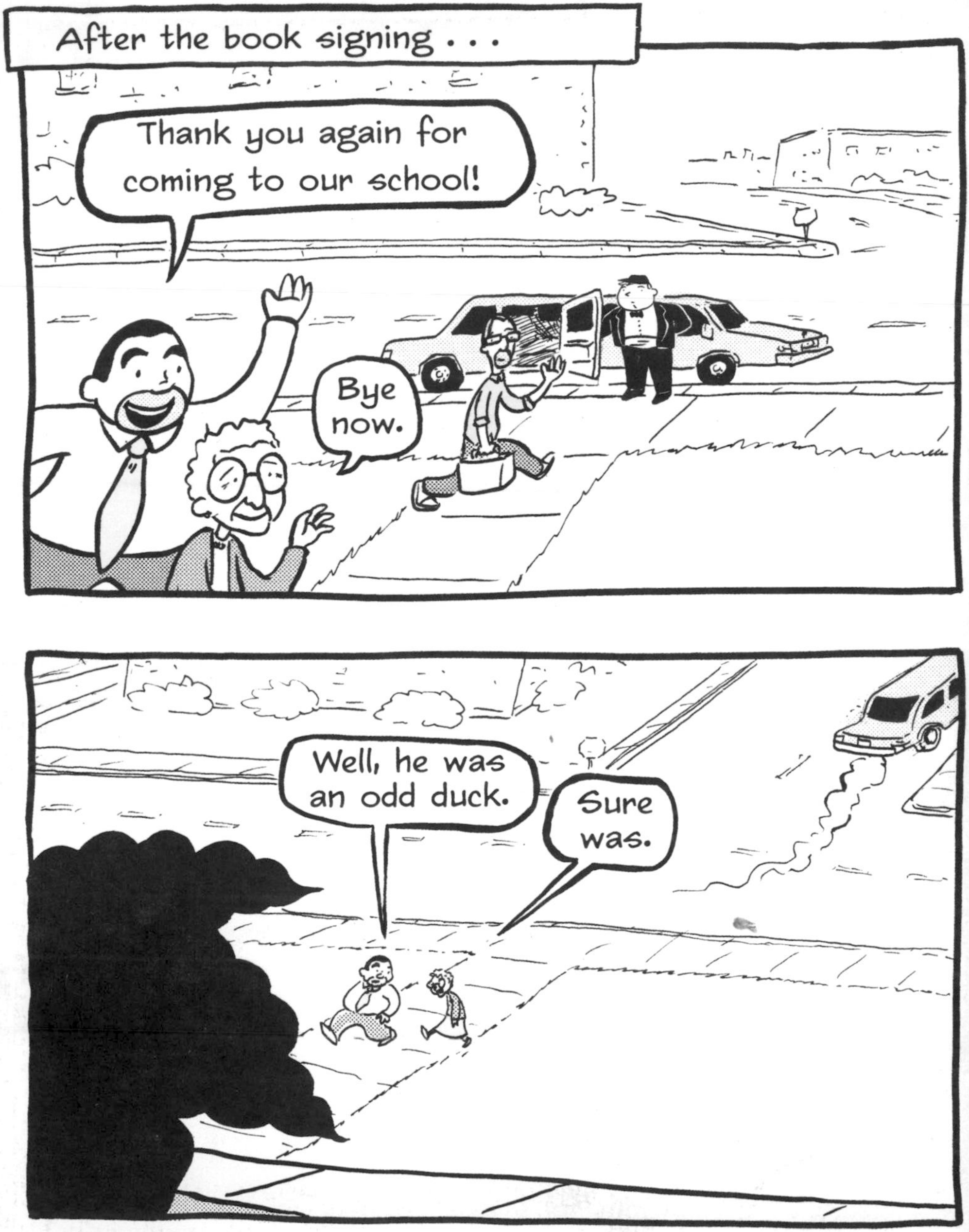
After the book signing . . .
Thank you again for coming to our school!
Bye now.
Well, he was an odd duck.
Sure was.

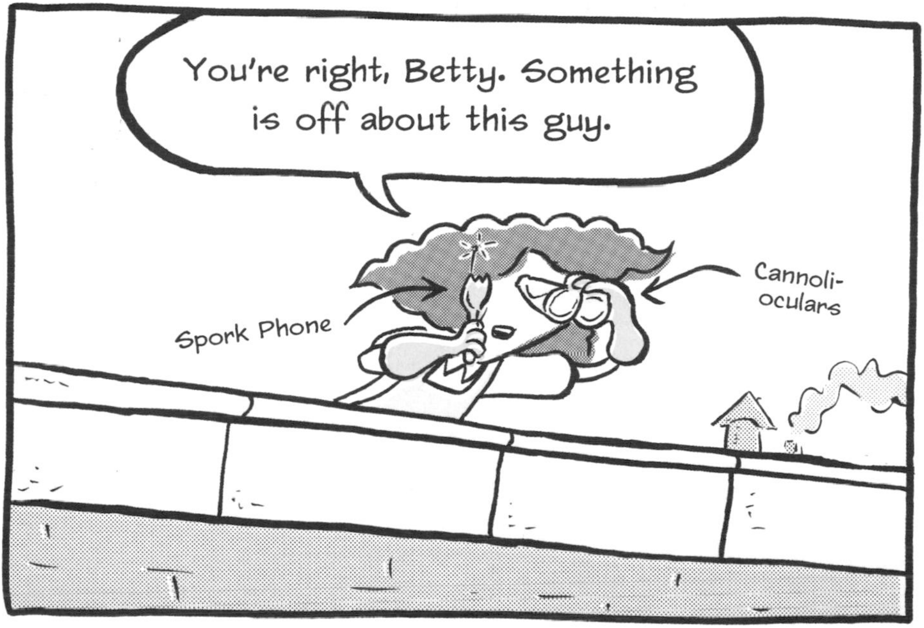
You're right, Betty. Something is off about this guy.
Spork Phone
Cannoli-oculars

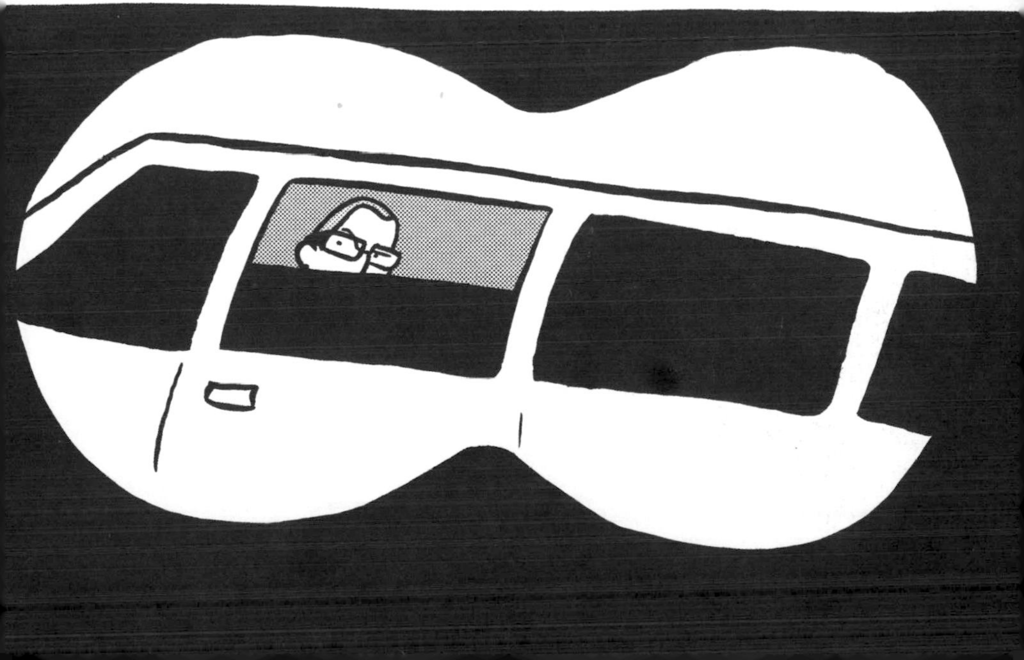

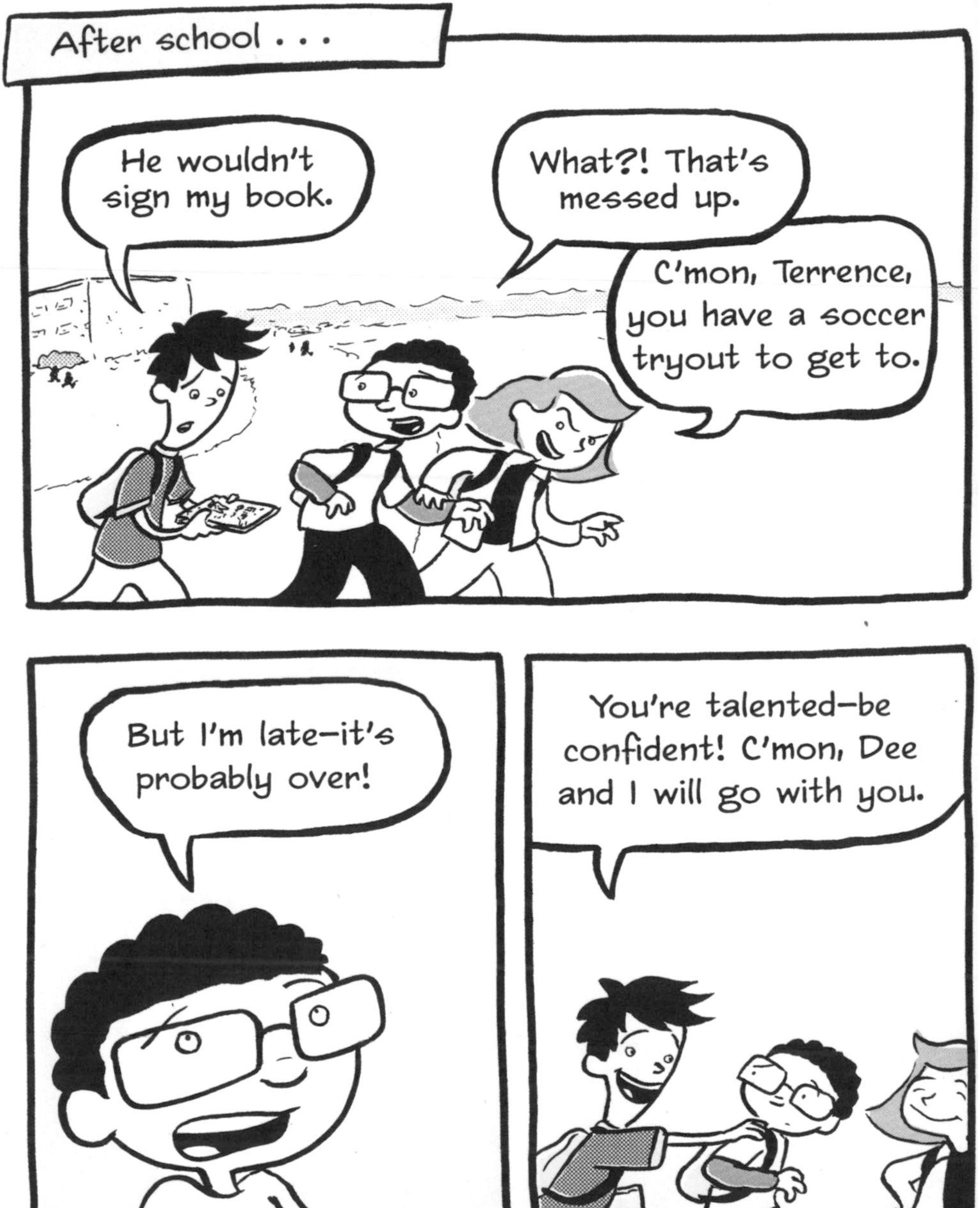
After school . . .
He wouldn't sign my book.
What?! That's messed up.
C'mon, Terrence, you have a soccer tryout to get to.
But I'm late–it's probably over!
You're talented–be confident! C'mon, Dee and I will go with you.

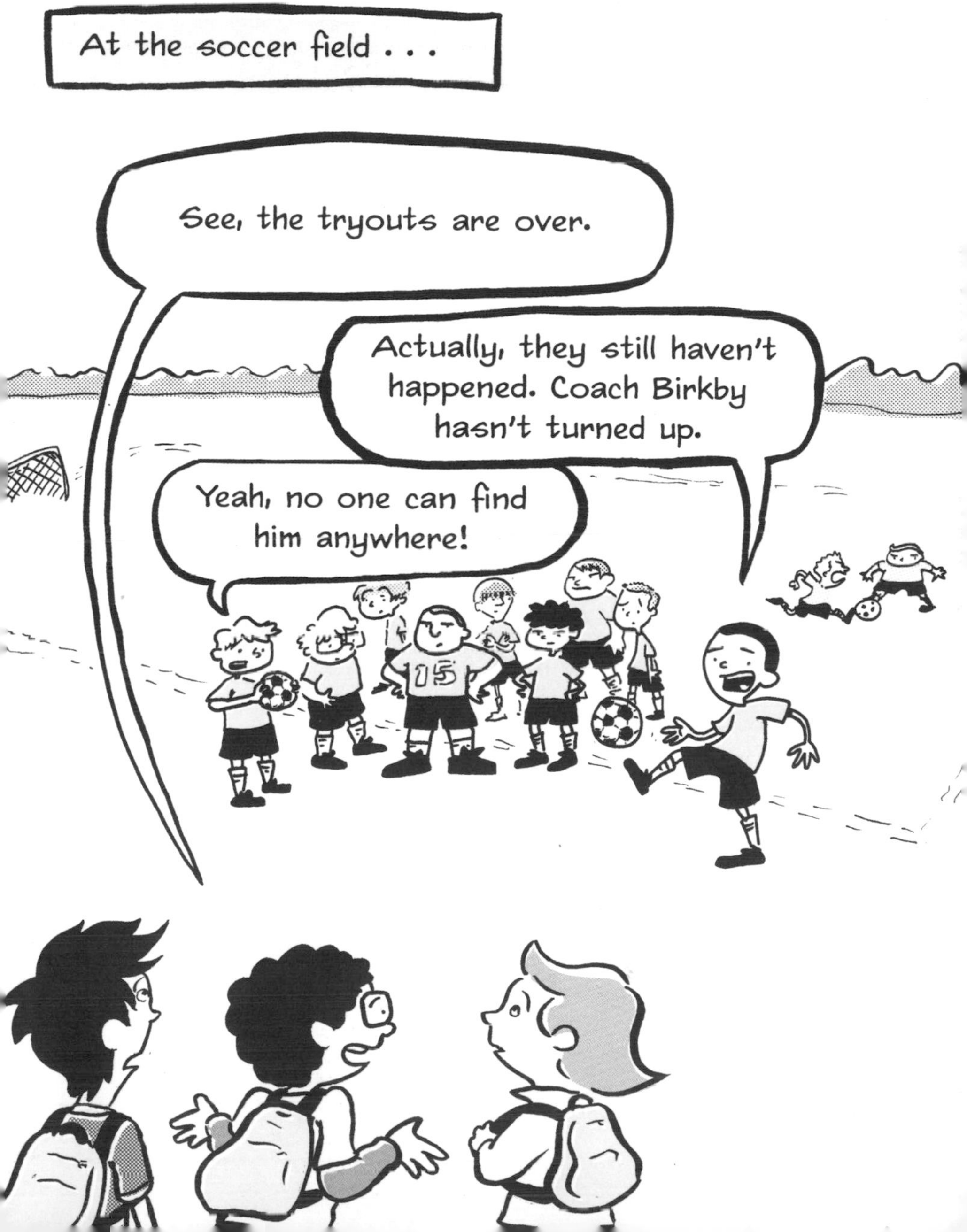

At the soccer field . . .
See, the tryouts are over.
Actually, they still haven't happened. Coach Birkby hasn't turned up.
Yeah, no one can find him anywhere!
15

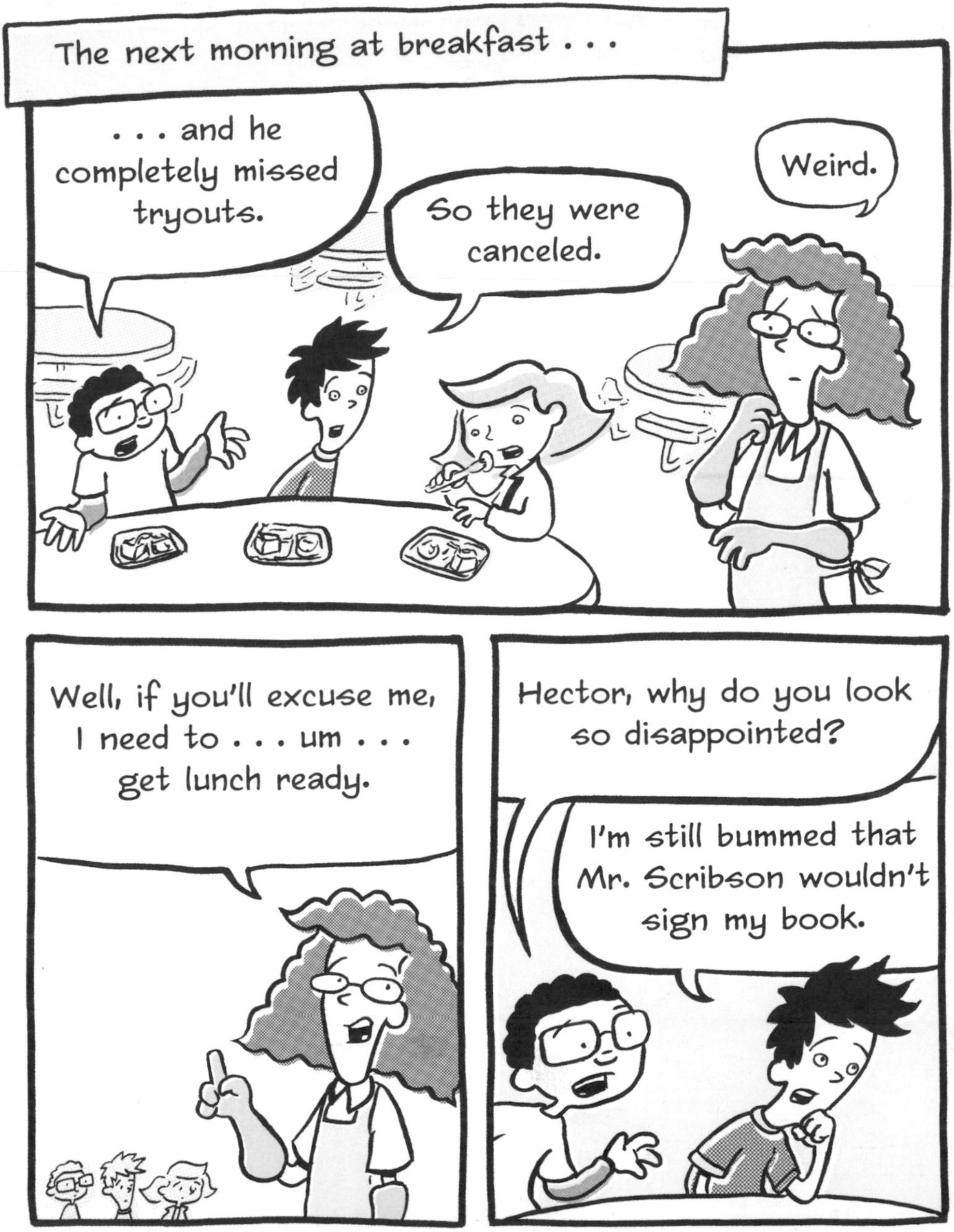
The next morning at breakfast . . .
. . . and he completely missed tryouts.
So they were canceled.
Weird.
Well, if you'll excuse me, I need to . . . um . . . get lunch ready.
Hector, why do you look so disappointed?
I'm still bummed that Mr. Scribson wouldn't sign my book.

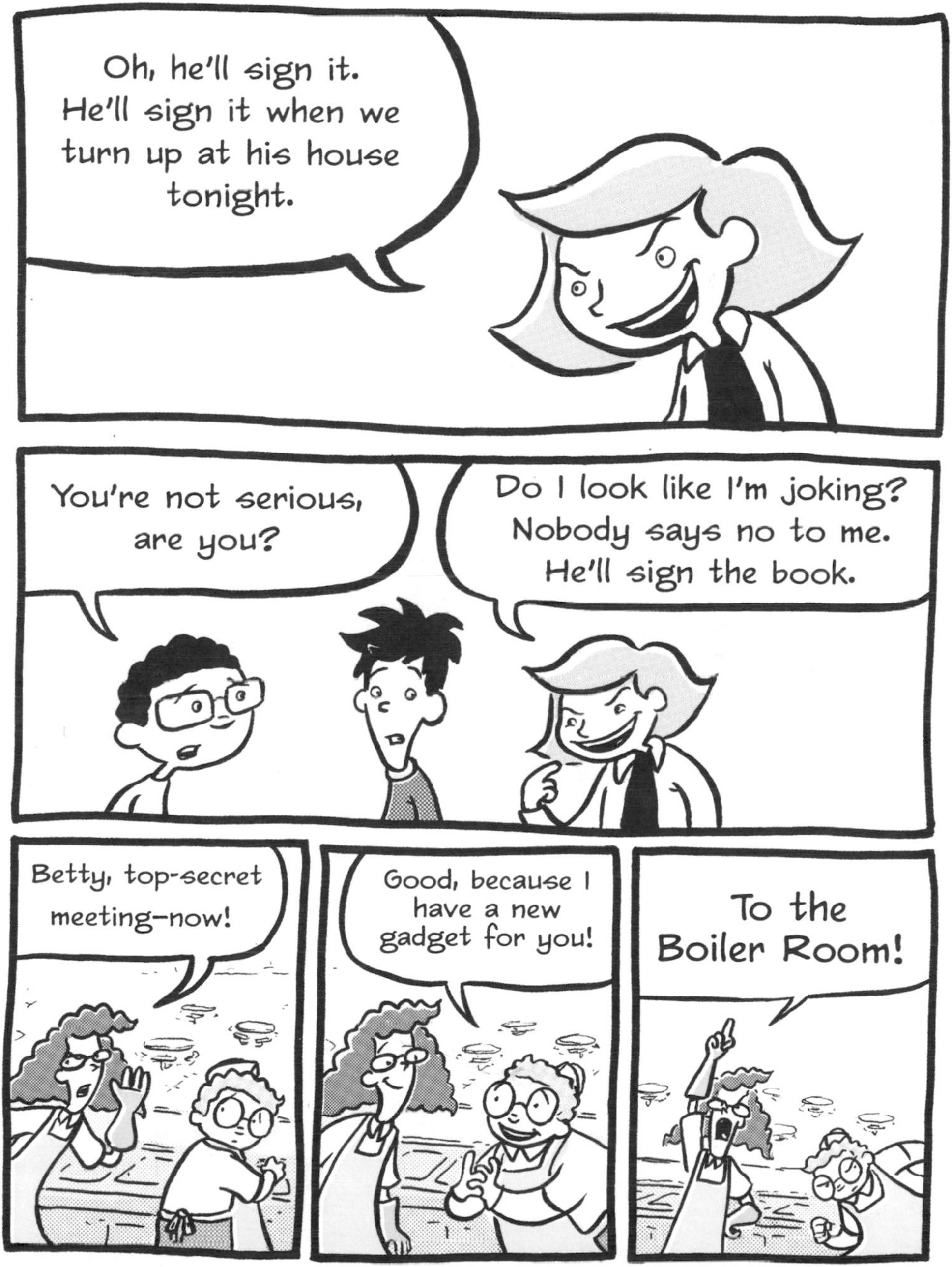
Oh, he'll sign it. He'll sign it when we turn up at his house tonight.
You're not serious, are you?
Do I look like I'm joking? Nobody says no to me. He'll sign the book.
Betty, top-secret meeting—now!
Good, because I have a new gadget for you!
To the Boiler Room!

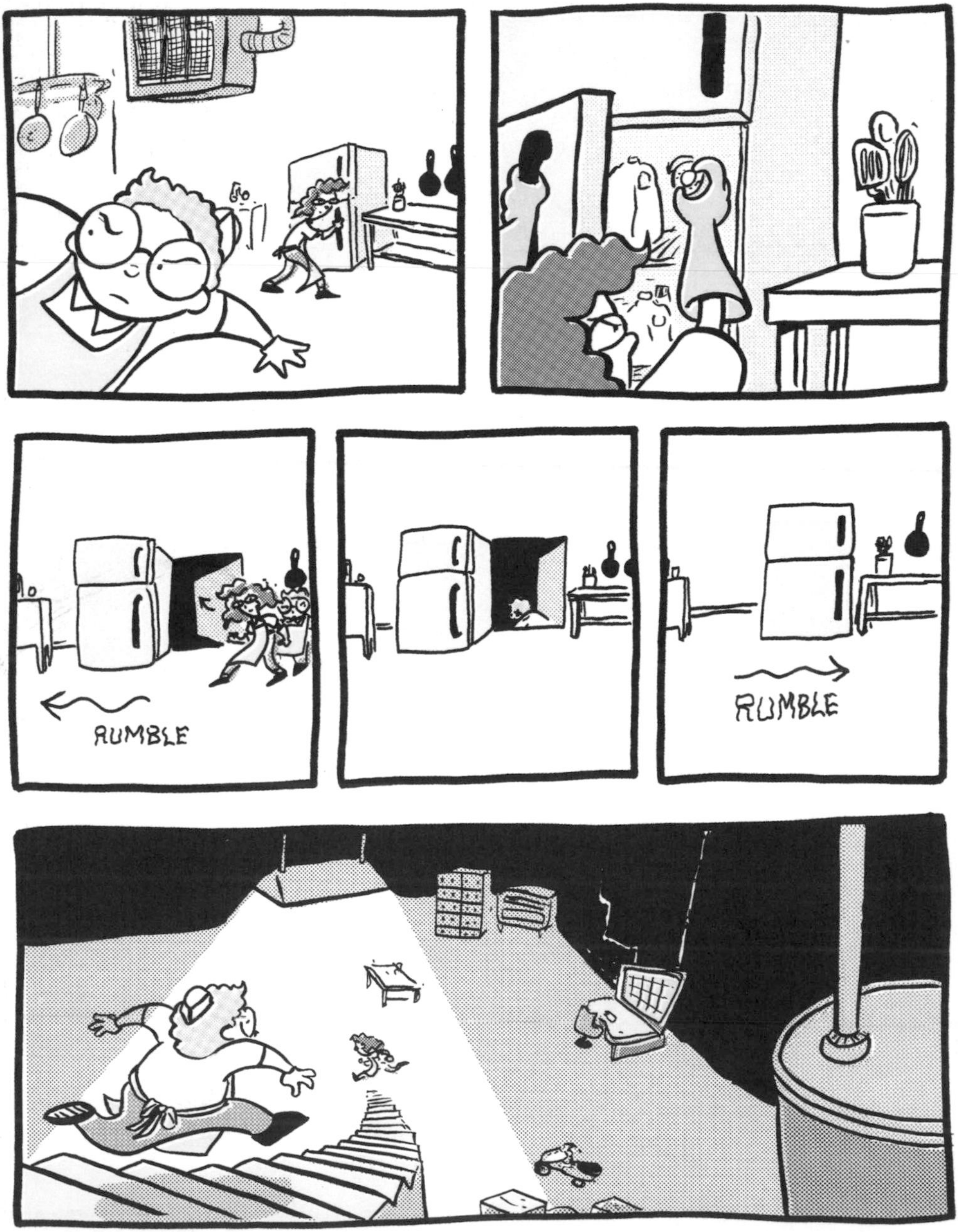
RUMBLE
RUMBLE

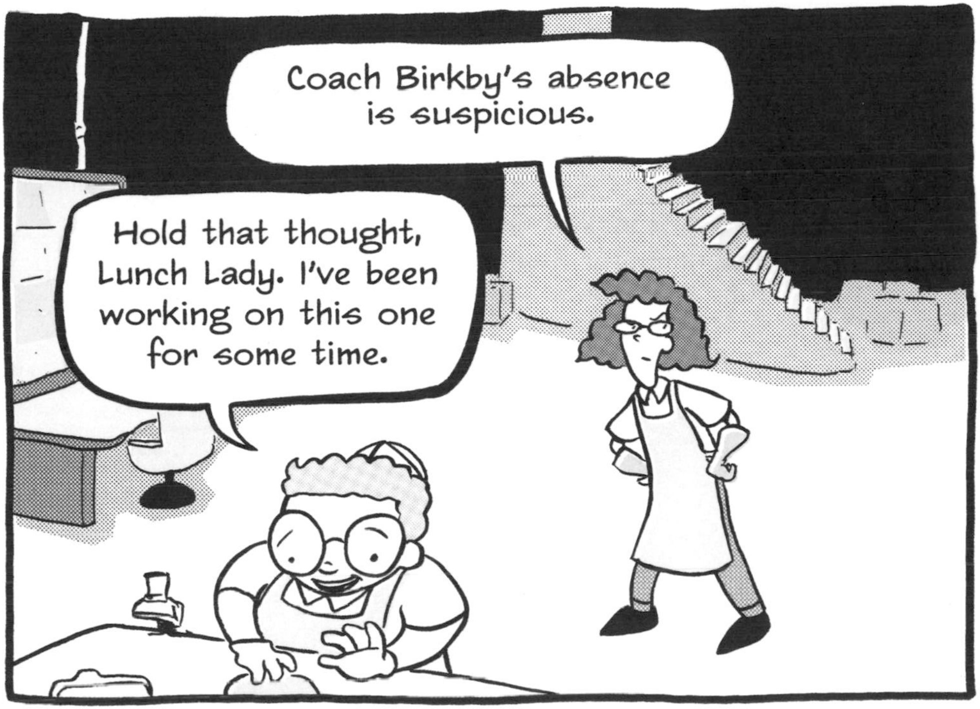
Coach Birkby's absence is suspicious.
Hold that thought, Lunch Lady. I've been working on this one for some time.

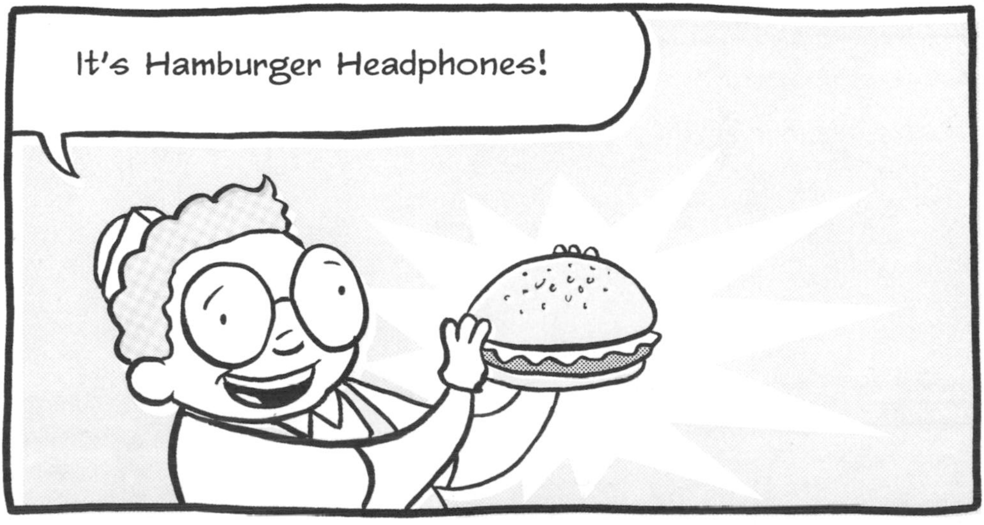
It's Hamburger Headphones!

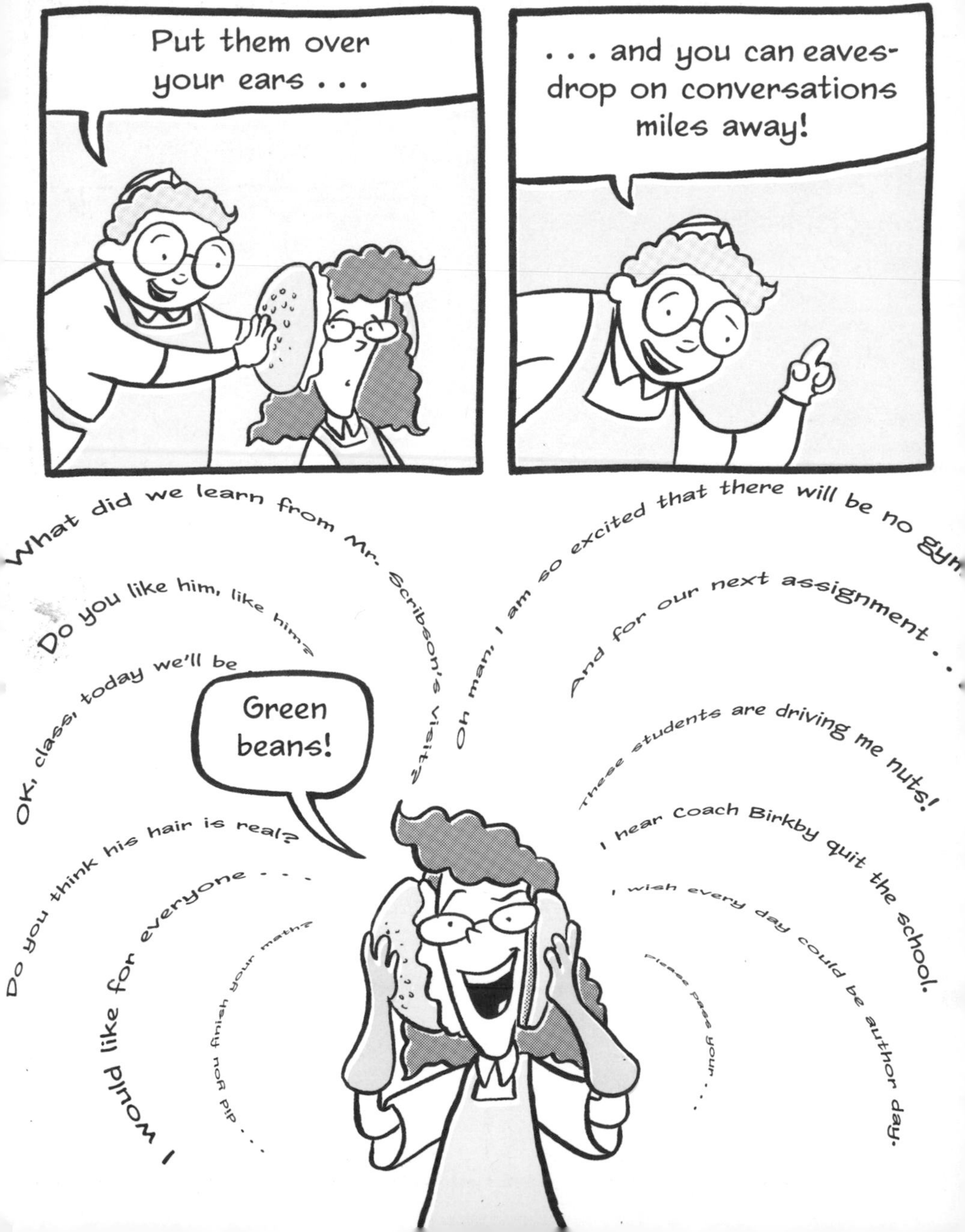

Put them over your ears . . .
. . . and you can eaves-drop on conversations miles away!
What did we learn from Mr. Scribson's visit?
Do you like him, like him?
OK, class, today we'll be . . .
Do you think his hair is real?
I would like for everyone . . .
. . . did you finish your math?
Green beans!
Oh man, I am so excited that there will be no gym
And for our next assignment . . .
These students are driving me nuts!
I hear Coach Birkby quit the school.
I wish every day could be author day.
Please pass your . . .

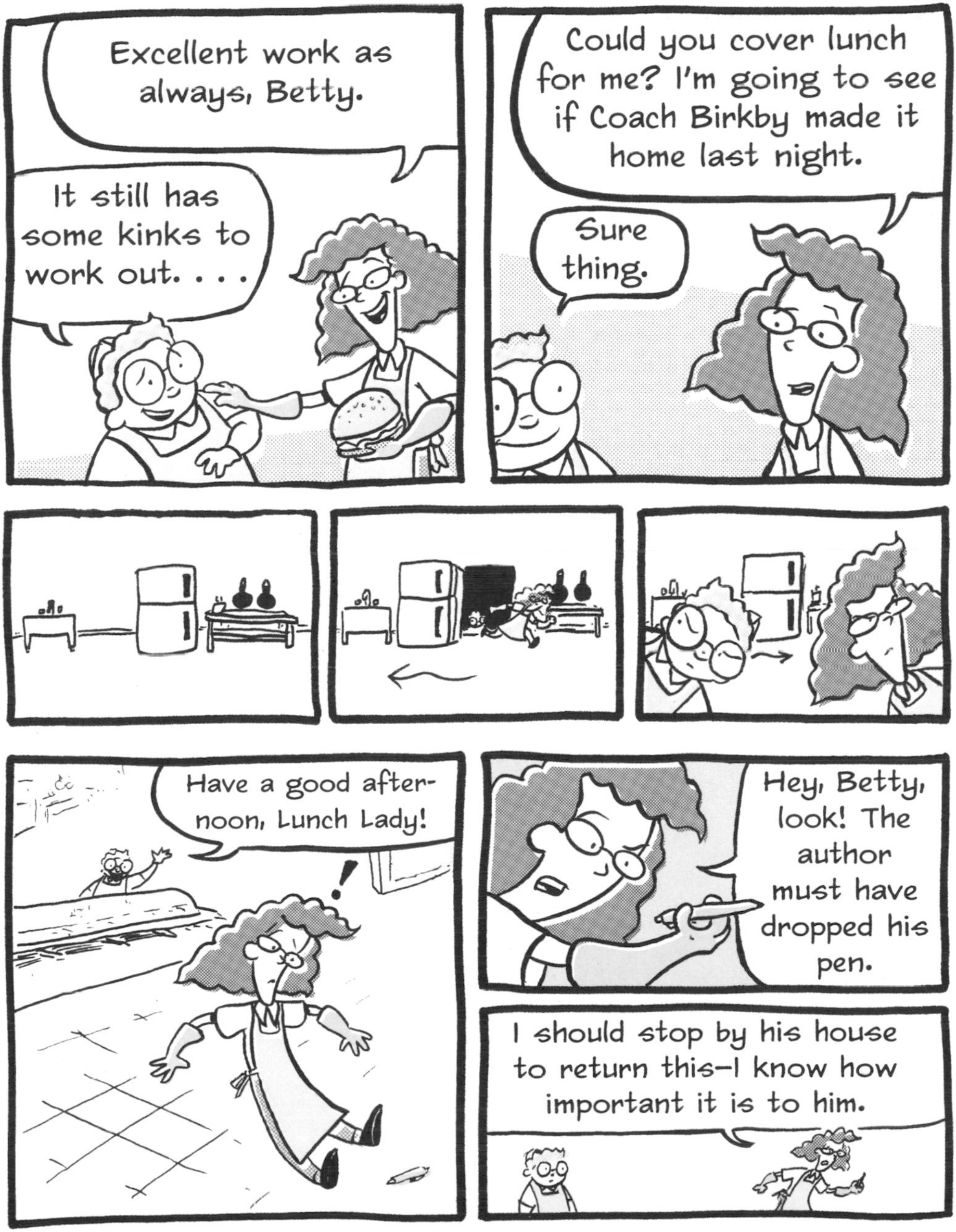

Excellent work as always, Betty.
It still has some kinks to work out. . . .
Could you cover lunch for me? I'm going to see if Coach Birkby made it home last night.
Sure thing.
Have a good after-noon, Lunch Lady!
!
Hey, Betty, look! The author must have dropped his pen.
I should stop by his house to return this—I know how important it is to him.

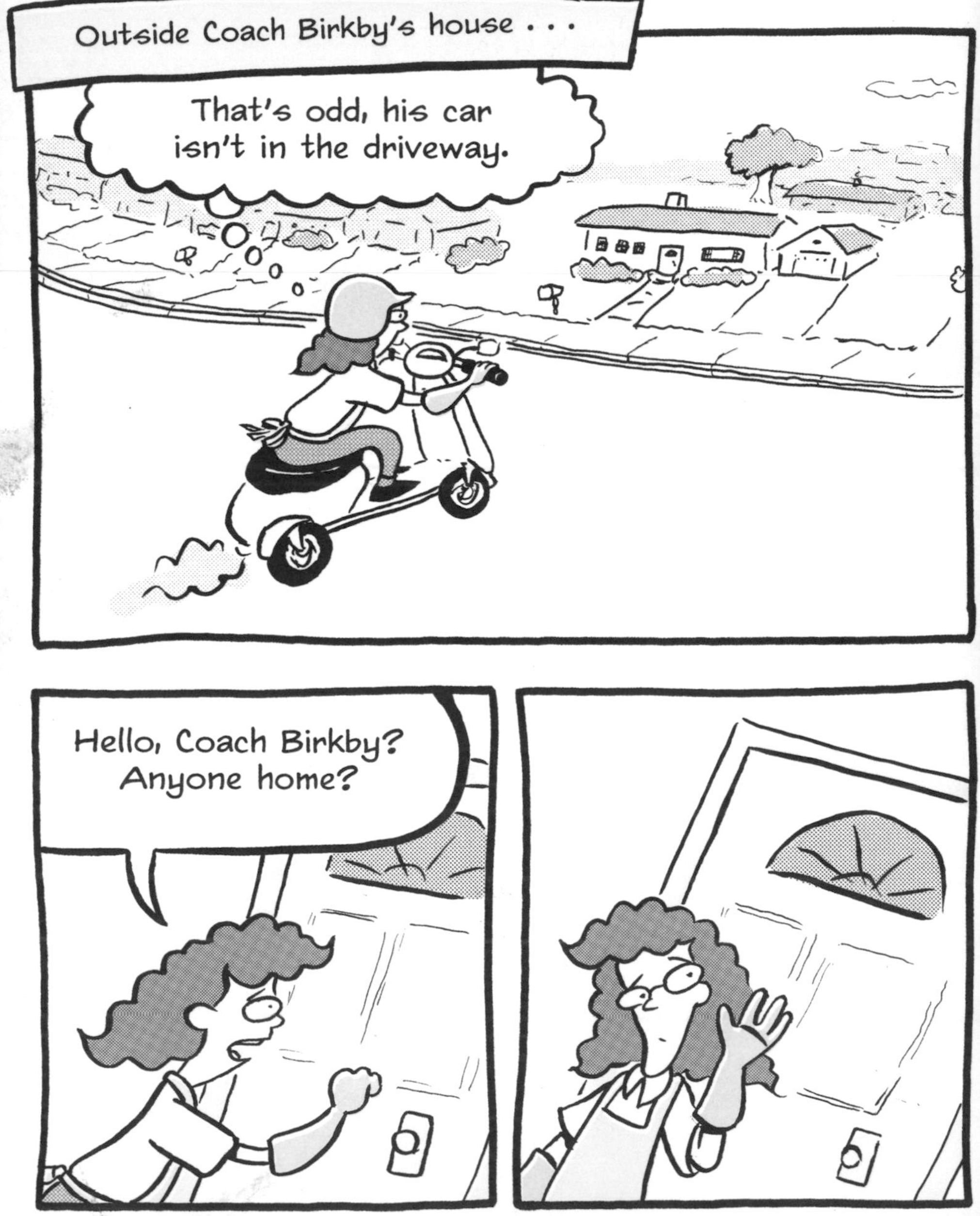

Outside Coach Birkby's house . . .
That's odd, his car isn't in the driveway.
Hello, Coach Birkby? Anyone home?

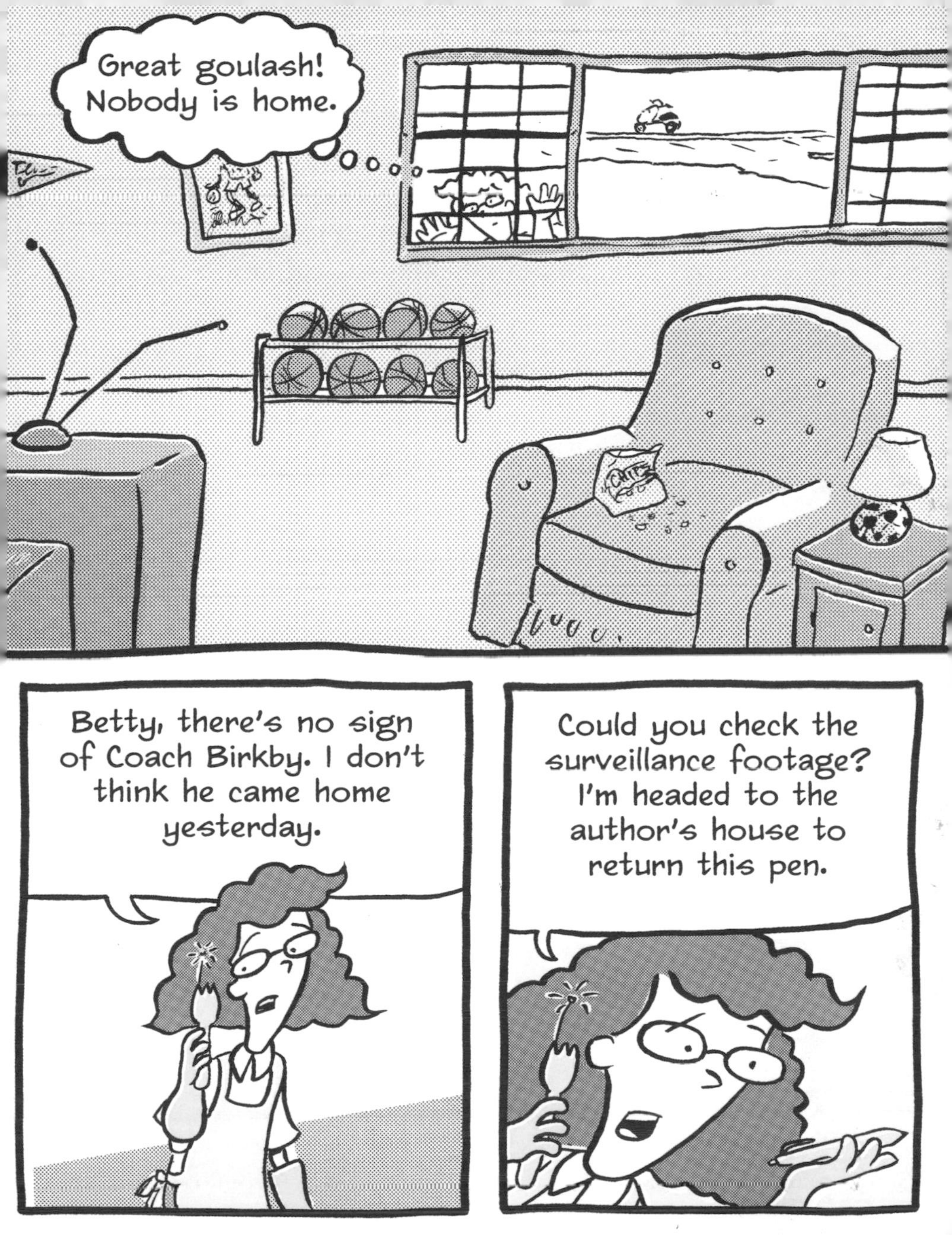
Great goulash! Nobody is home.
CHIPS
Betty, there's no sign of Coach Birkby. I don't think he came home yesterday.
Could you check the surveillance footage? I'm headed to the author's house to return this pen.

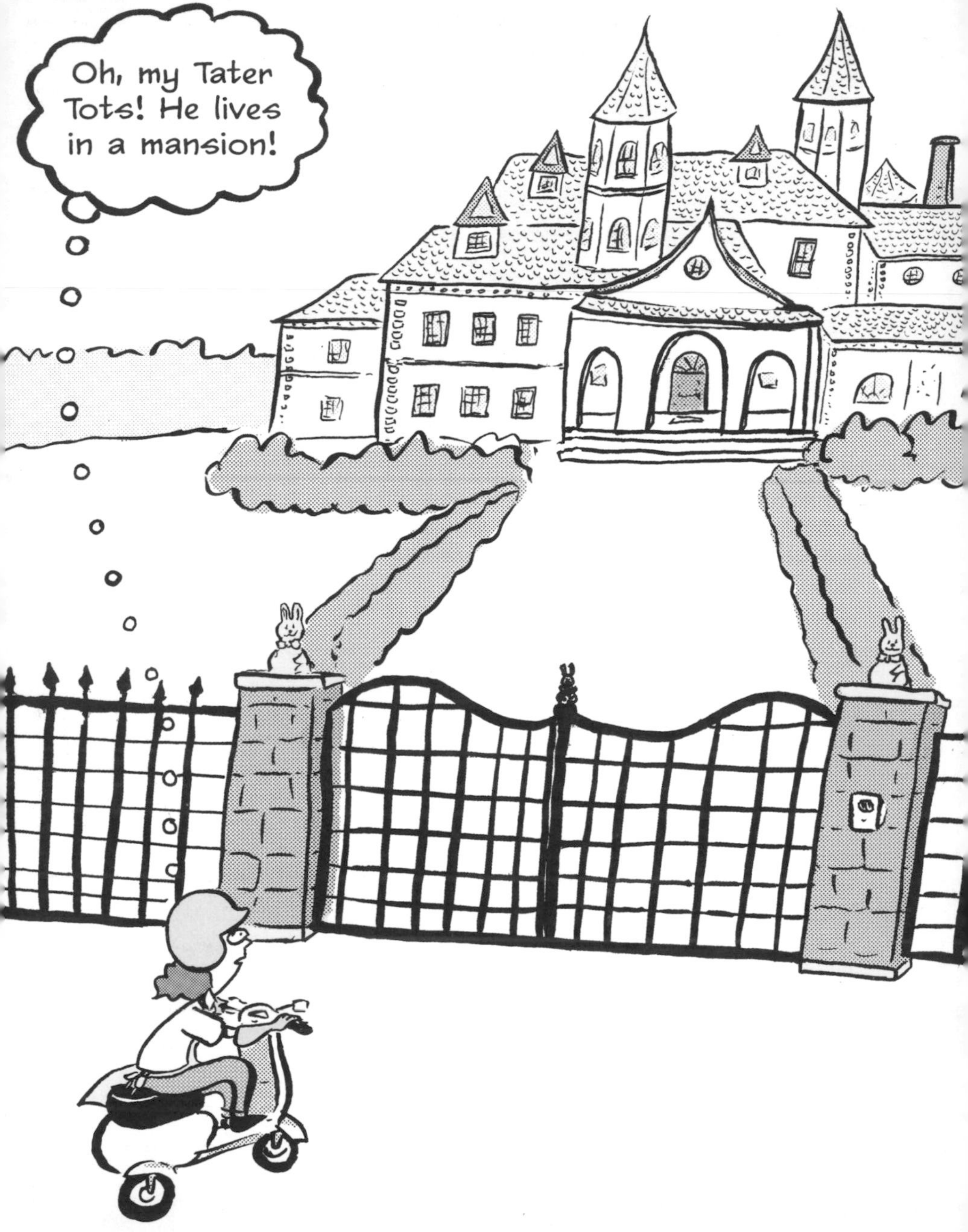
Oh, my Tater Tots! He lives in a mansion!

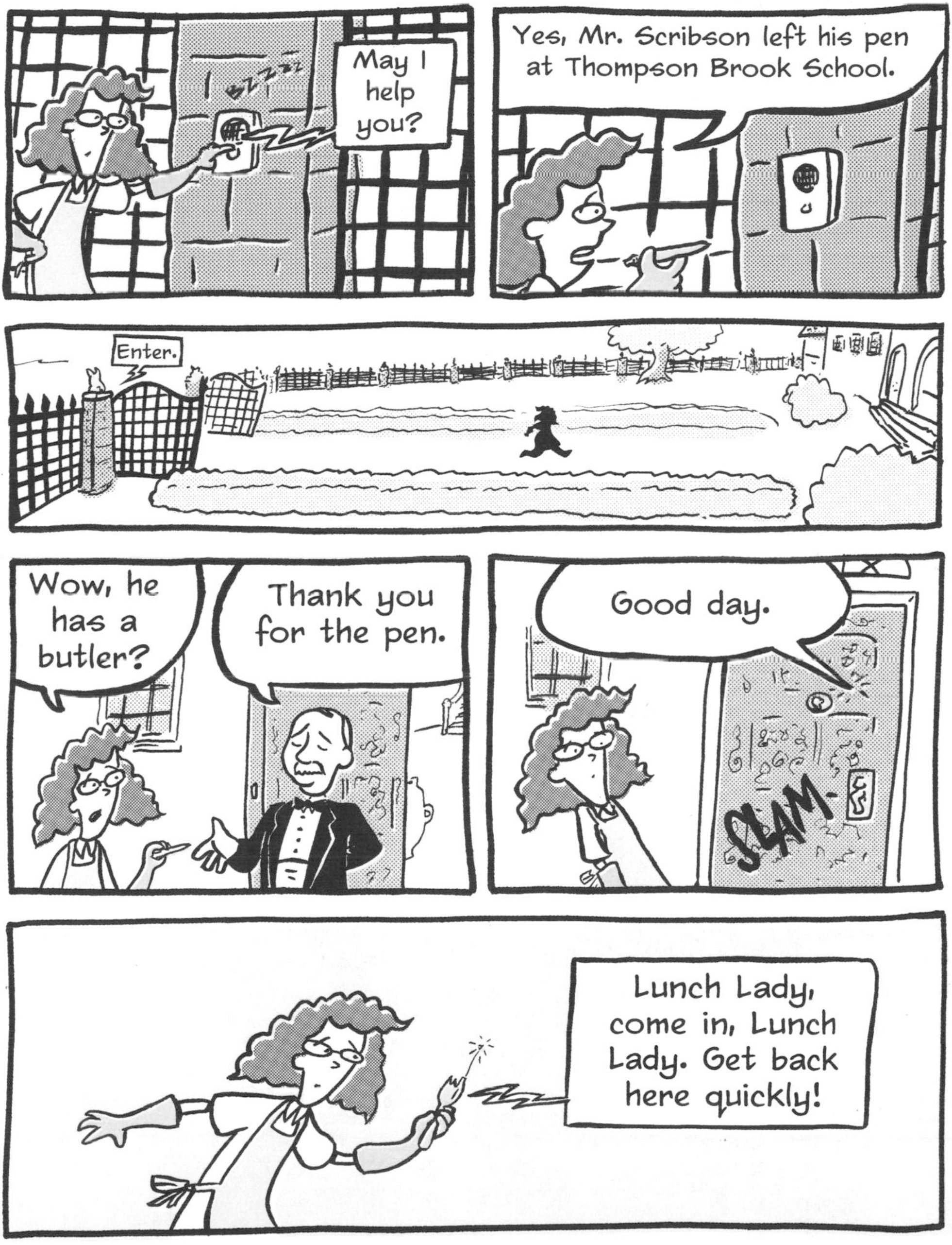
May I help you?
Yes, Mr. Scribson left his pen at Thompson Brook School.
Enter.
Wow, he has a butler?
Thank you for the pen.
Good day.
SLAM
Lunch Lady, come in, Lunch Lady. Get back here quickly!

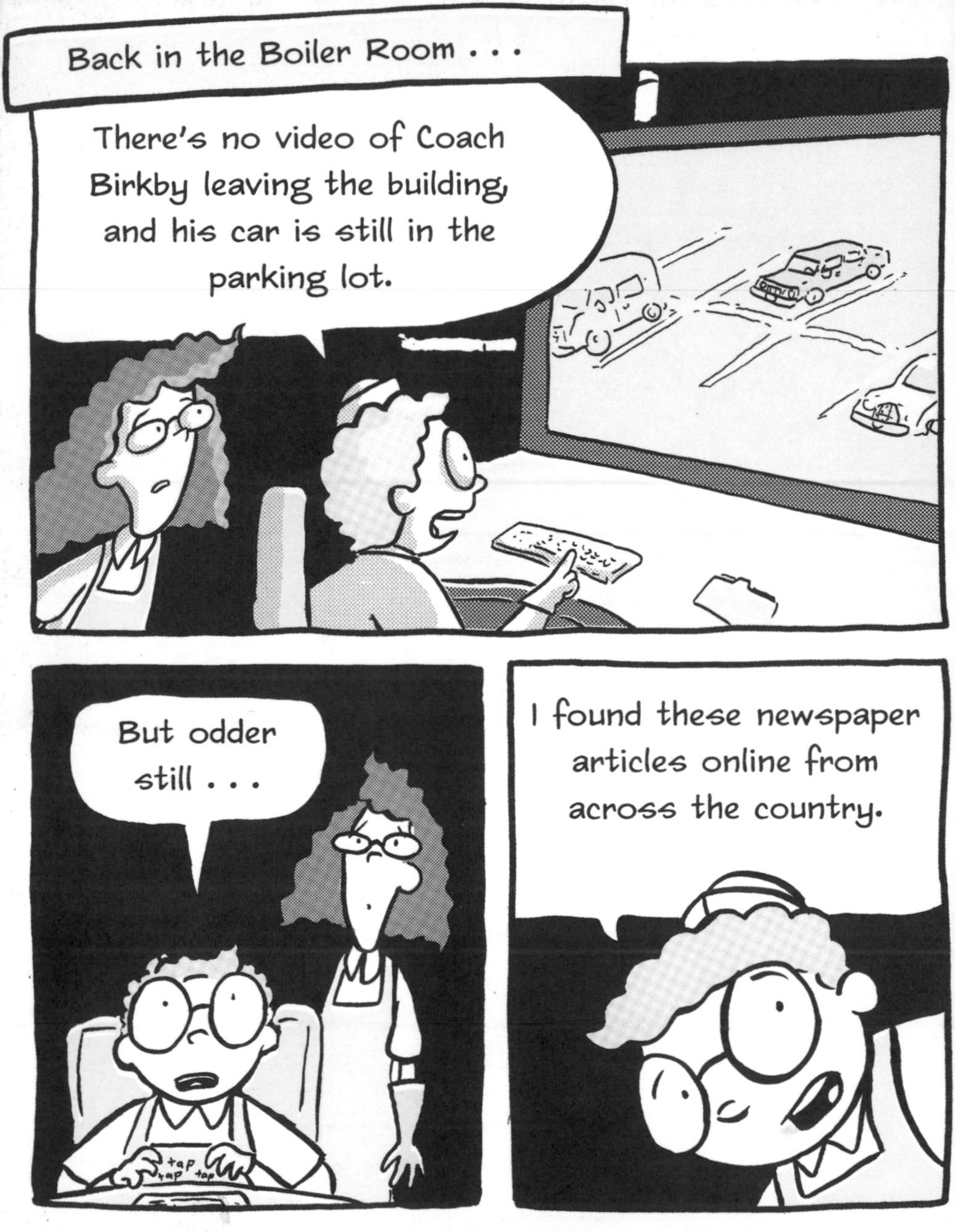
Back in the Boiler Room . . .
There's no video of Coach Birkby leaving the building, and his car is still in the parking lot.
But odder still . . .
tap tap tap
I found these newspaper articles online from across the country.

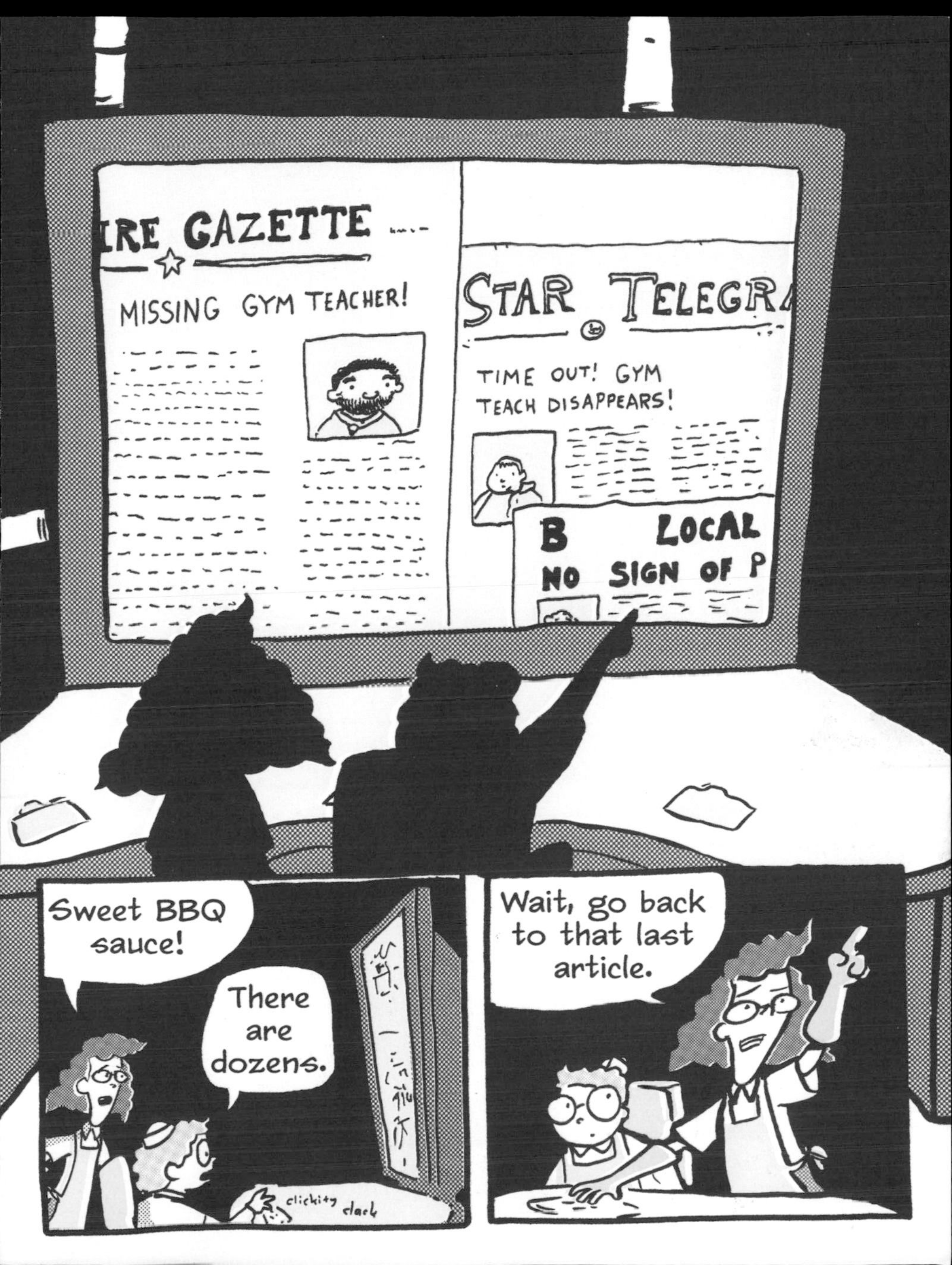
IRE GAZETTE
MISSING GYM TEACHER!
STAR TELEGRA
TIME OUT! GYM TEACH DISAPPEARS!
B LOCAL
NO SIGN OF P
Sweet BBQ sauce!
There are dozens.
clickity clack
Wait, go back to that last article.

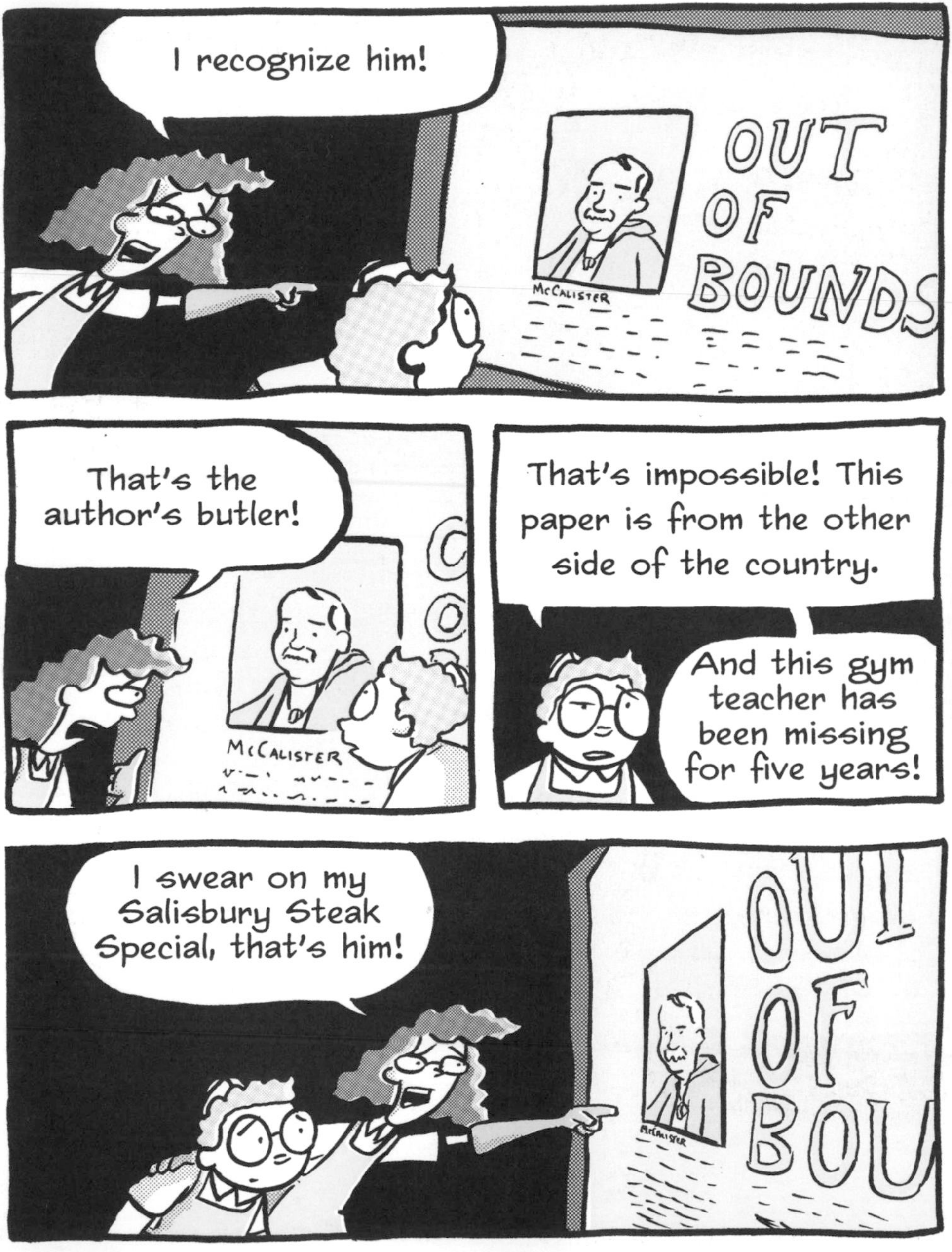
I recognize him!
OUT OF BOUNDS
McCALISTER
That's the author's butler!
McCALISTER
That's impossible! This paper is from the other side of the country.
And this gym teacher has been missing for five years!
I swear on my Salisbury Steak Special, that's him!
OF
BOU
McCALISTER

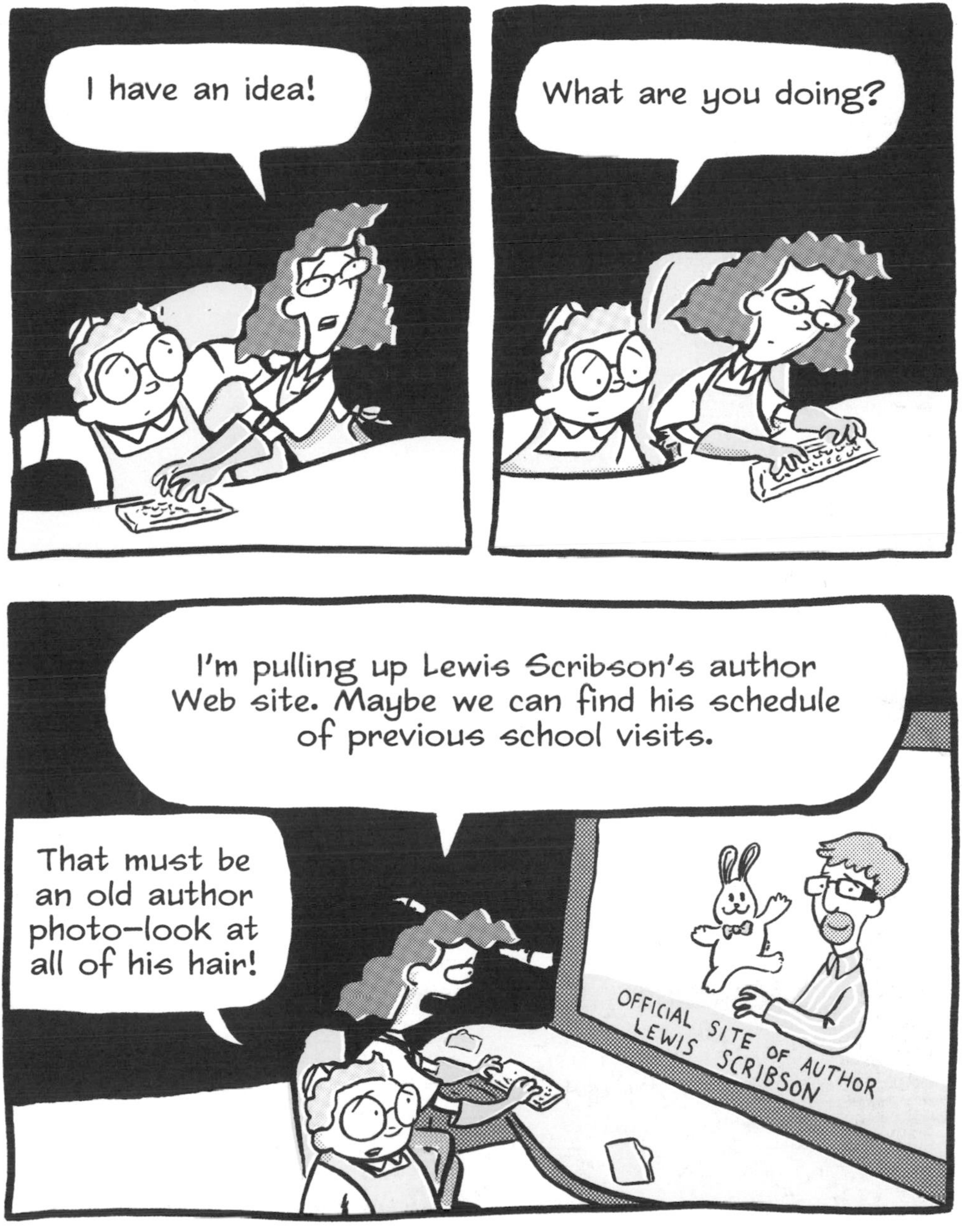
I have an idea!
What are you doing?
I'm pulling up Lewis Scribson's author Web site. Maybe we can find his schedule of previous school visits.
That must be an old author photo—look at all of his hair!
OFFICIAL SITE OF AUTHOR LEWIS SCRIBSON

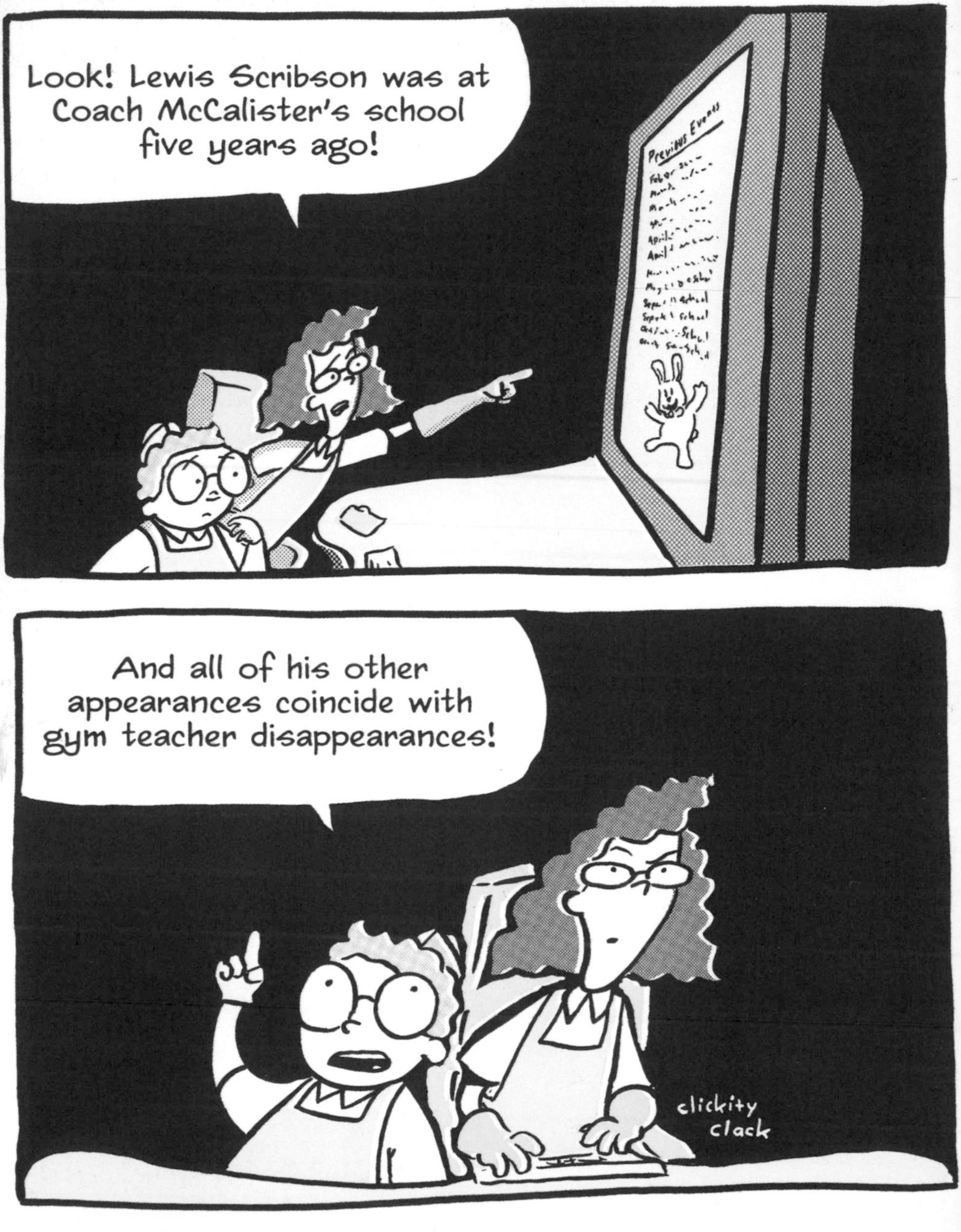
Look! Lewis Scribson was at Coach McCalister's school five years ago!
Previous Events
And all of his other appearances coincide with gym teacher disappearances!
clickity clack

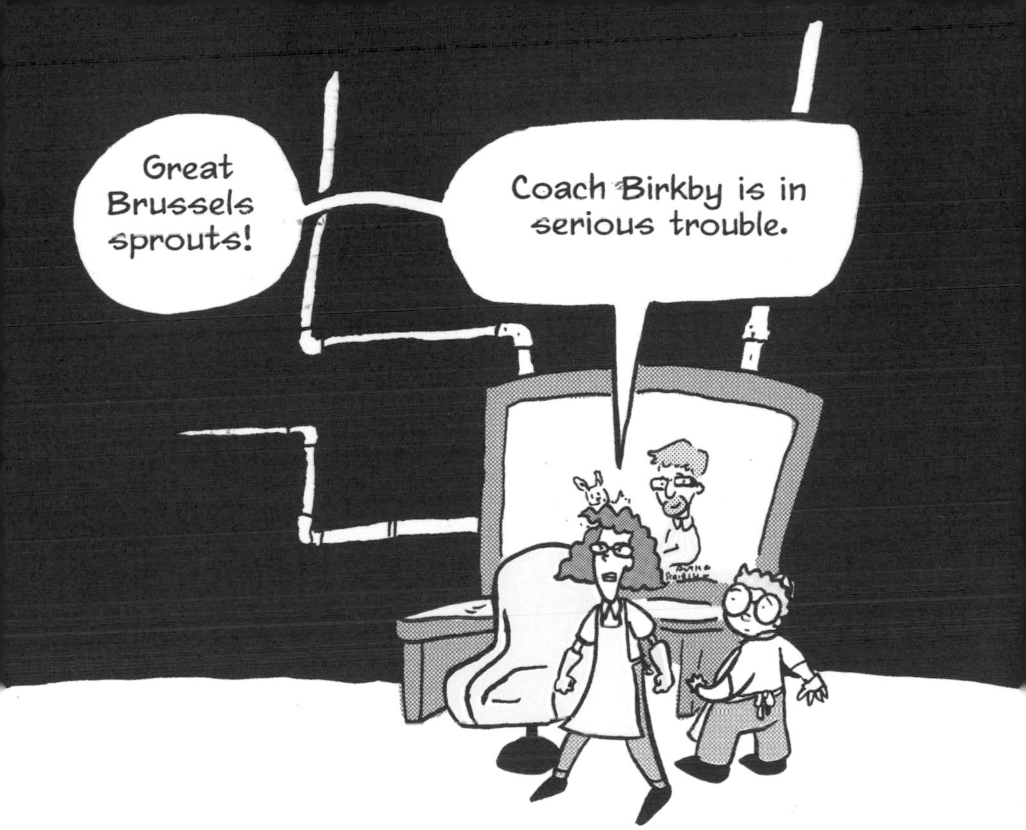
Great Brussels sprouts!
Coach Birkby is in serious trouble.

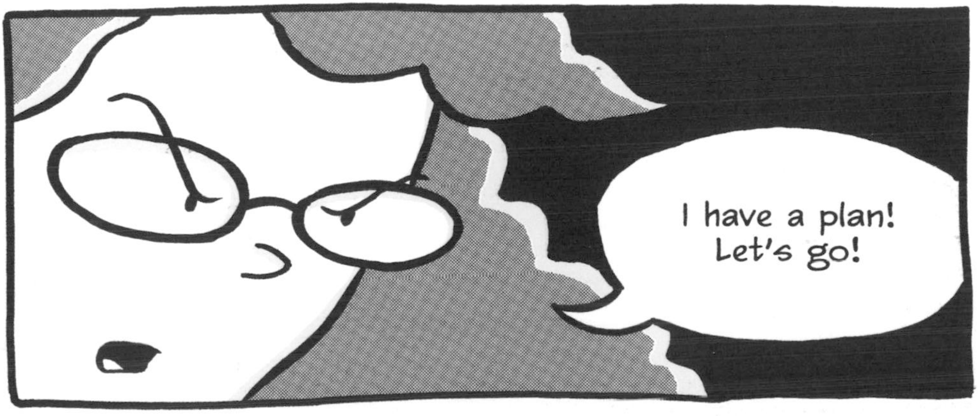
I have a plan! Let's go!

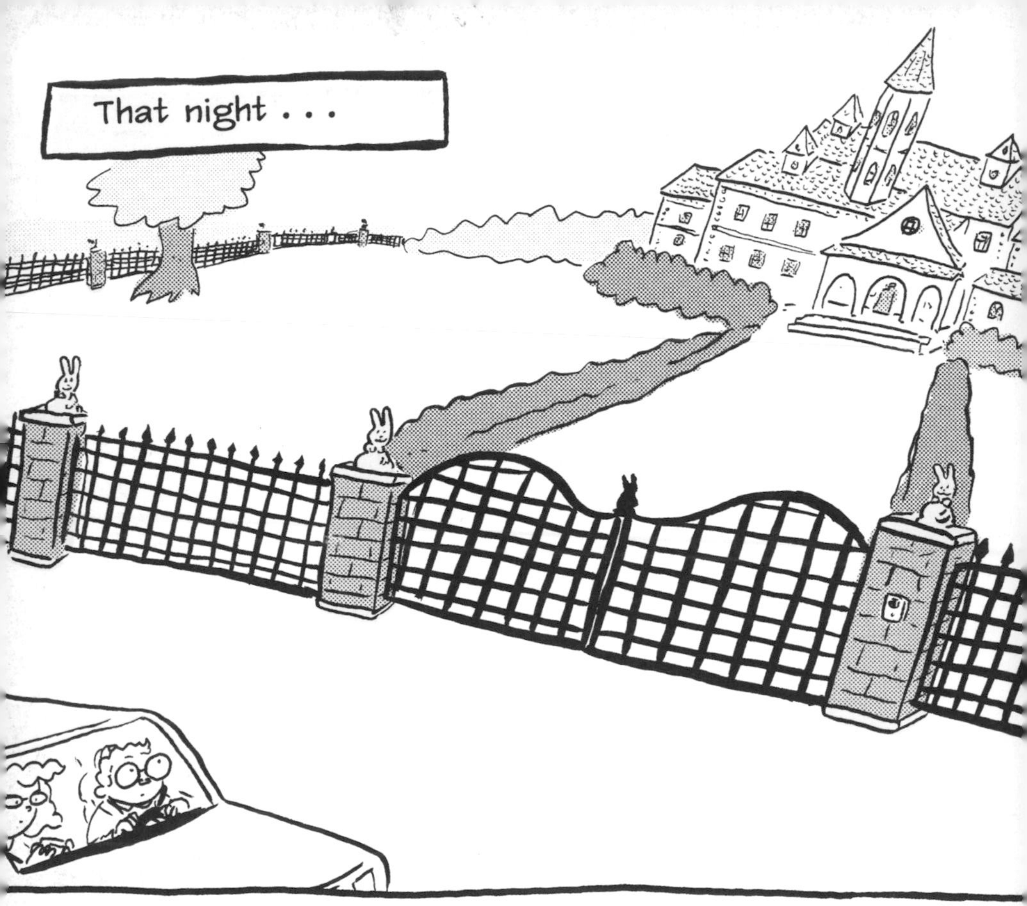
That night . . .

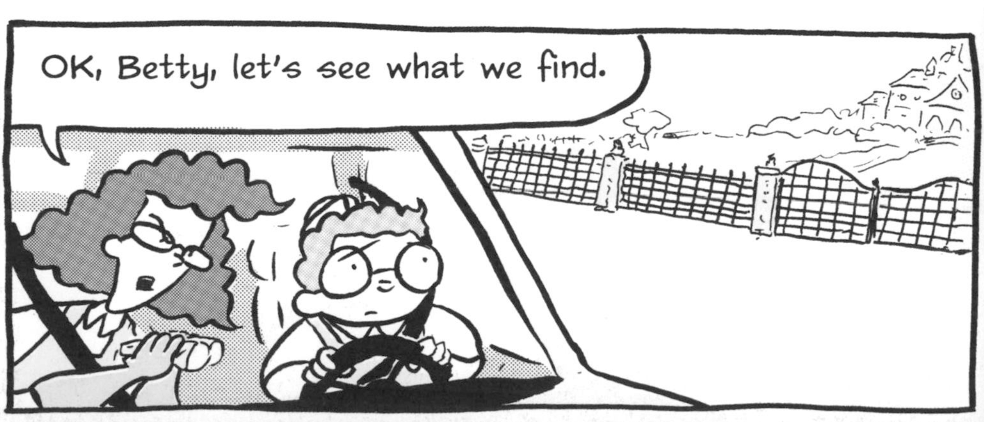
OK, Betty, let's see what we find.

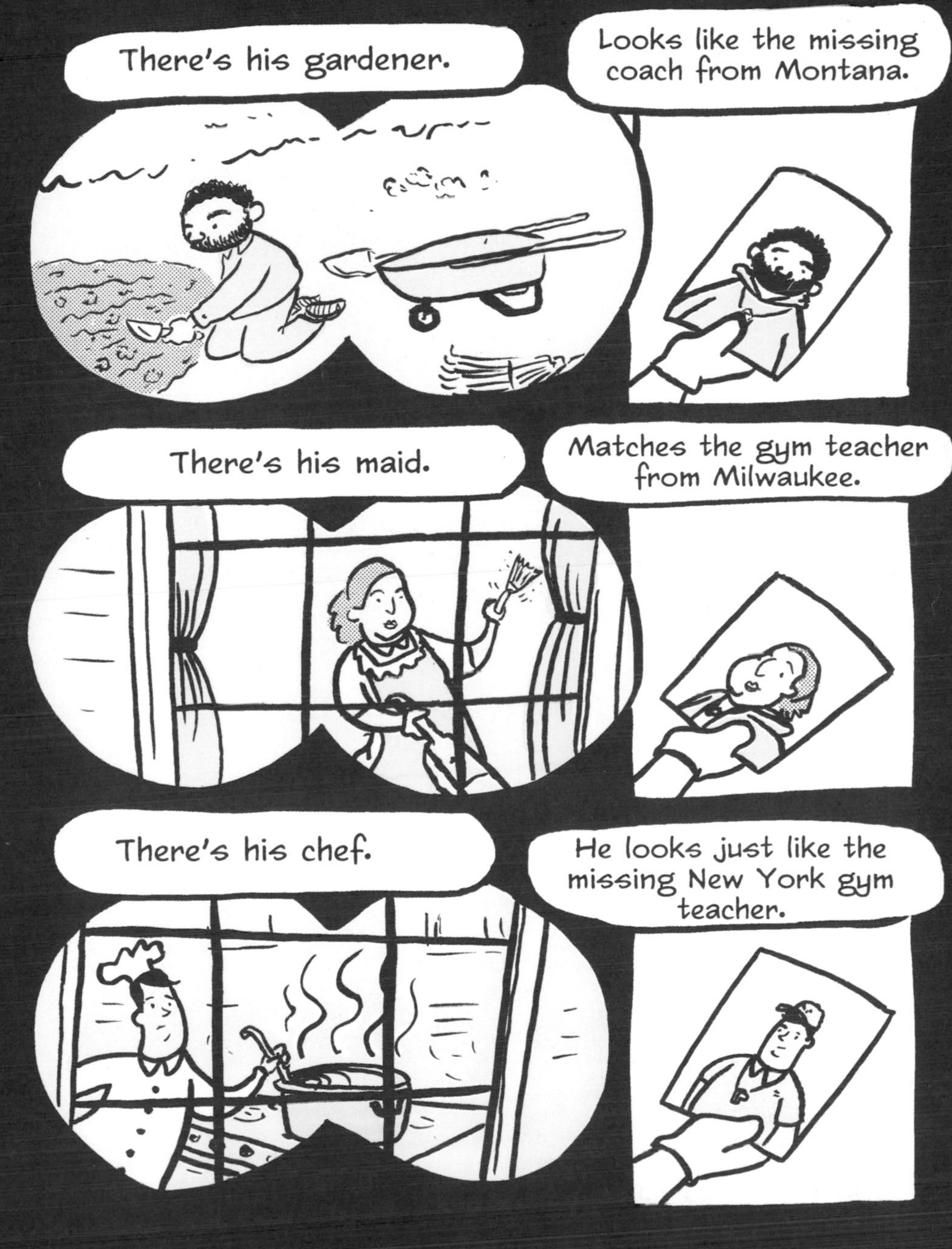
There's his gardener.
Looks like the missing coach from Montana.
There's his maid.
Matches the gym teacher from Milwaukee.
There's his chef.
He looks just like the missing New York gym teacher.

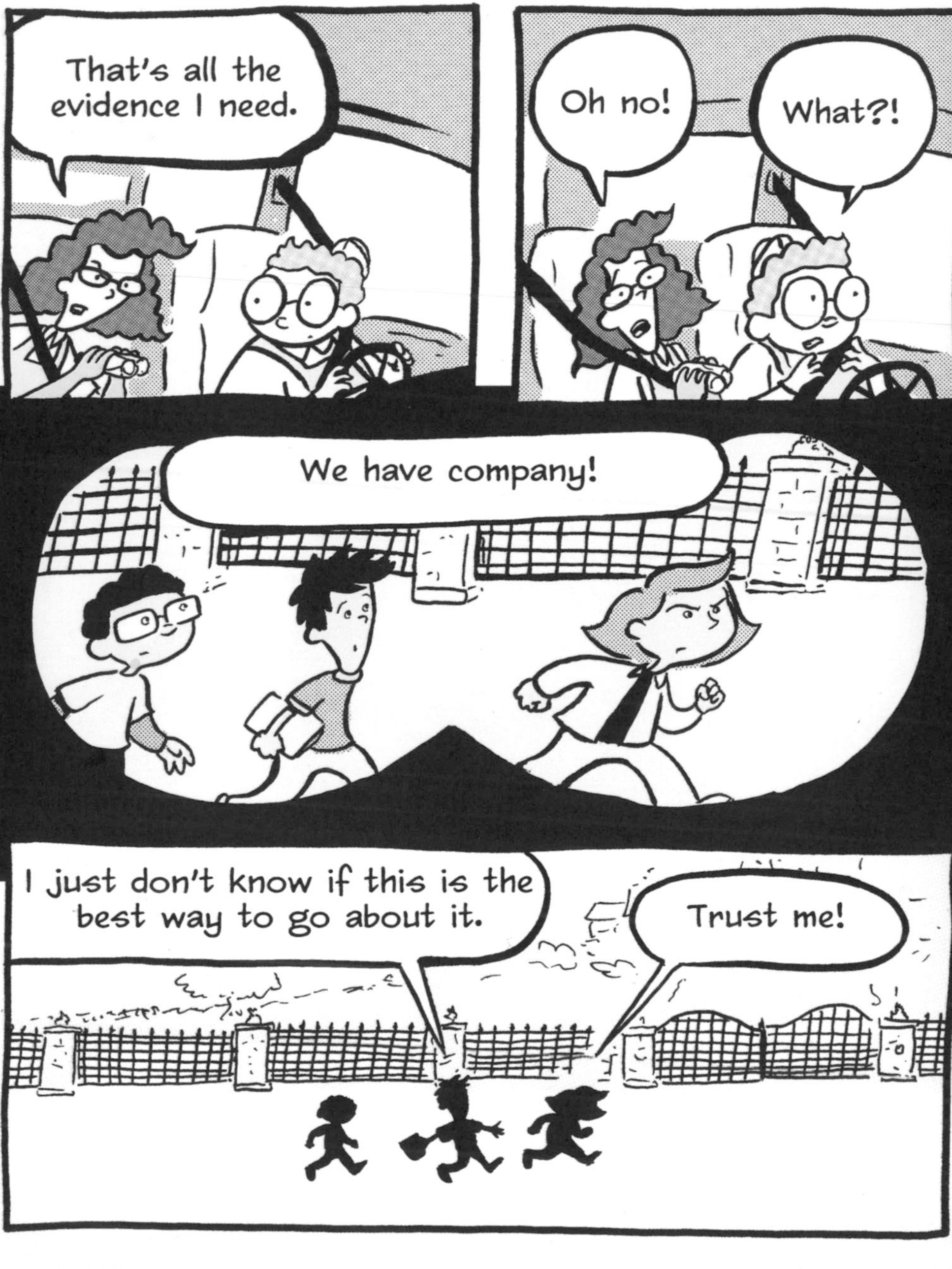
That's all the evidence I need.
Oh no!
What?!
We have company!
I just don't know if this is the best way to go about it.
Trust me!

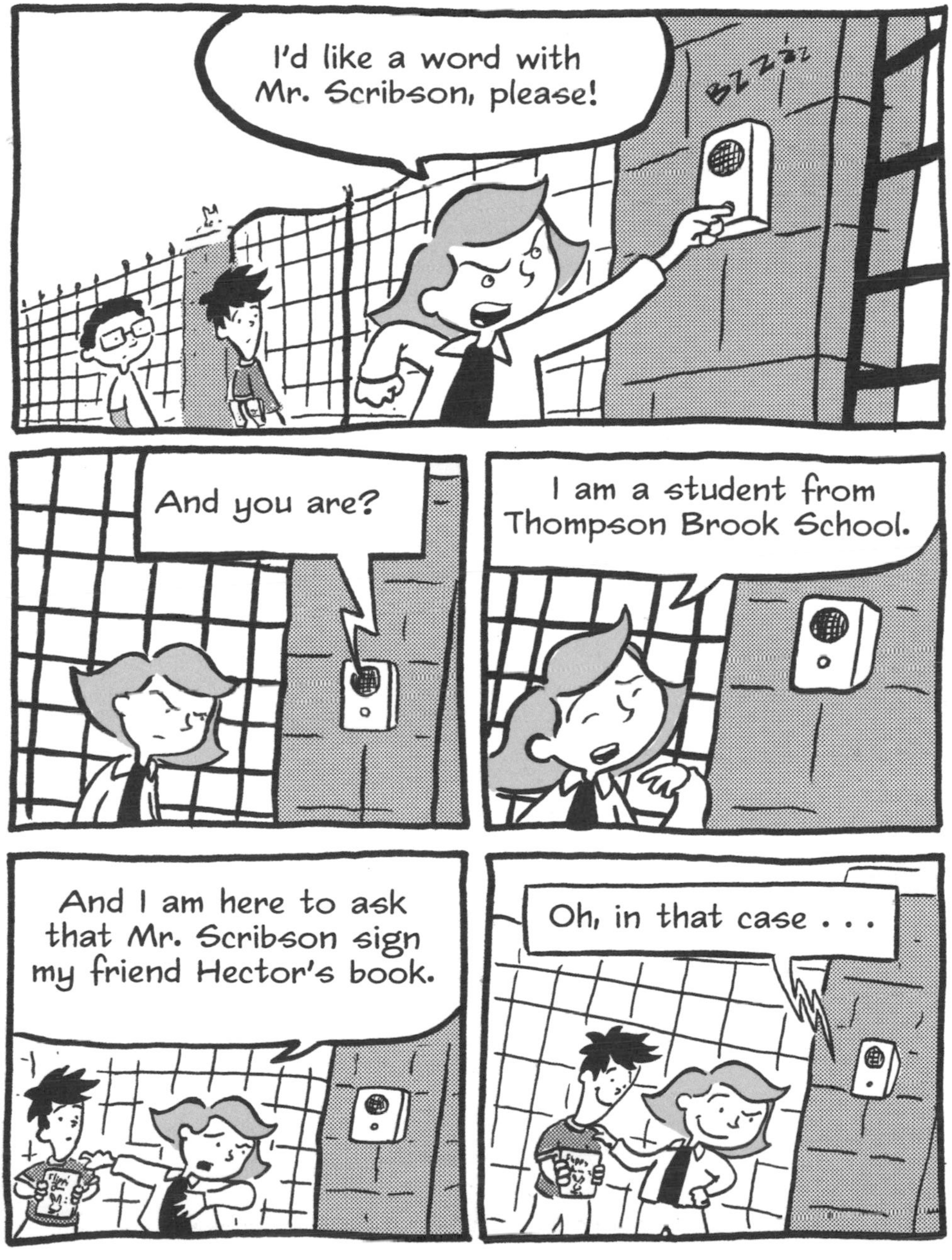
I'd like a word with Mr. Scribson, please!
BZZZzz
And you are?
I am a student from Thompson Brook School.
And I am here to ask that Mr. Scribson sign my friend Hector's book.
Oh, in that case . . .

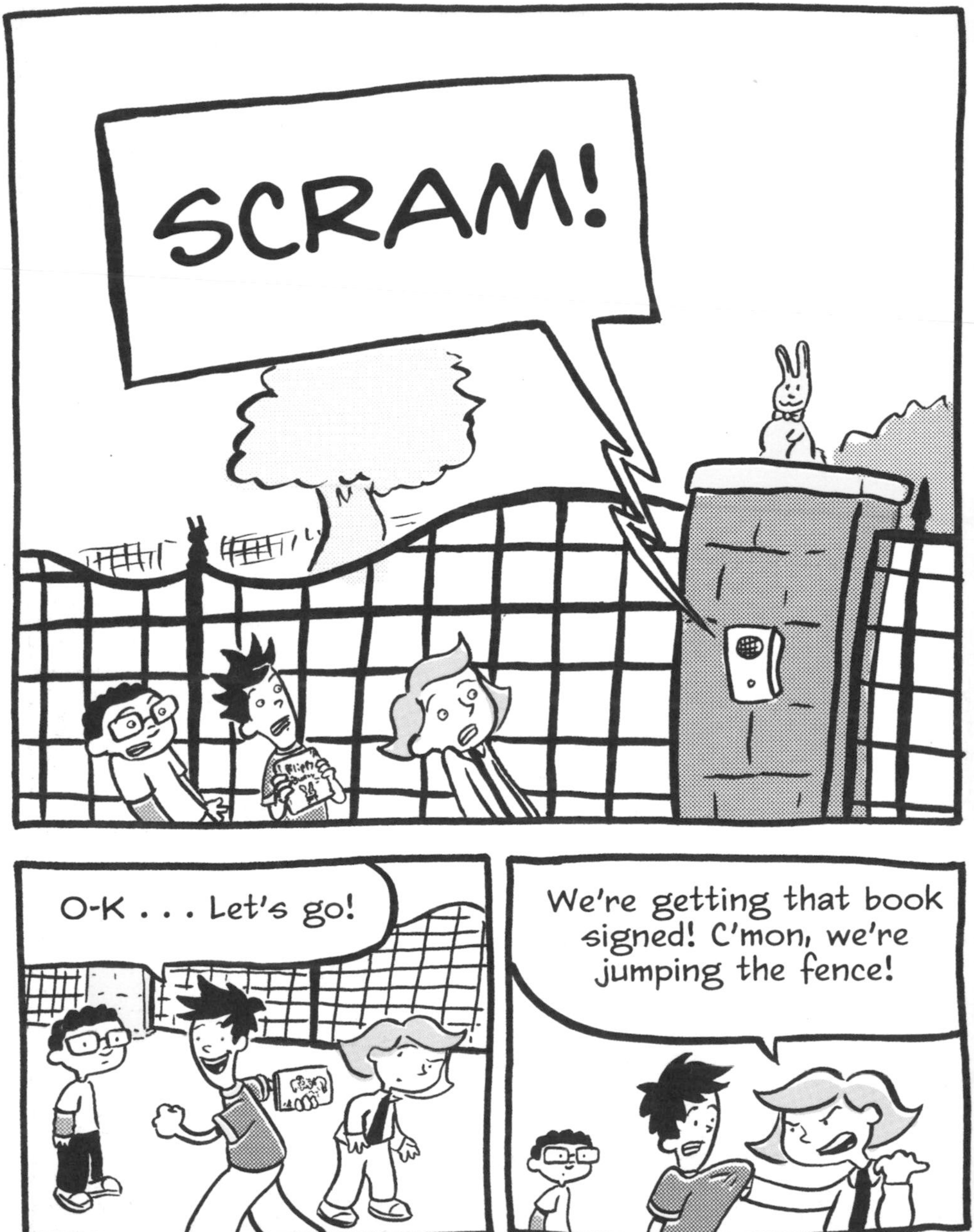
SCRAM!
O-K . . . Let's go!
We're getting that book signed! C'mon, we're jumping the fence!

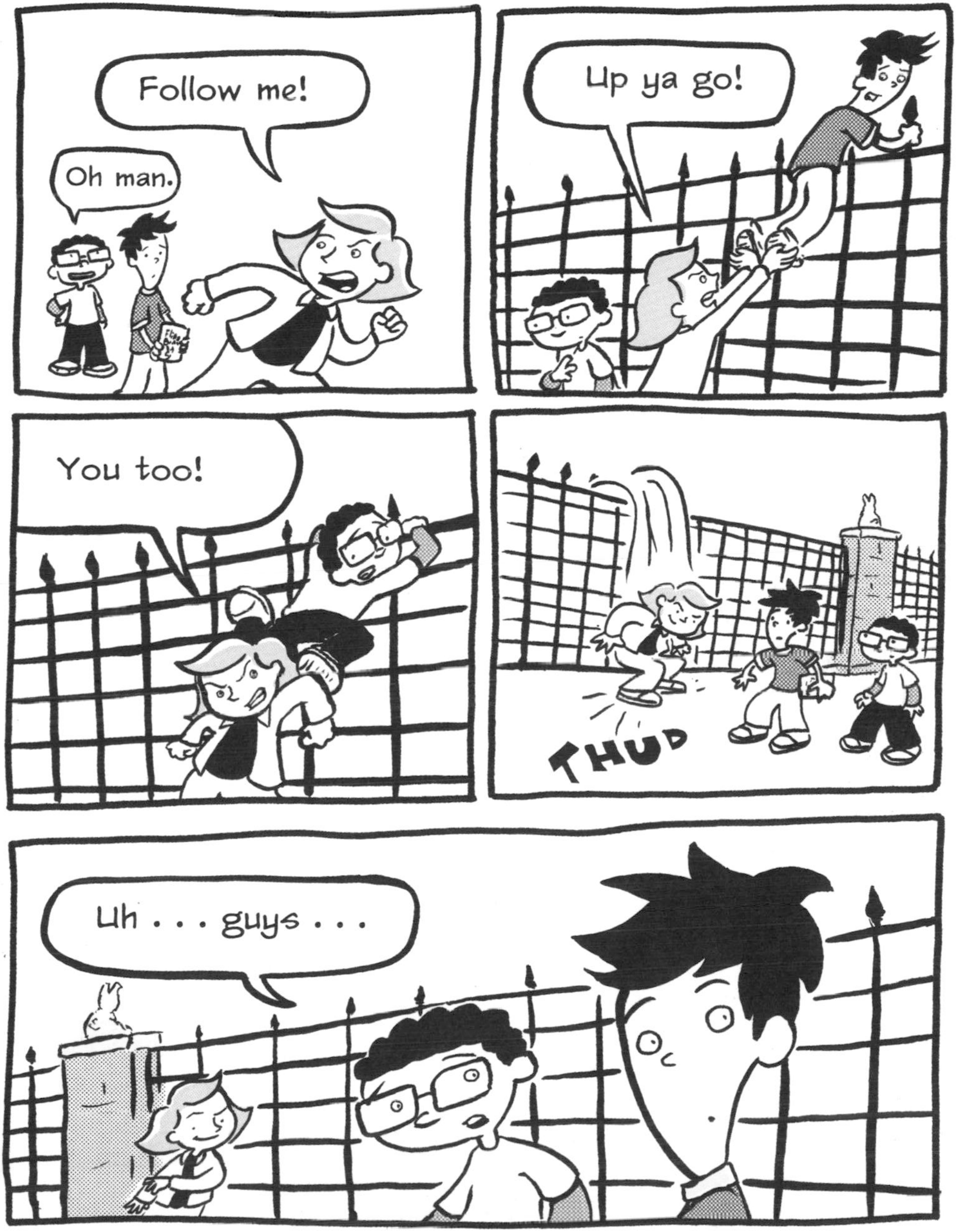
Oh man.
Follow me!
Up ya go!
You too!
THUD
Uh . . . guys . . .

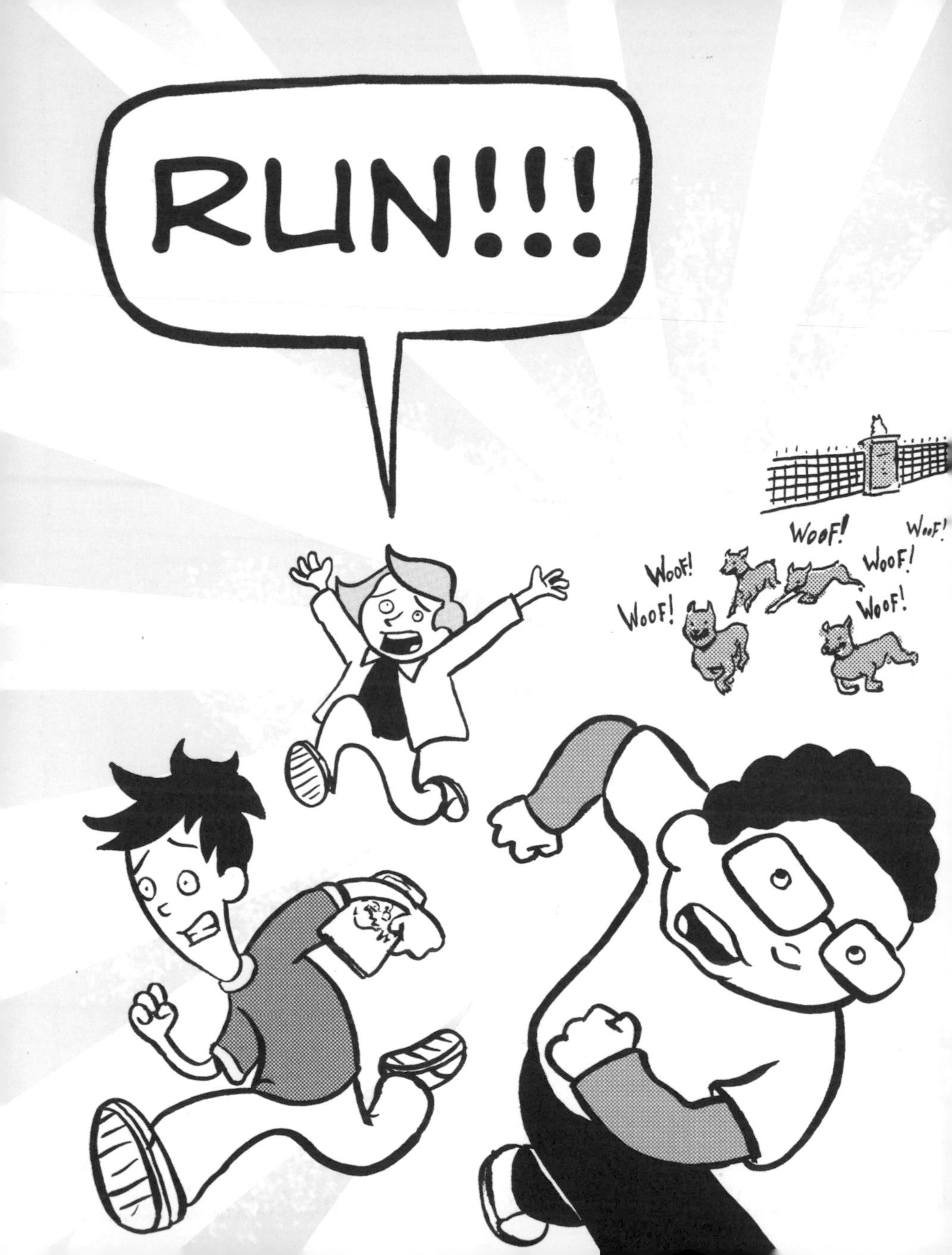
RUN!!!
WOOF!
WOOF!
WOOF!
WOOF!
WOOF!
WOOF!

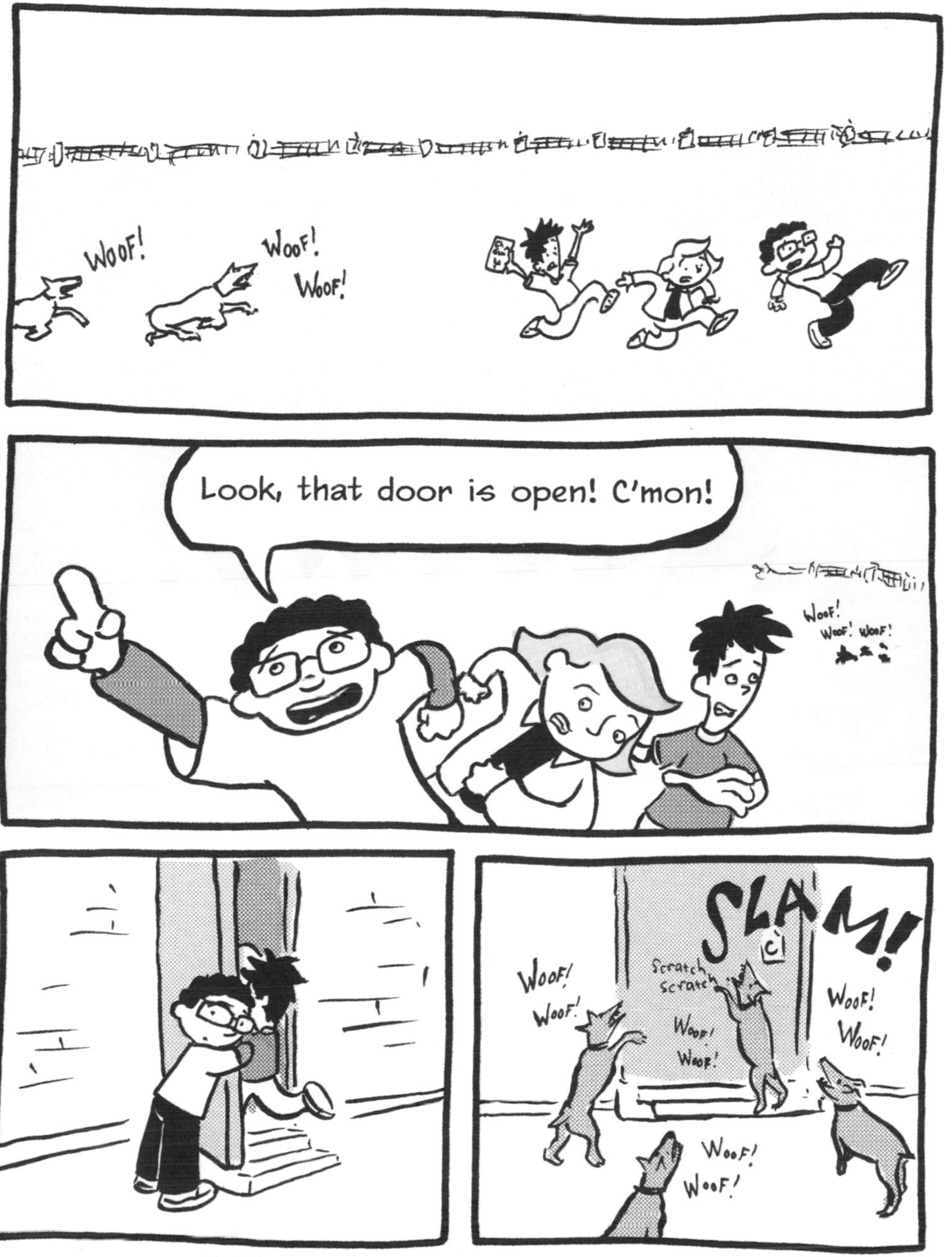
WOOF!
WOOF!
WOOF!
Look, that door is open! C'mon!
WOOF! WOOF! WOOF!
SLAM!
WOOF! WOOF!
Scratch scratch
WOOF! WOOF!
WOOF! WOOF!
WOOF! WOOF!

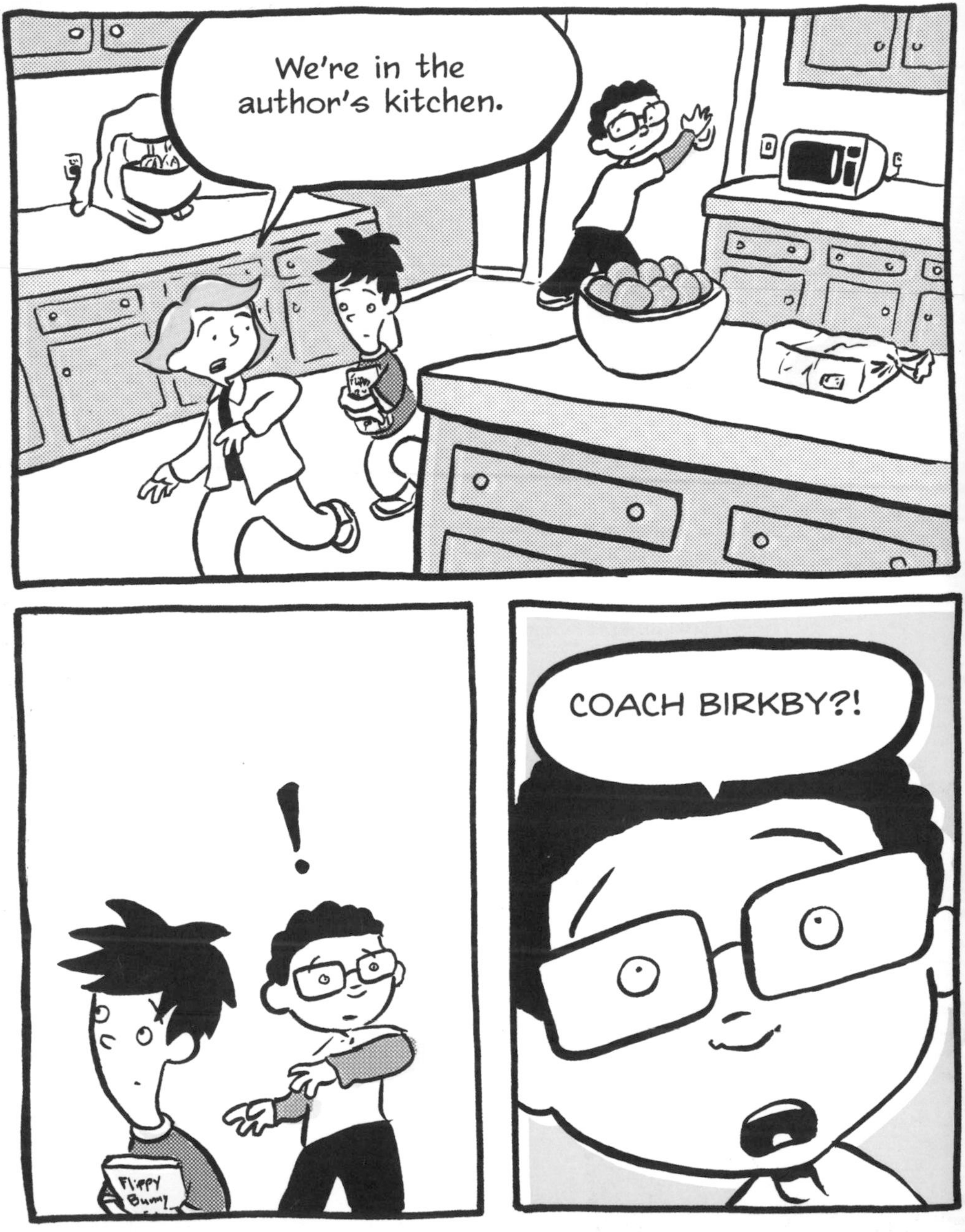
We're in the author's kitchen.
!
Flippy Bunny
COACH BIRKBY?!

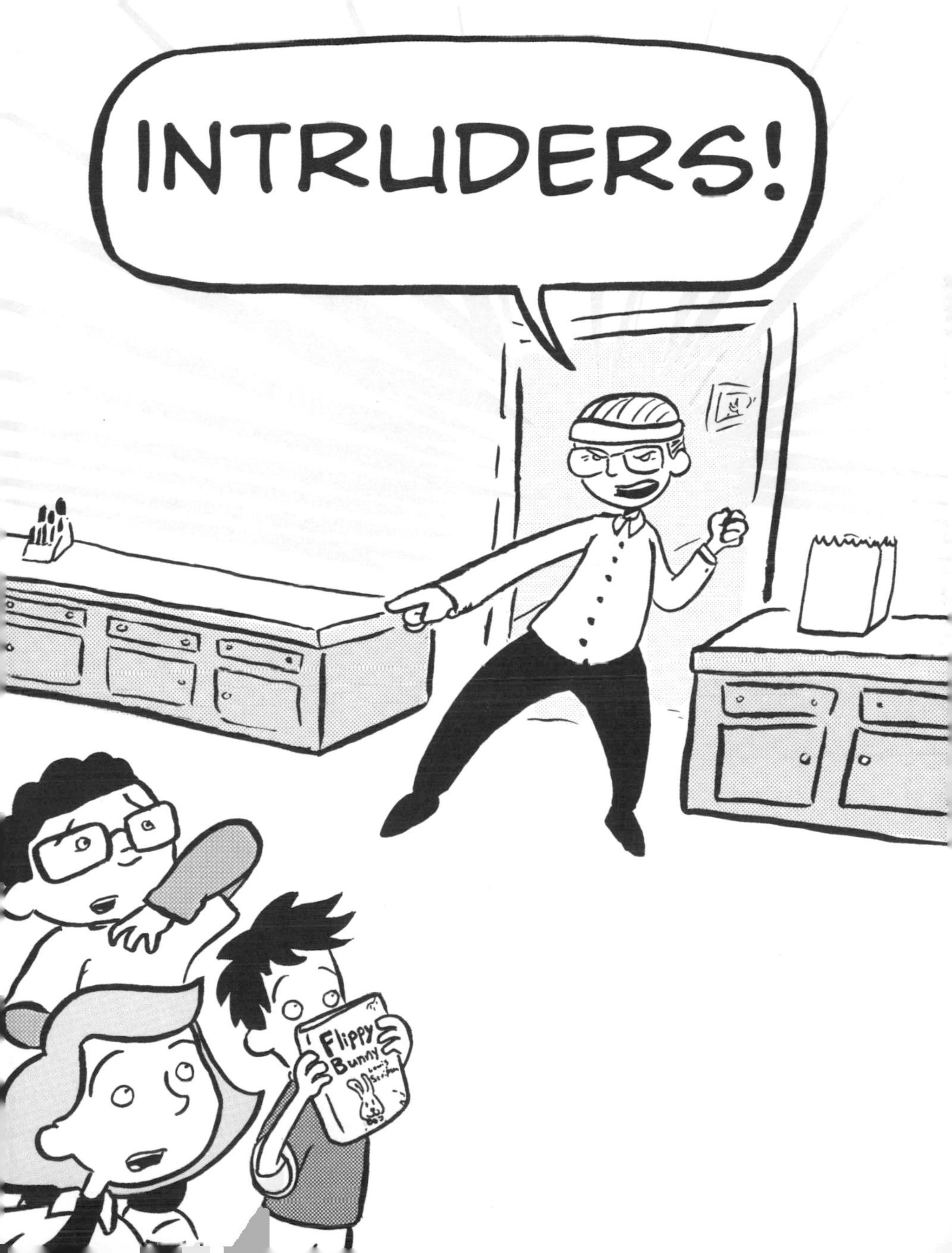
INTRUDERS!
Flippy Bunny

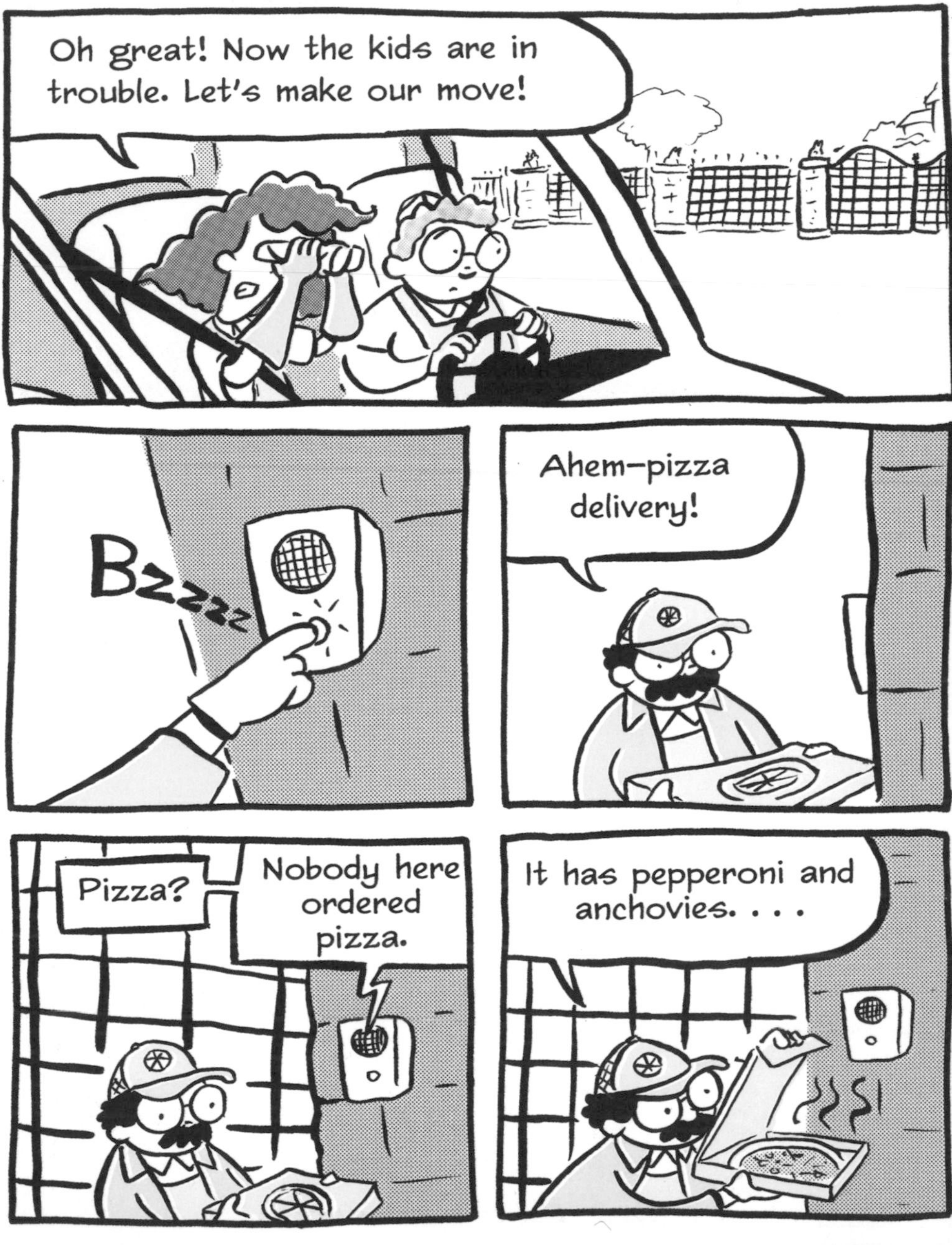
Oh great! Now the kids are in trouble. Let's make our move!
Bzzzzz
Ahem—pizza delivery!
Pizza?
Nobody here ordered pizza.
It has pepperoni and anchovies. . . .

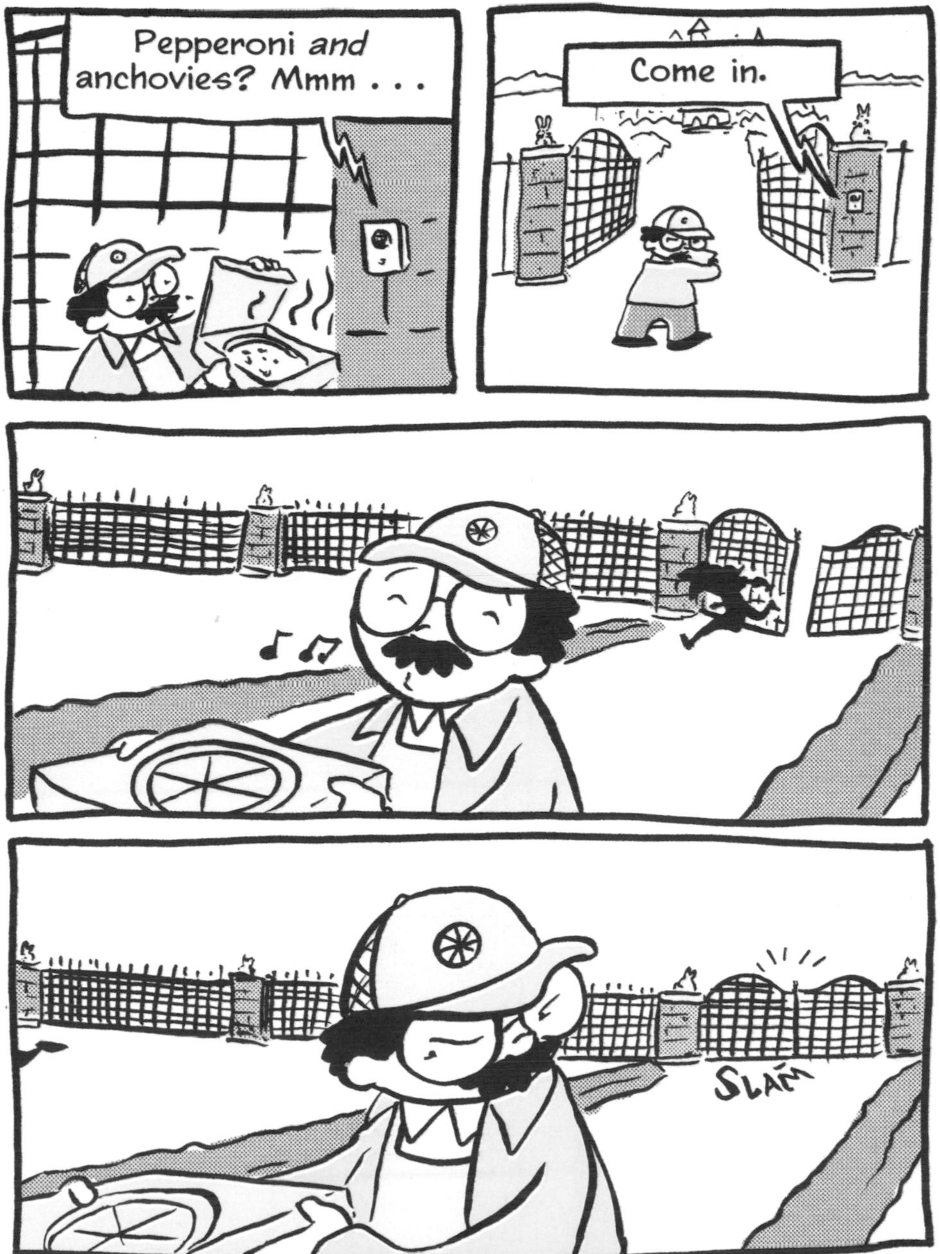
Pepperoni *and* anchovies? Mmm . . .
Come in.
SLAM

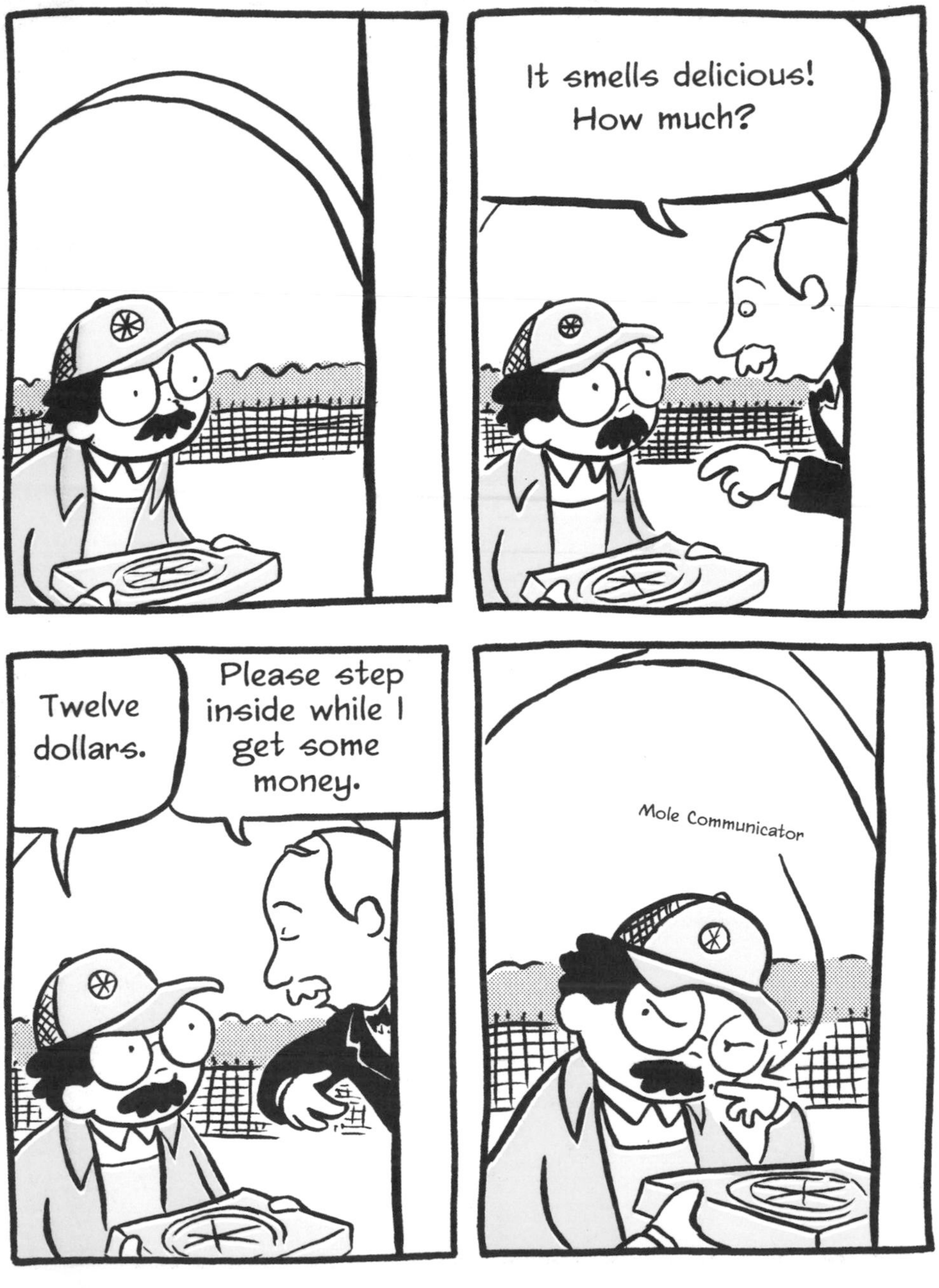
It smells delicious! How much?
Twelve dollars.
Please step inside while I get some money.
Mole Communicator

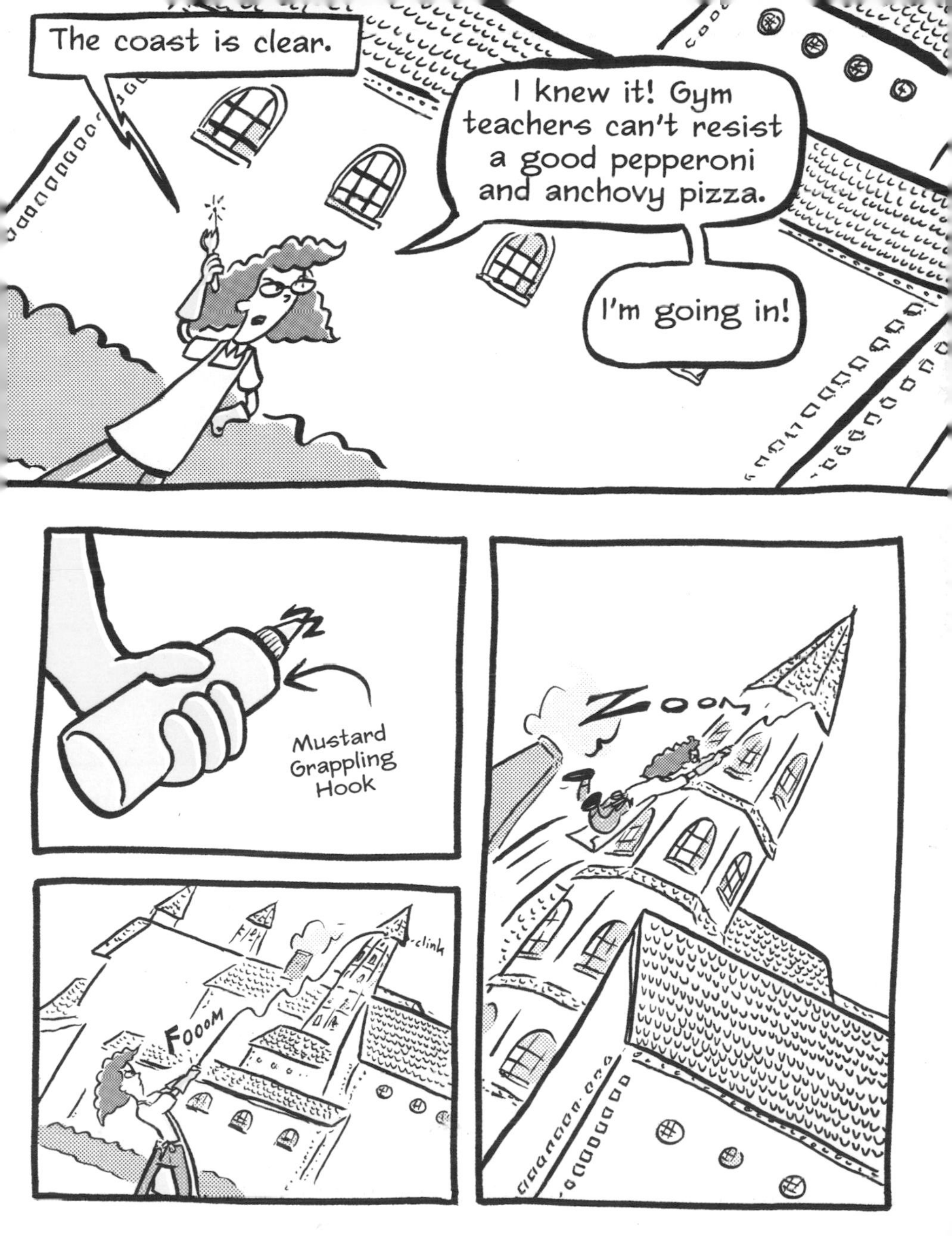

The coast is clear.
I knew it! Gym teachers can't resist a good pepperoni and anchovy pizza.
I'm going in!
Mustard Grappling Hook
ZOOM
FOOOM
clink

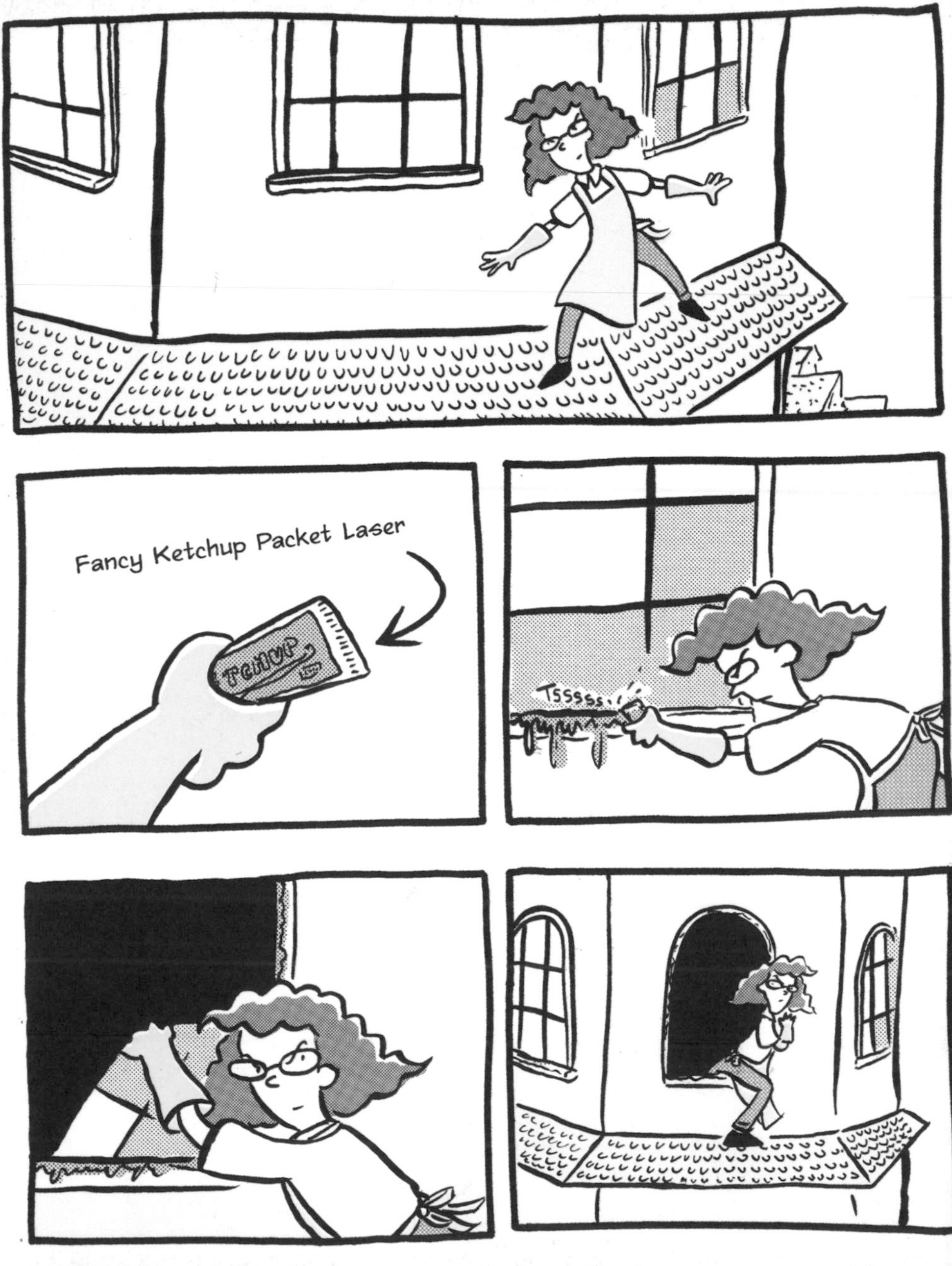
Fancy Ketchup Packet Laser
Tsssss

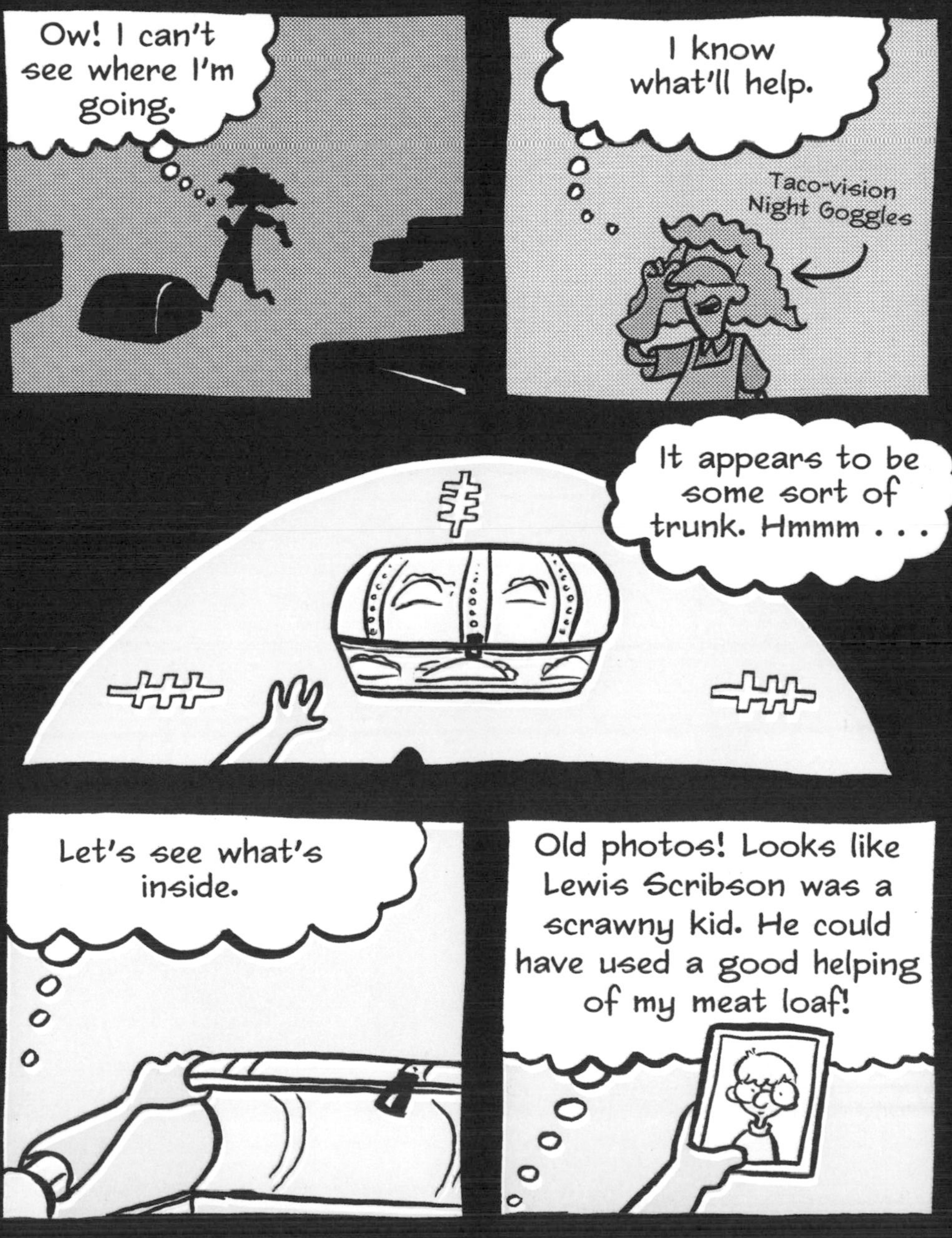
Ow! I can't see where I'm going.
I know what'll help.
Taco-vision Night Goggles
It appears to be some sort of trunk. Hmmm . . .
Let's see what's inside.
Old photos! Looks like Lewis Scribson was a scrawny kid. He could have used a good helping of my meat loaf!

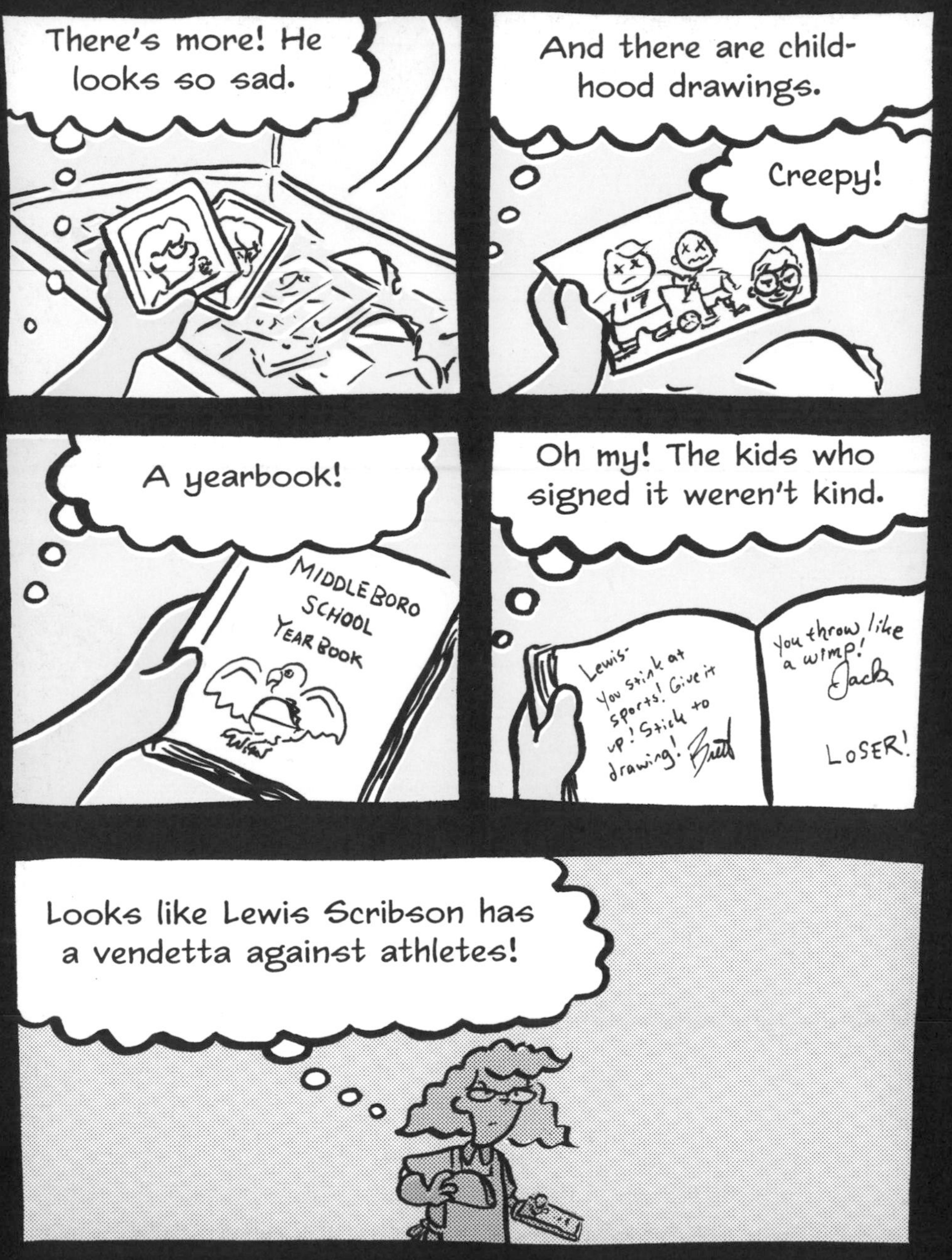

There's more! He looks so sad.
And there are child-hood drawings.
Creepy!
A yearbook!
MIDDLE BORO SCHOOL YEAR BOOK
Oh my! The kids who signed it weren't kind.
Lewis- You stink at sports! Give it up! Stick to drawing!
You throw like a wimp!
LOSER!
Looks like Lewis Scribson has a vendetta against athletes!

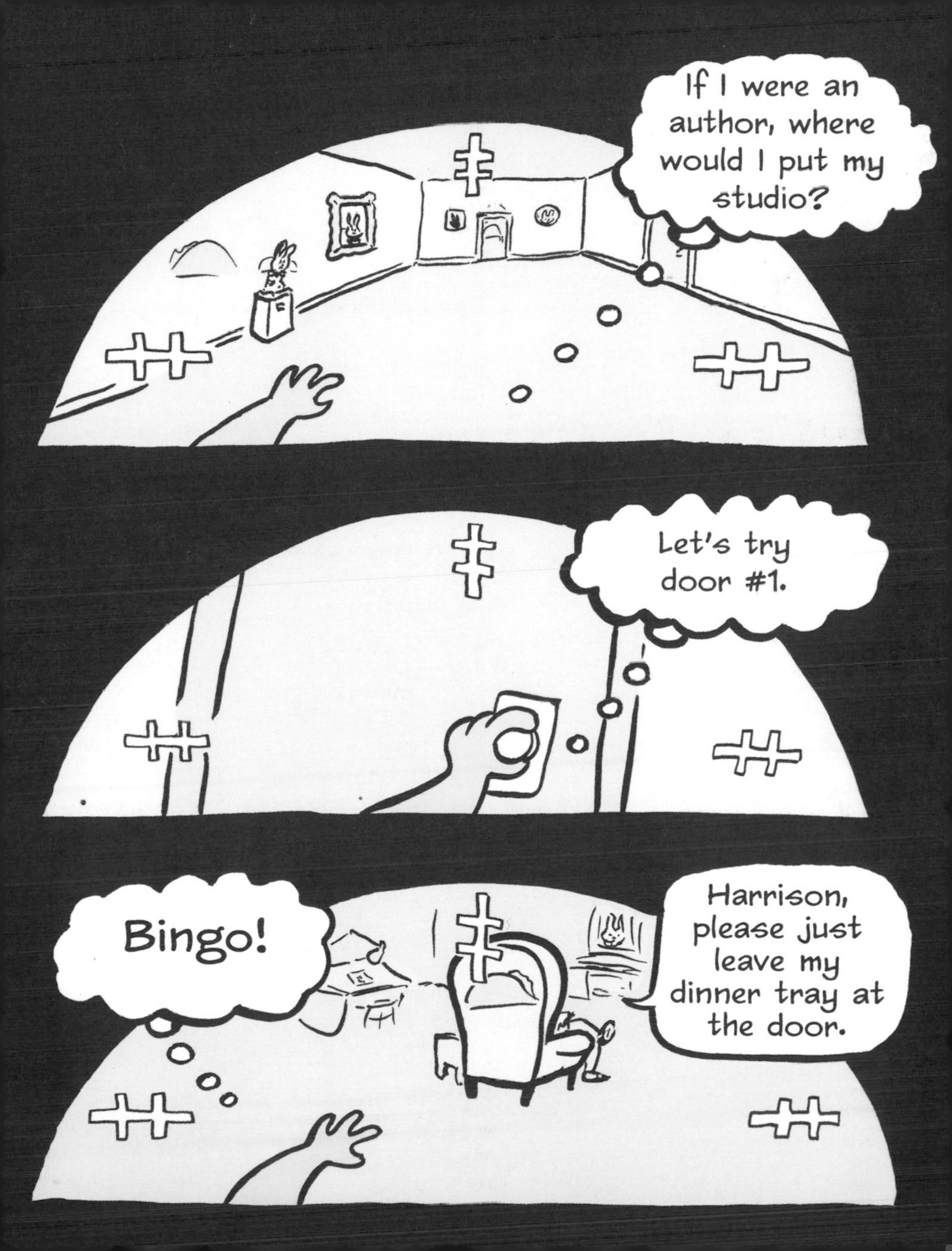
If I were an author, where would I put my studio?
Let's try door #1.
Bingo!
Harrison, please just leave my dinner tray at the door.

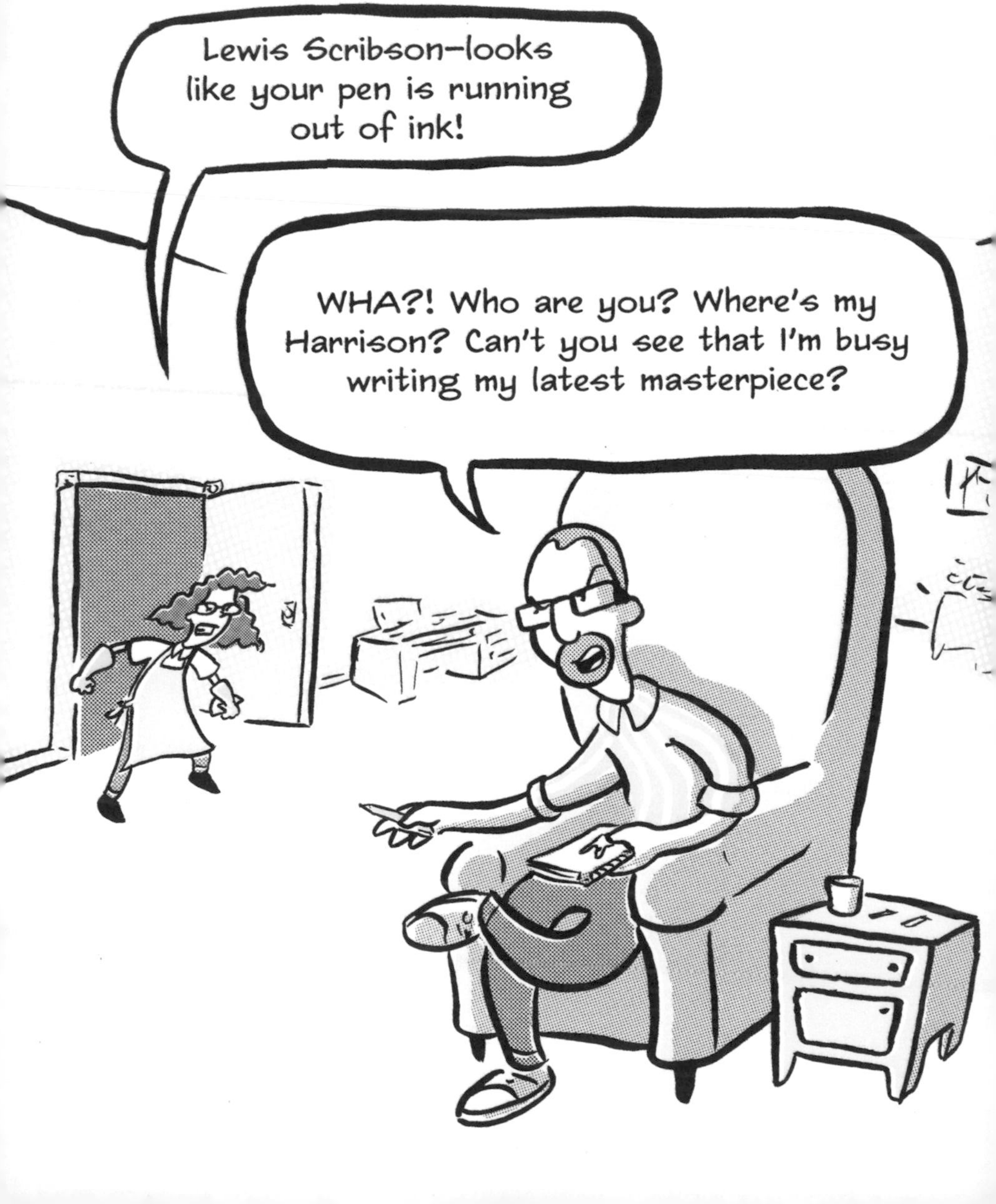
Lewis Scribson—looks like your pen is running out of ink!
WHA?! Who are you? Where's my Harrison? Can't you see that I'm busy writing my latest masterpiece?

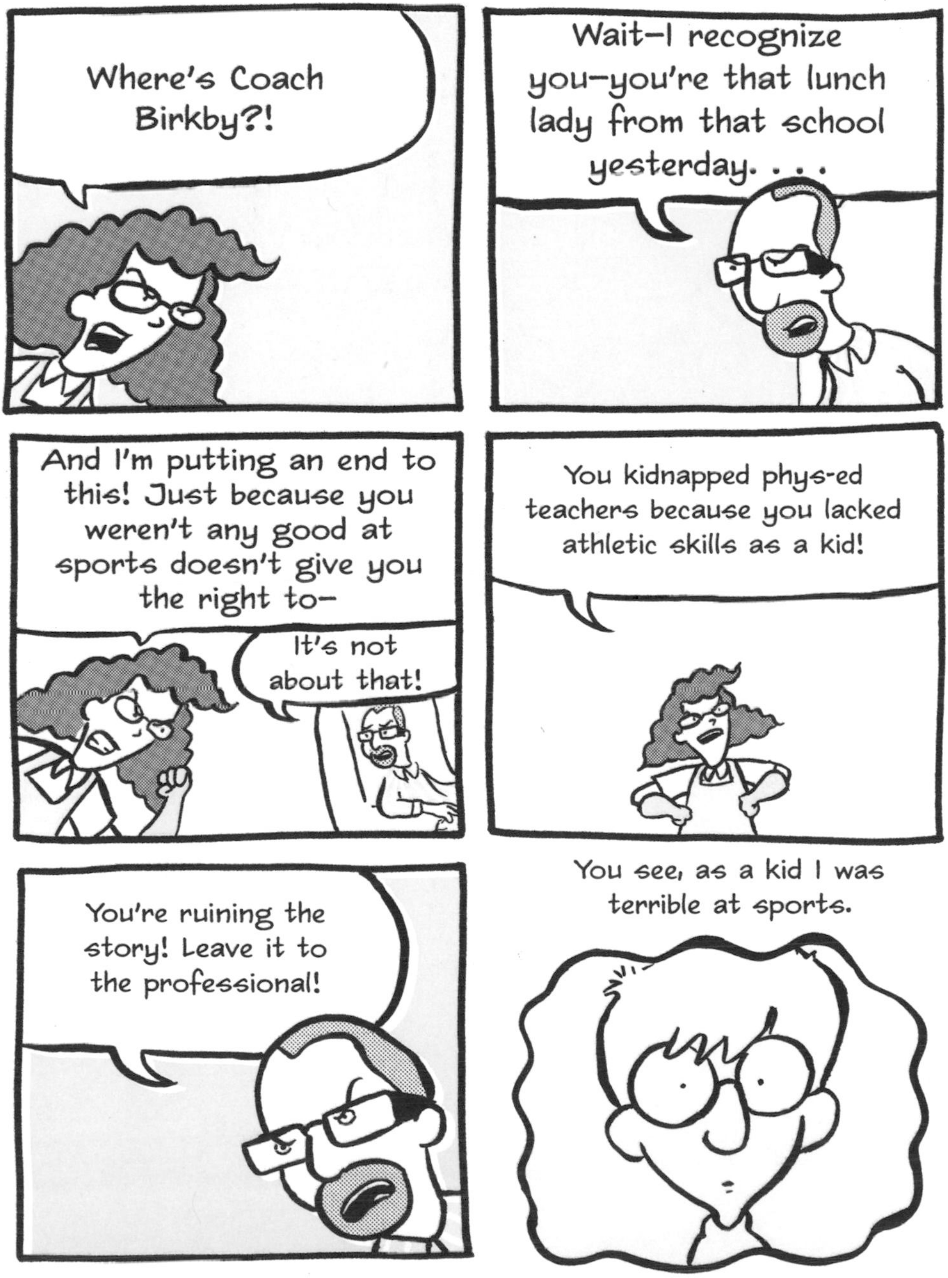

Where's Coach Birkby?!
Wait—I recognize you—you're that lunch lady from that school yesterday. . . .
And I'm putting an end to this! Just because you weren't any good at sports doesn't give you the right to—
It's not about that!
You kidnapped phys-ed teachers because you lacked athletic skills as a kid!
You're ruining the story! Leave it to the professional!
You see, as a kid I was terrible at sports.

Do you know the pain of
being picked last for teams?

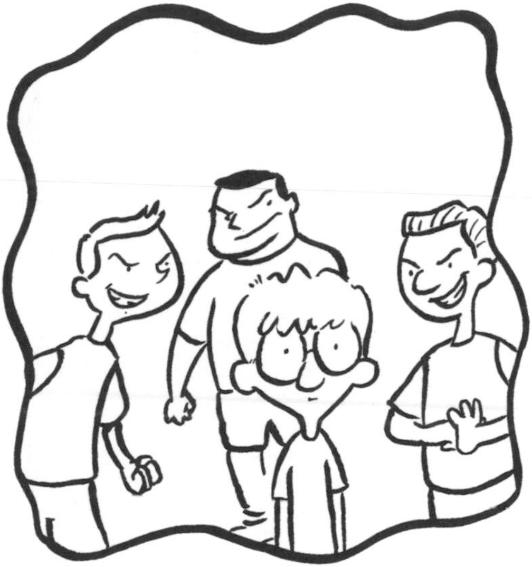

My gym teacher, Mr. Zatyrka,
only made it worse.

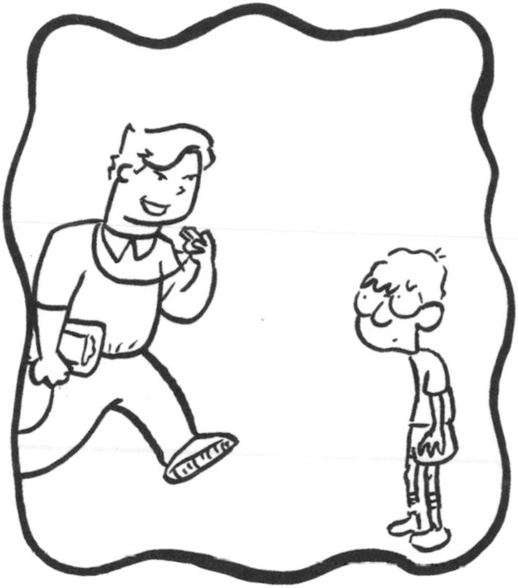

He made me play
dodgeball . . .

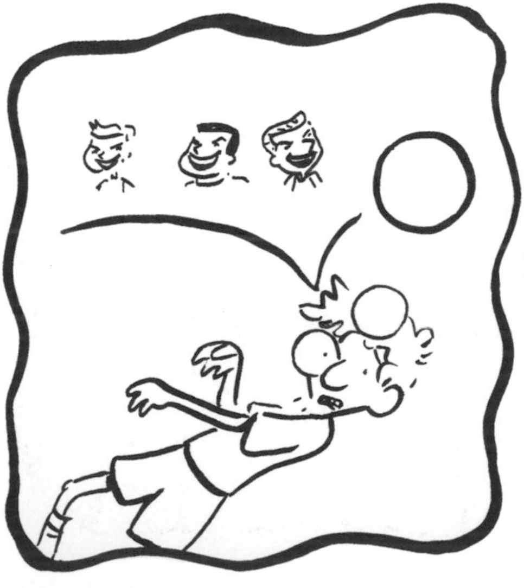

. . . and football.
It was dreadful!

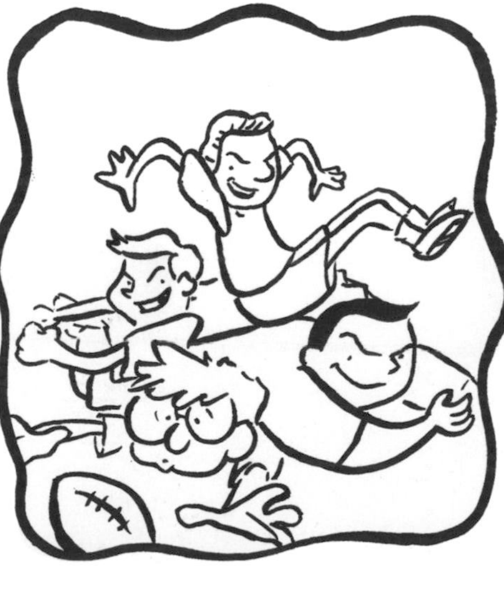

I had to climb the ropes . . .

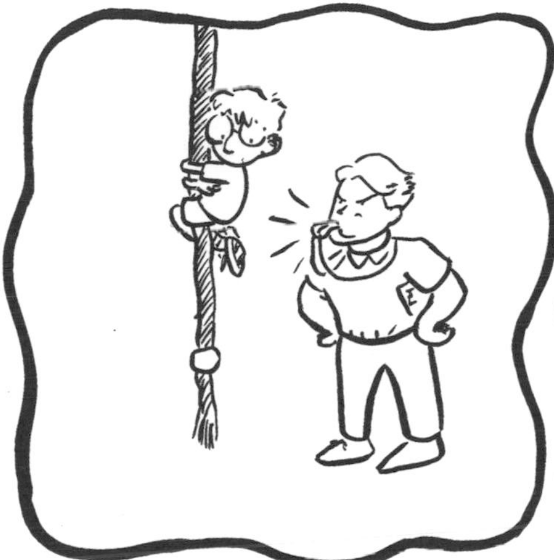

. . . and when I would fall . . .

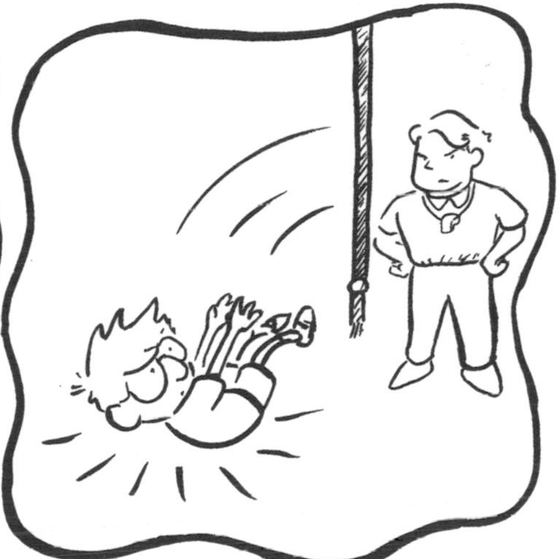

. . . he would make fun of me with all the other kids.

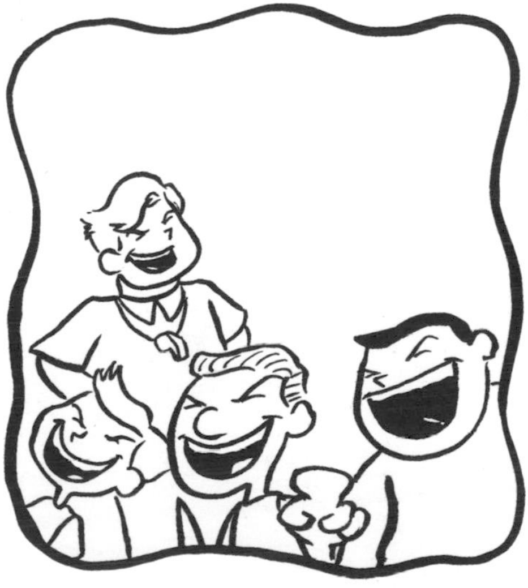

How I *hated* him.

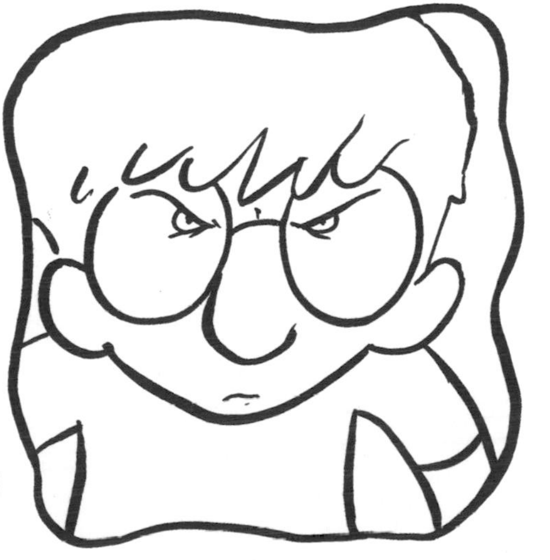

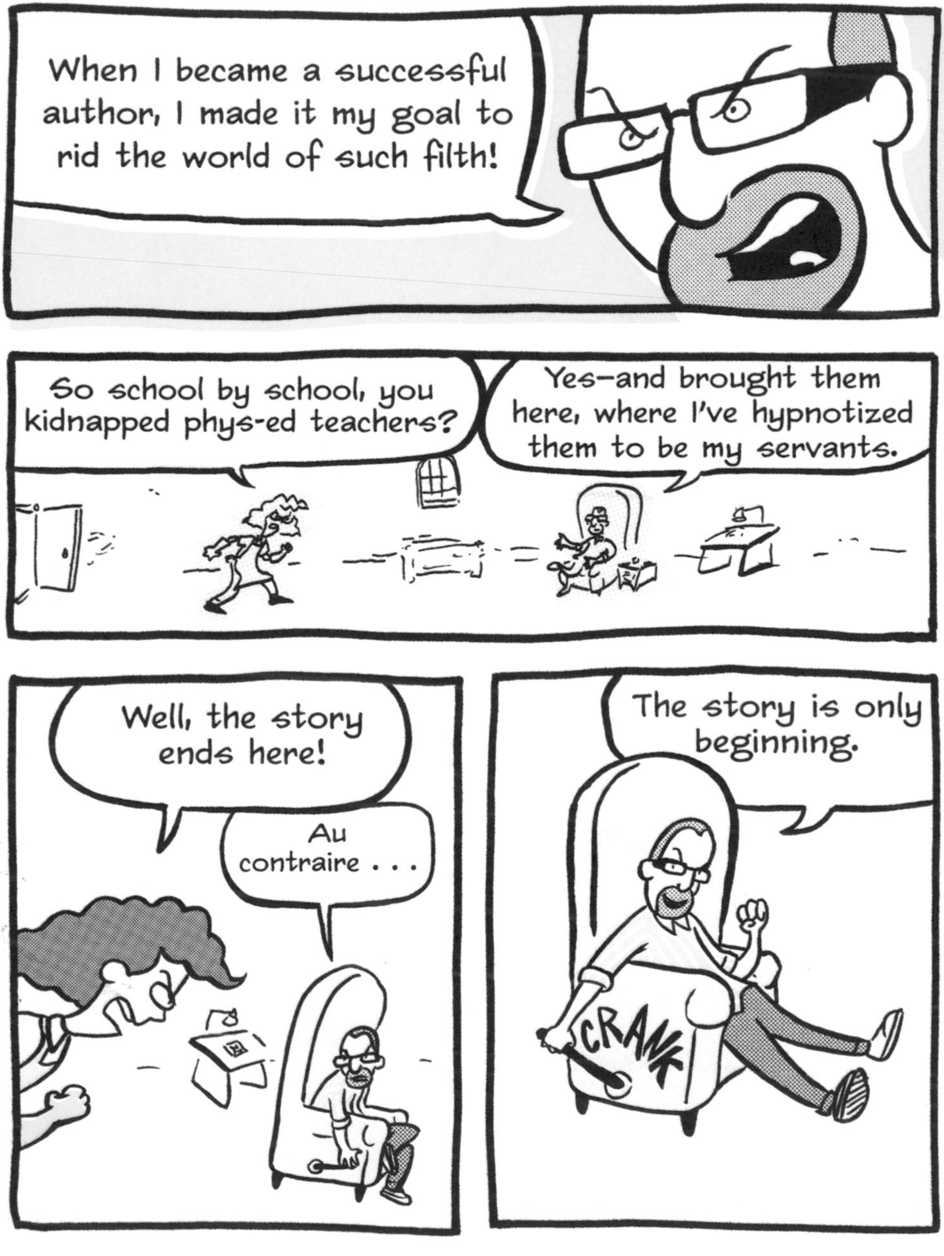
When I became a successful author, I made it my goal to rid the world of such filth!
So school by school, you kidnapped phys-ed teachers?
Yes—and brought them here, where I've hypnotized them to be my servants.
Well, the story ends here!
Au contraire . . .
The story is only beginning.
CRANK

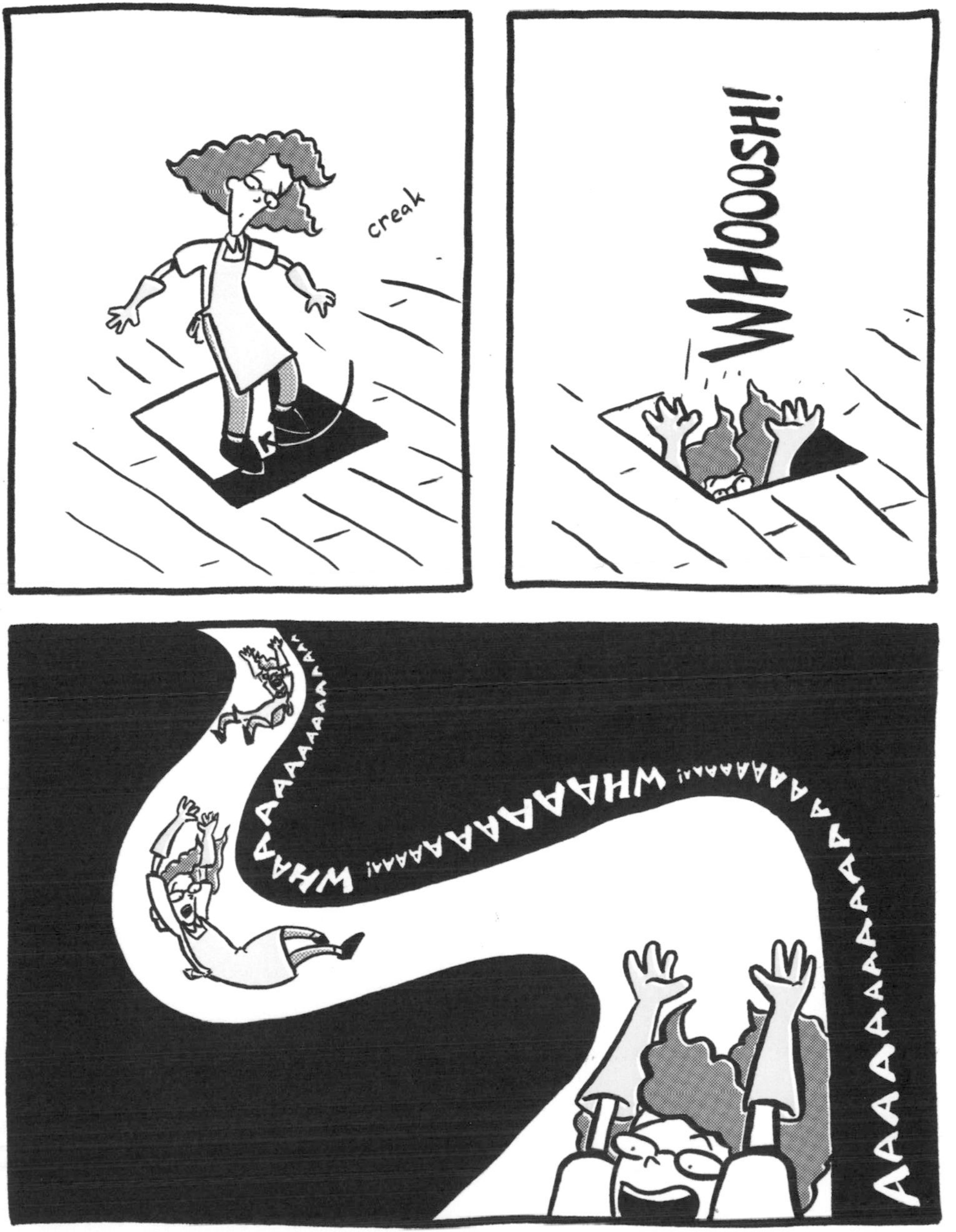
creak
WHOOOOSH!

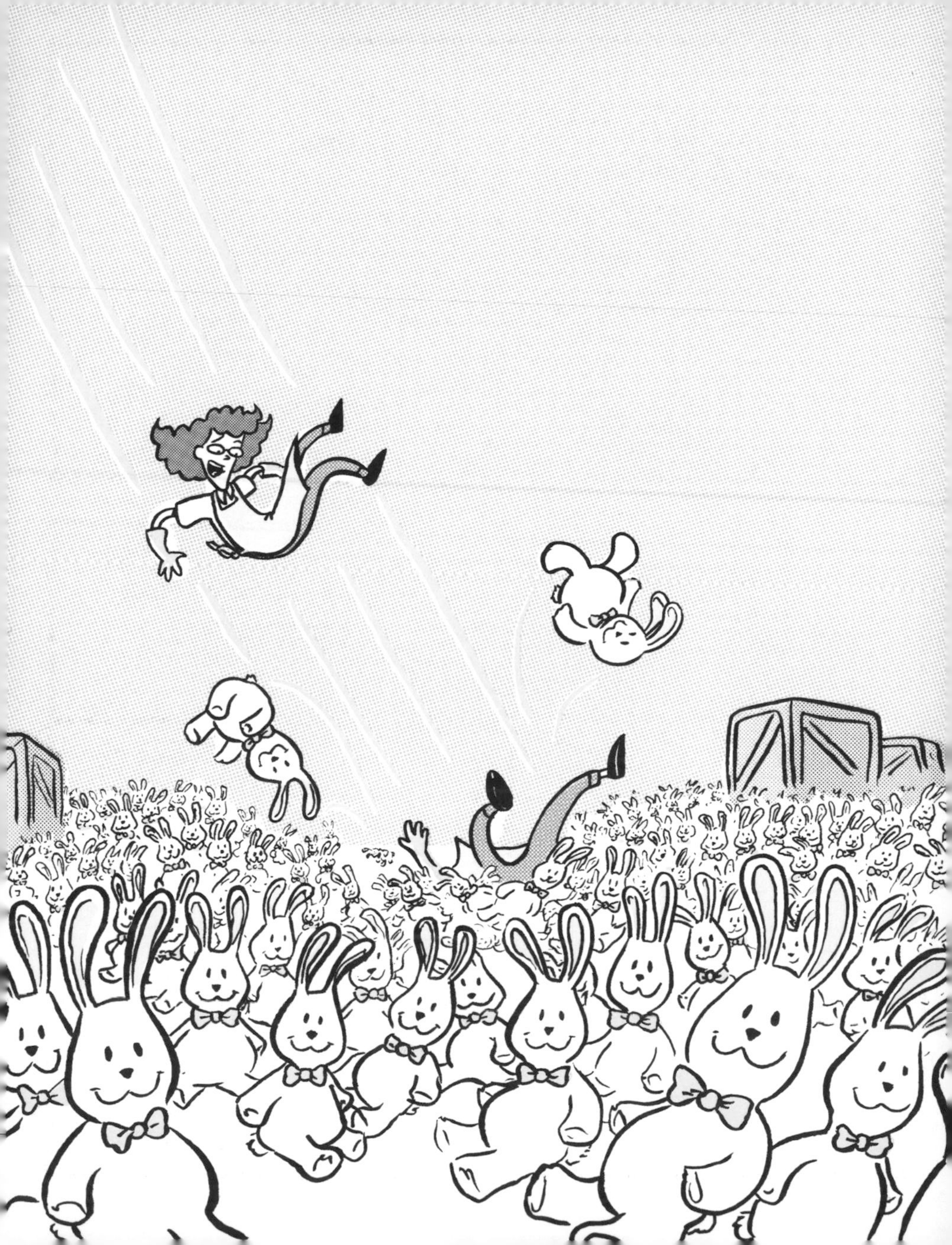

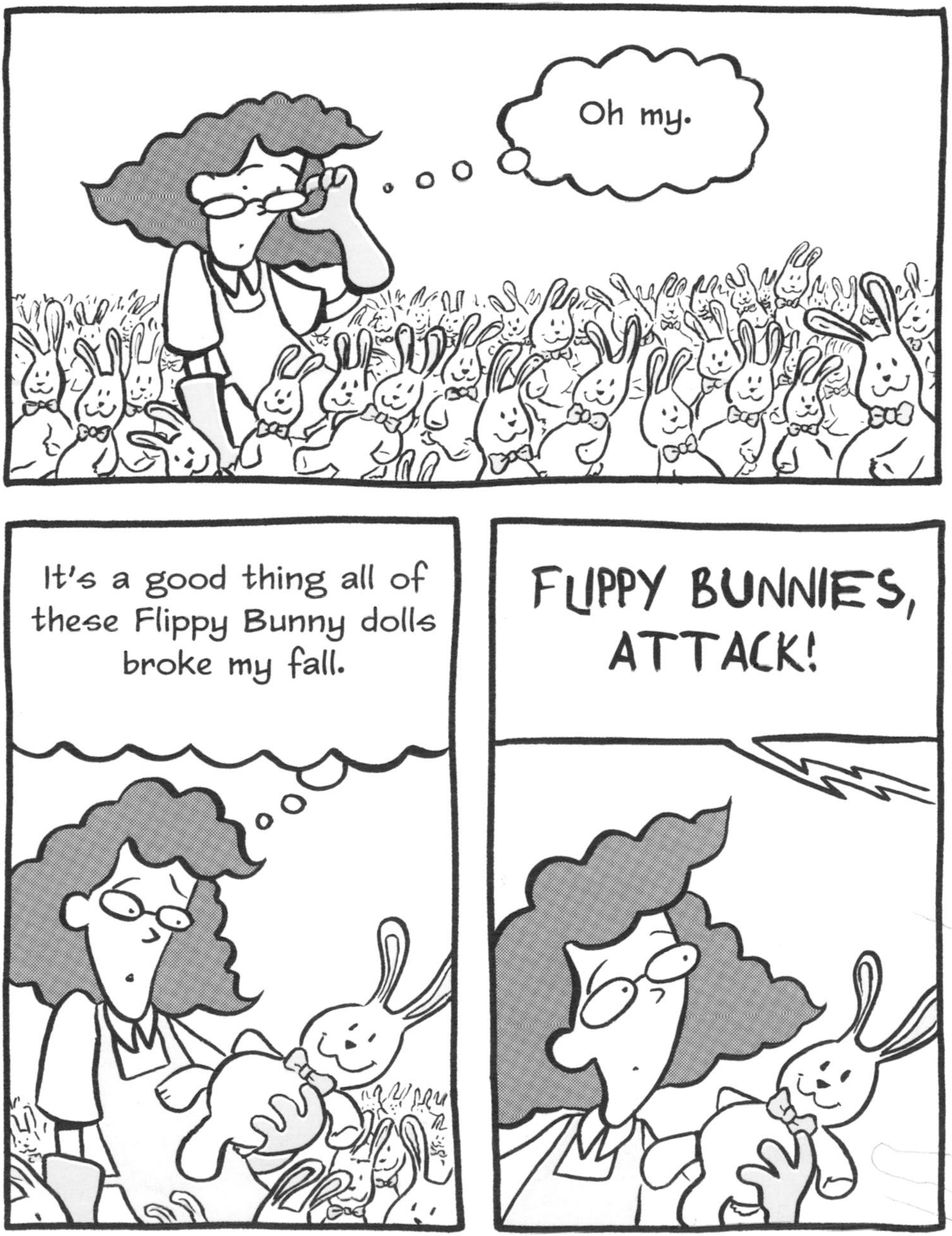
Oh my.
It's a good thing all of these Flippy Bunny dolls broke my fall.
FLIPPY BUNNIES, ATTACK!

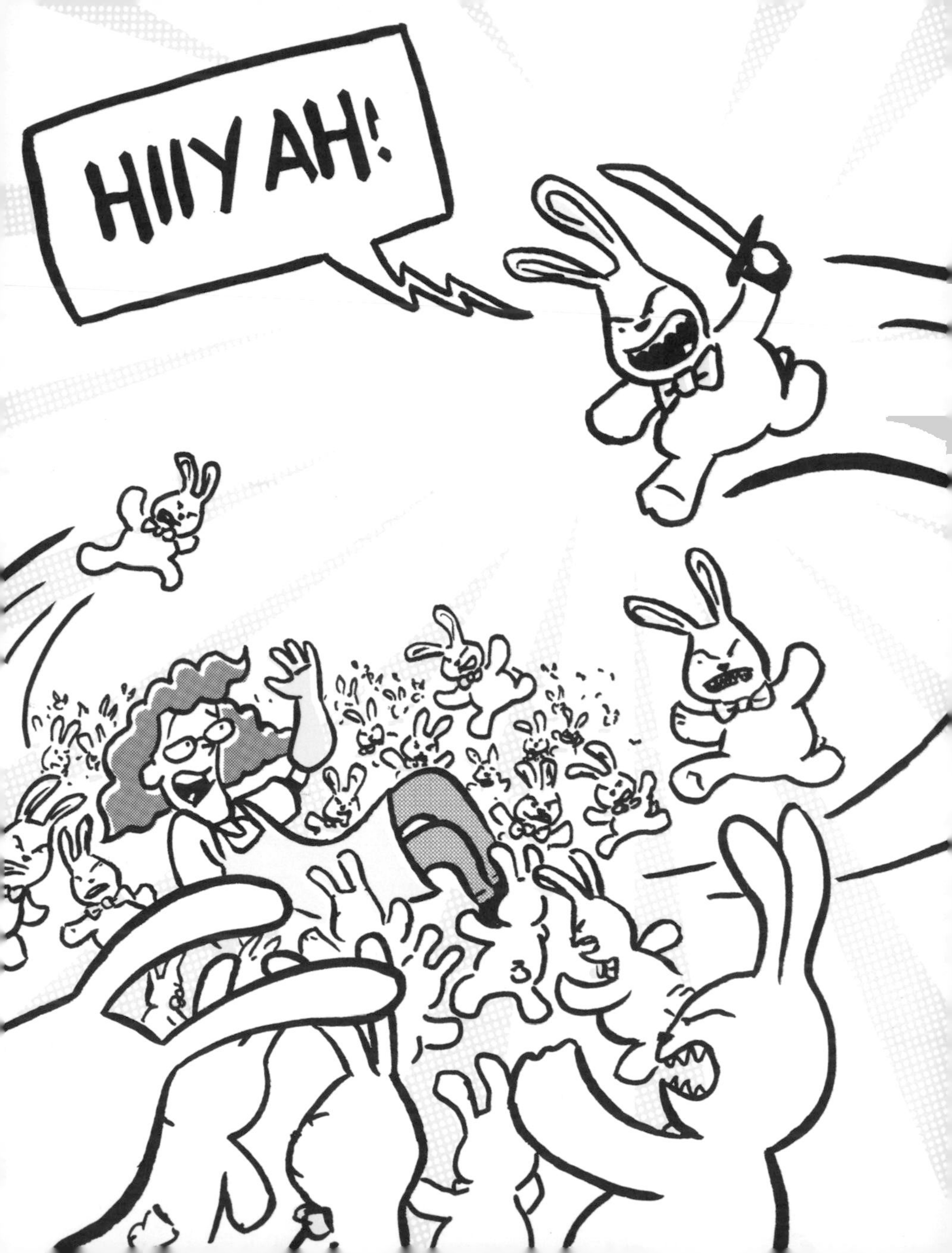
HIIYAH!

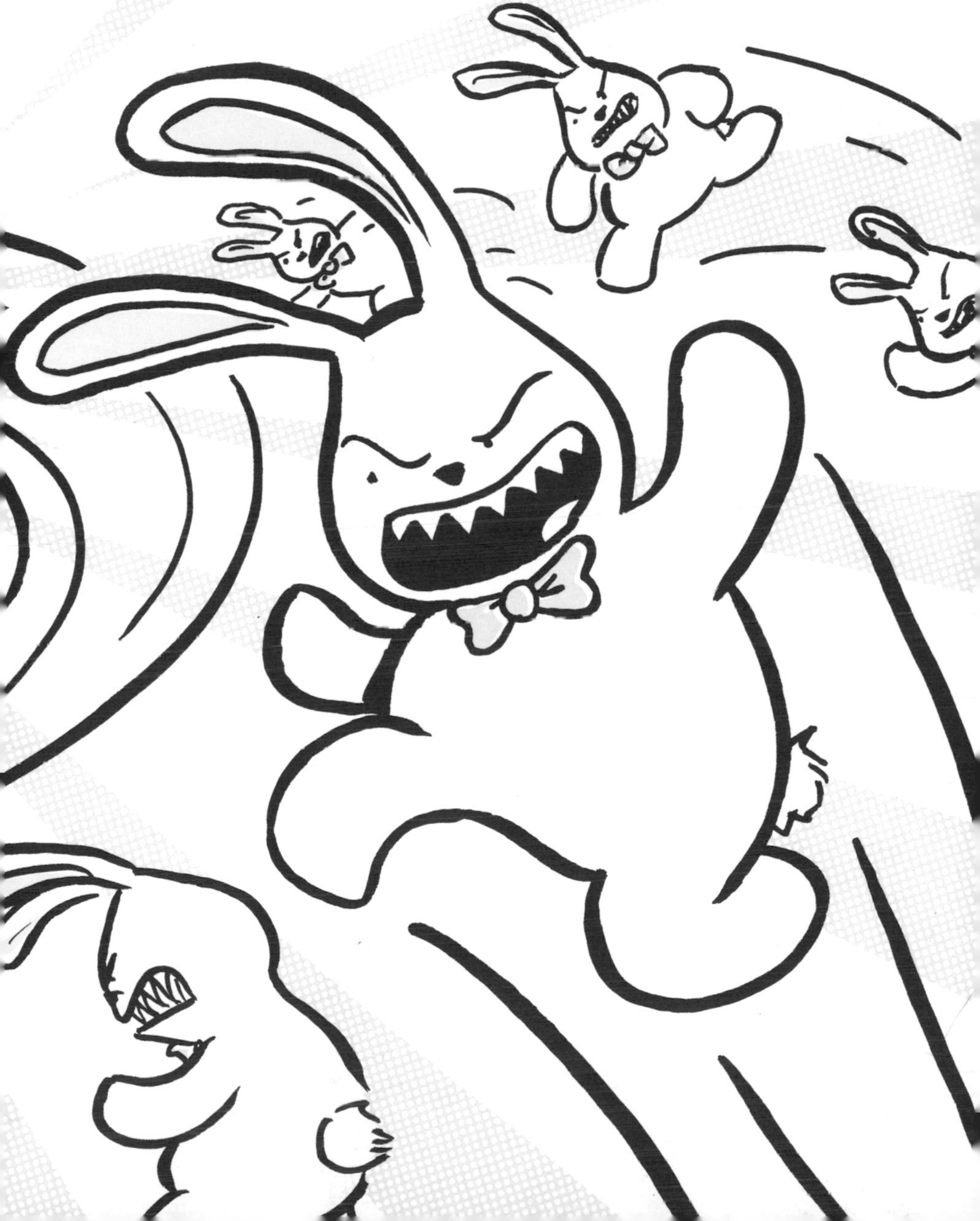

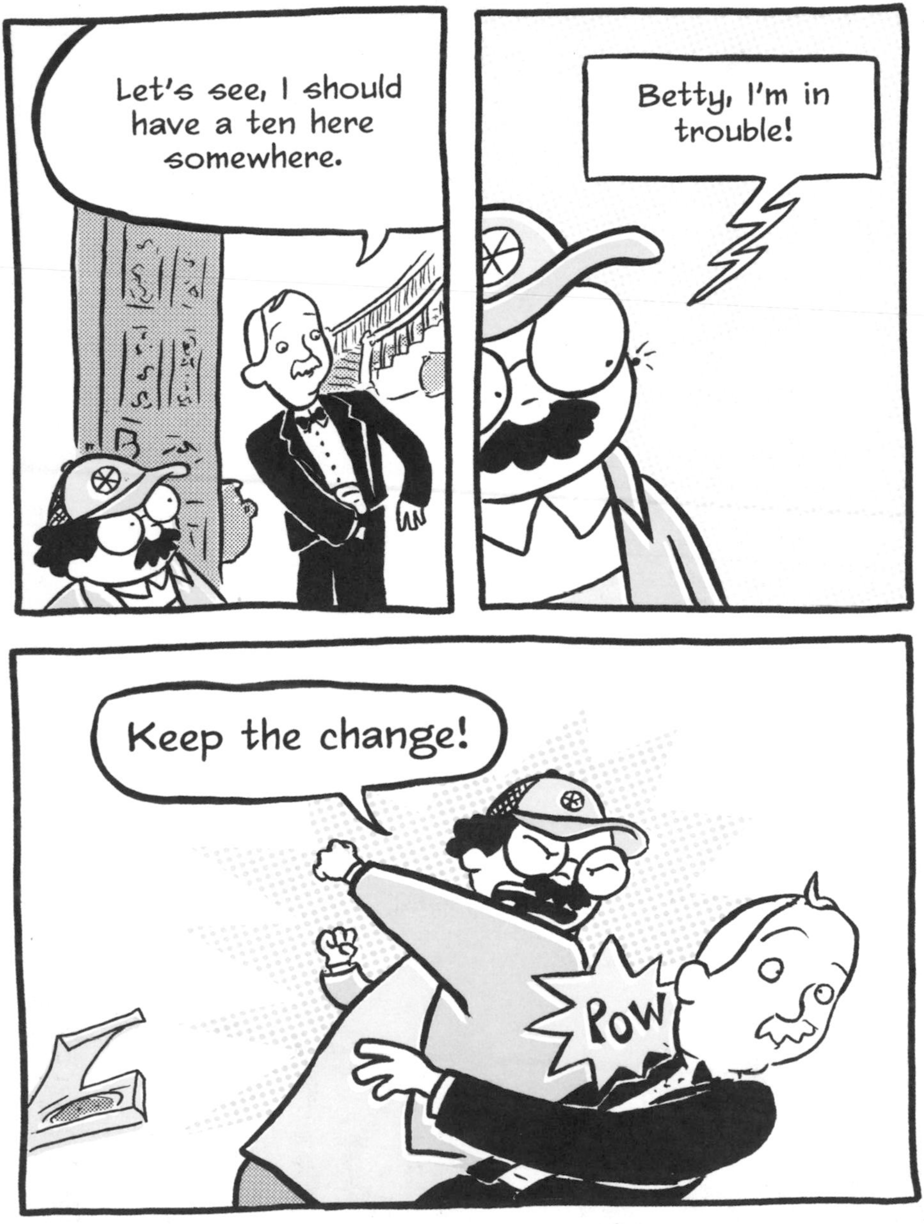
Let's see, I should have a ten here somewhere.
Betty, I'm in trouble!
Keep the change!
POW

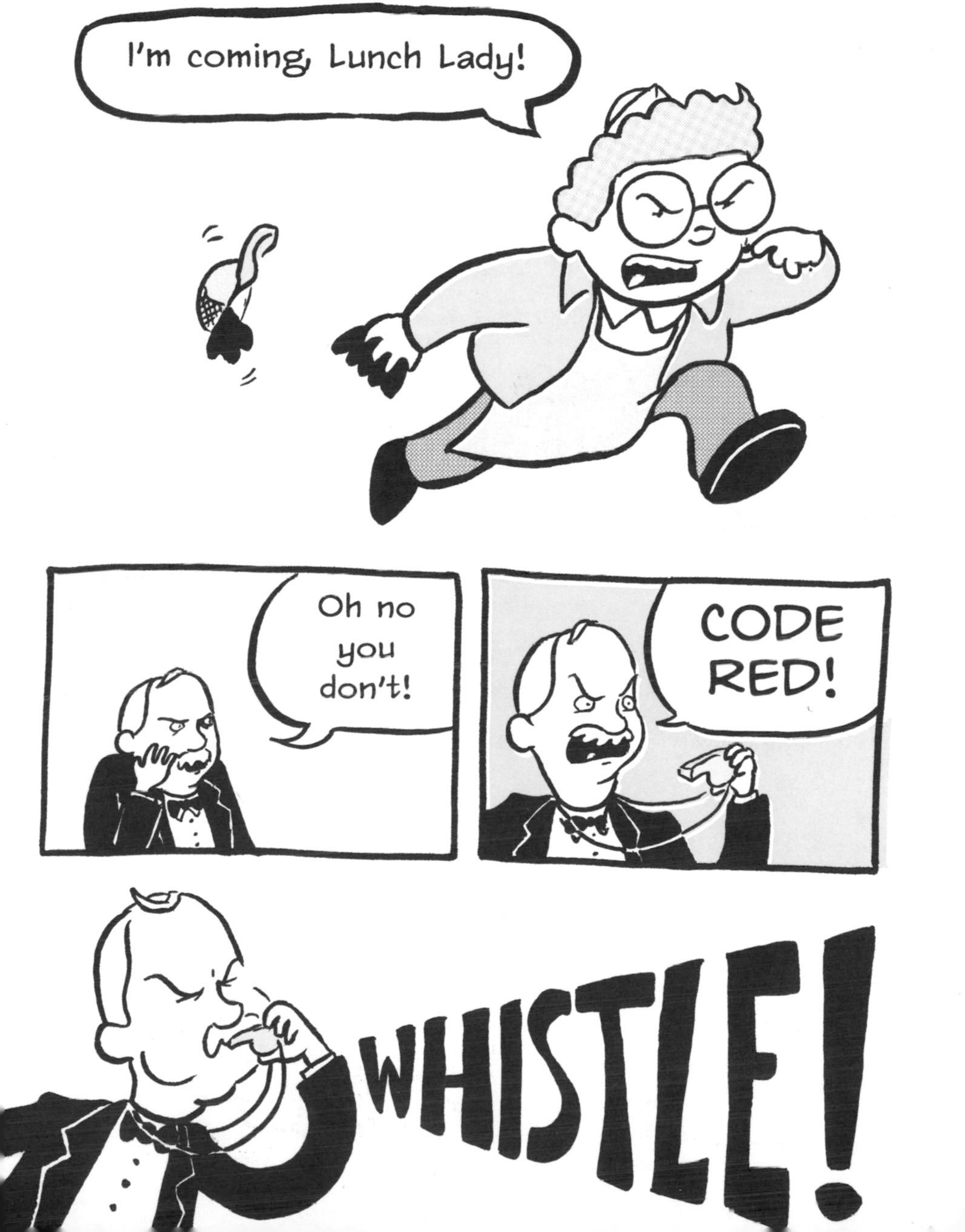
I'm coming, Lunch Lady!
Oh no you don't!
CODE RED!
WHISTLE!

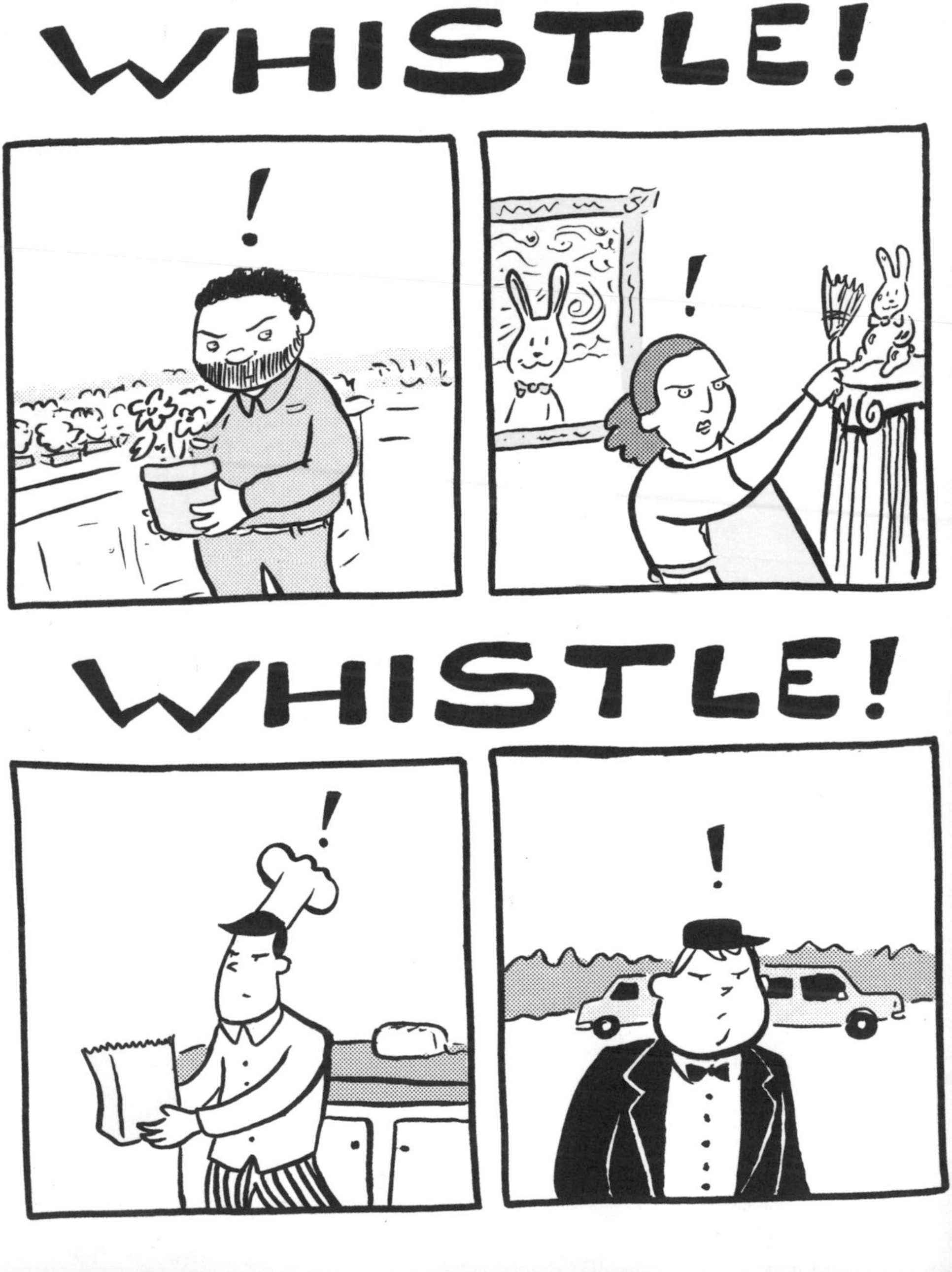
WHISTLE!
!
!
WHISTLE!
!
!

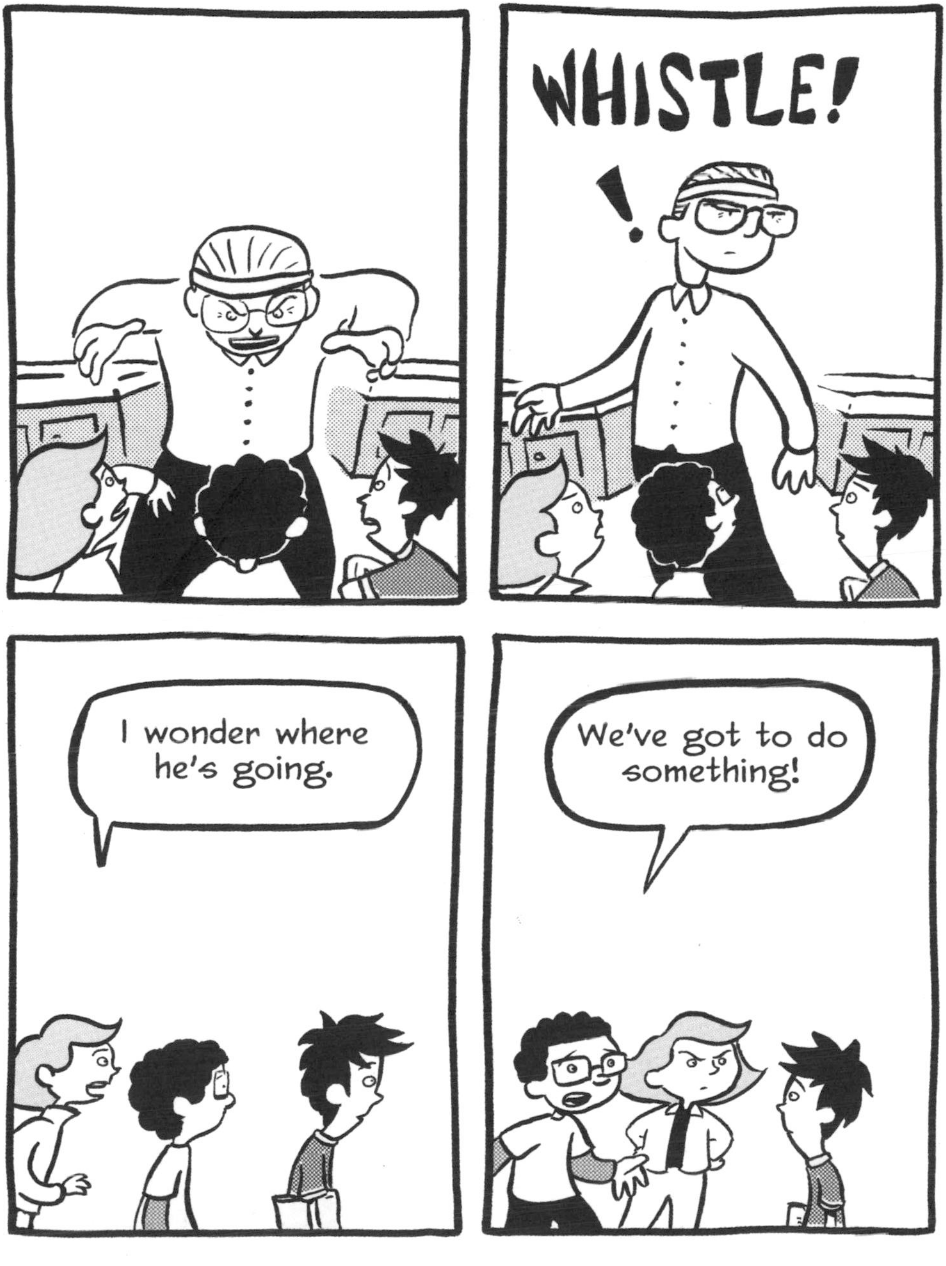
WHISTLE!
!
I wonder where he's going.
We've got to do something!

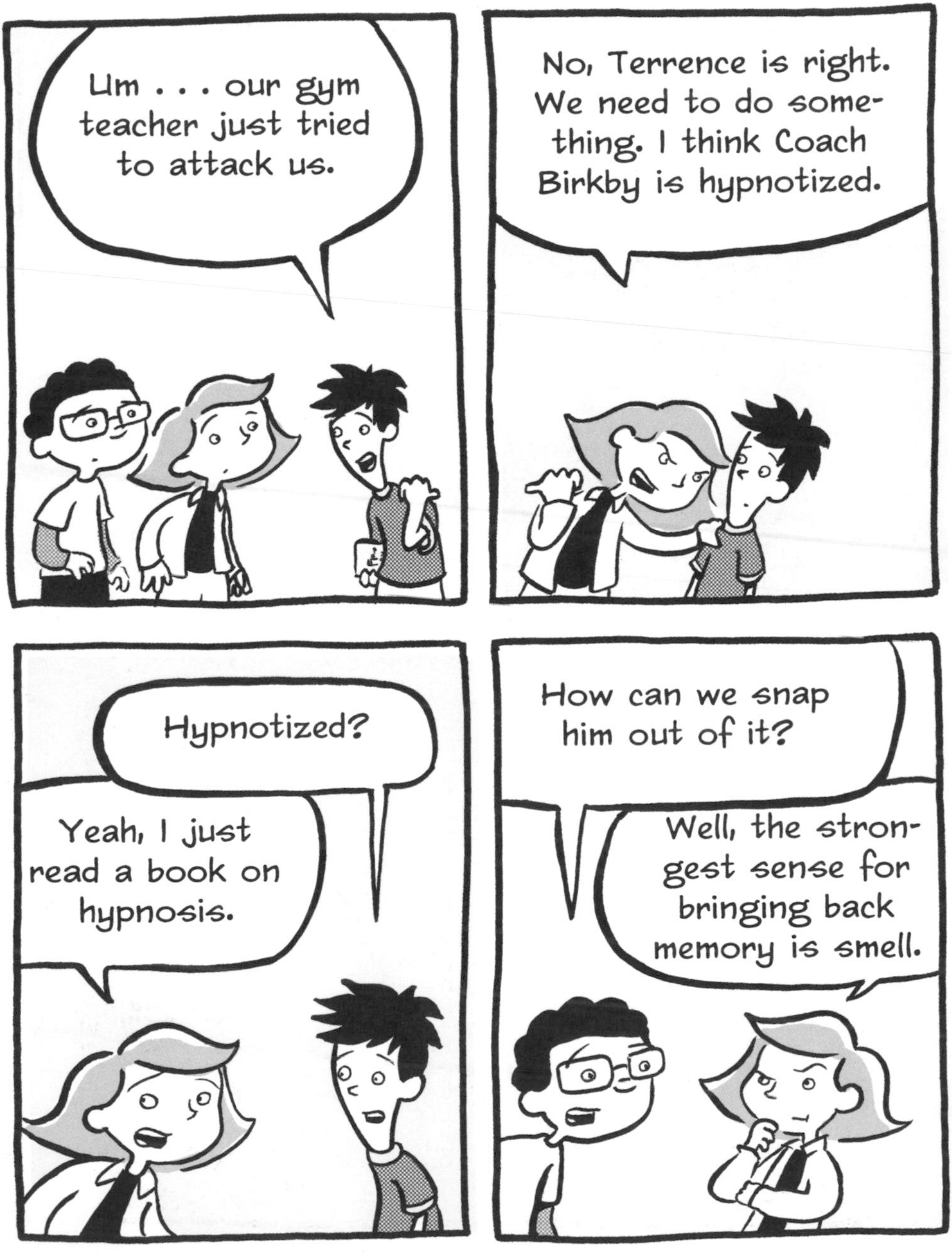
Um . . . our gym teacher just tried to attack us.
No, Terrence is right. We need to do something. I think Coach Birkby is hypnotized.
Hypnotized?
Yeah, I just read a book on hypnosis.
How can we snap him out of it?
Well, the strongest sense for bringing back memory is smell.

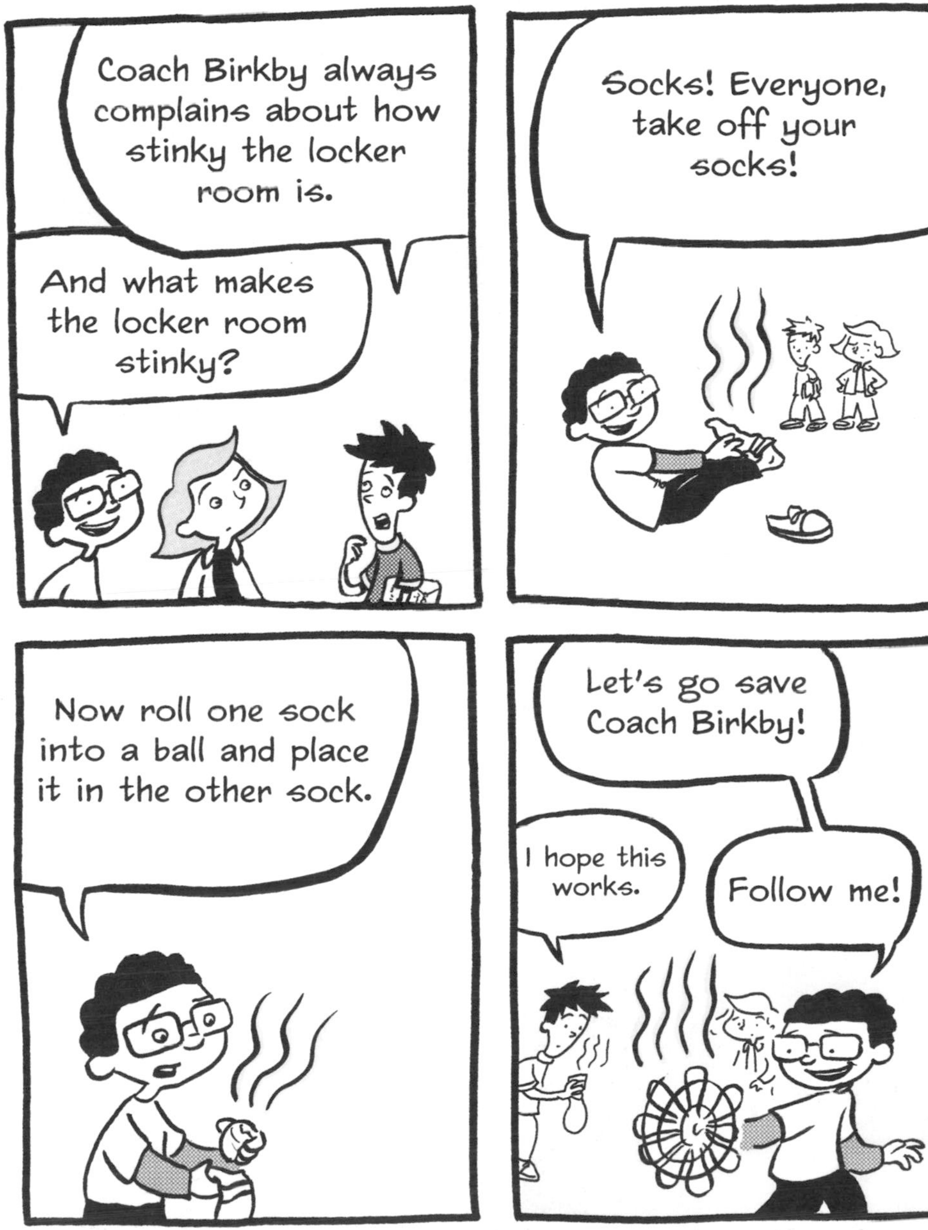
Coach Birkby always complains about how stinky the locker room is.
And what makes the locker room stinky?
Socks! Everyone, take off your socks!
Now roll one sock into a ball and place it in the other sock.
Let's go save Coach Birkby!
I hope this works.
Follow me!

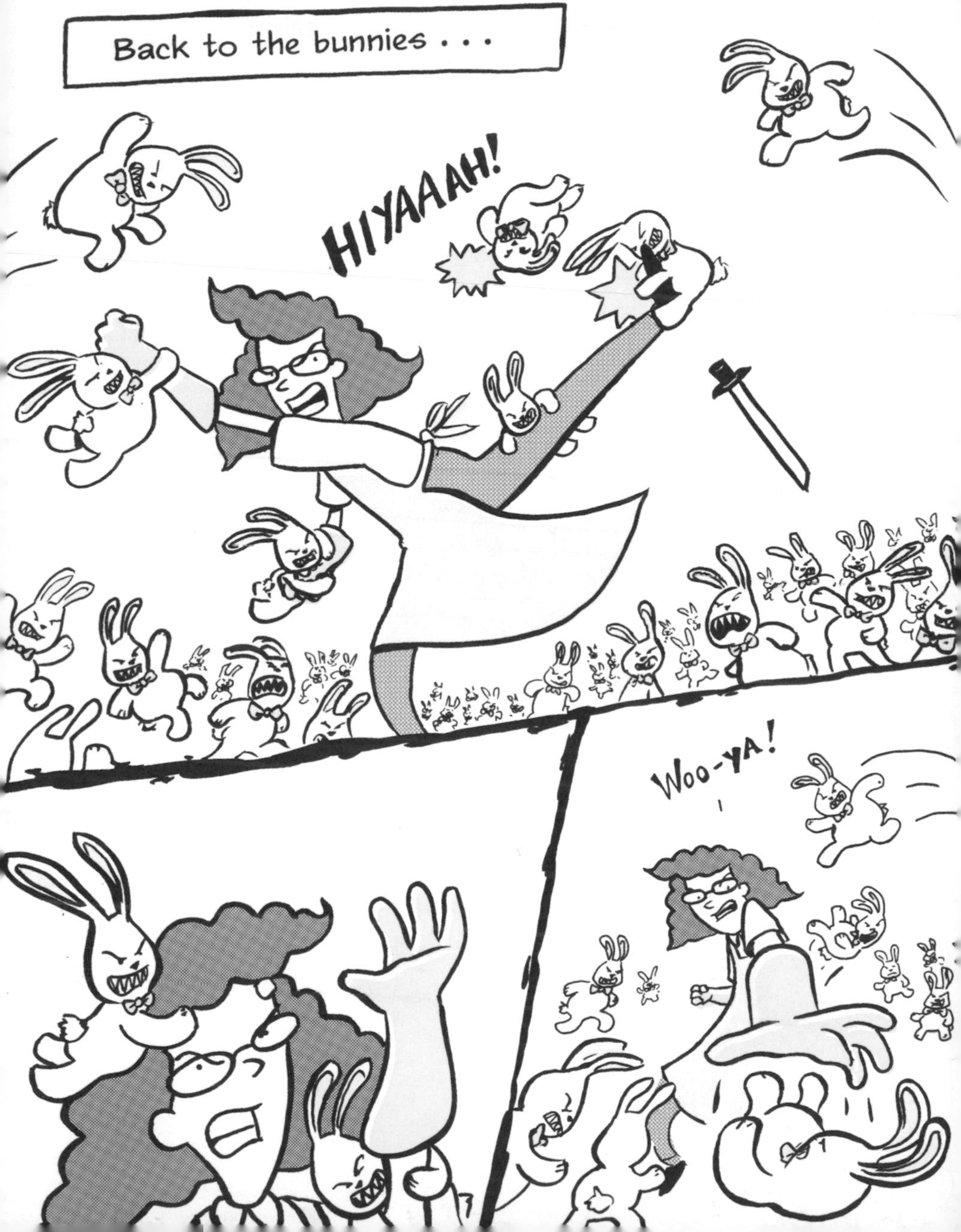
Back to the bunnies . . .
HIYAAAH!
WOO-YA!

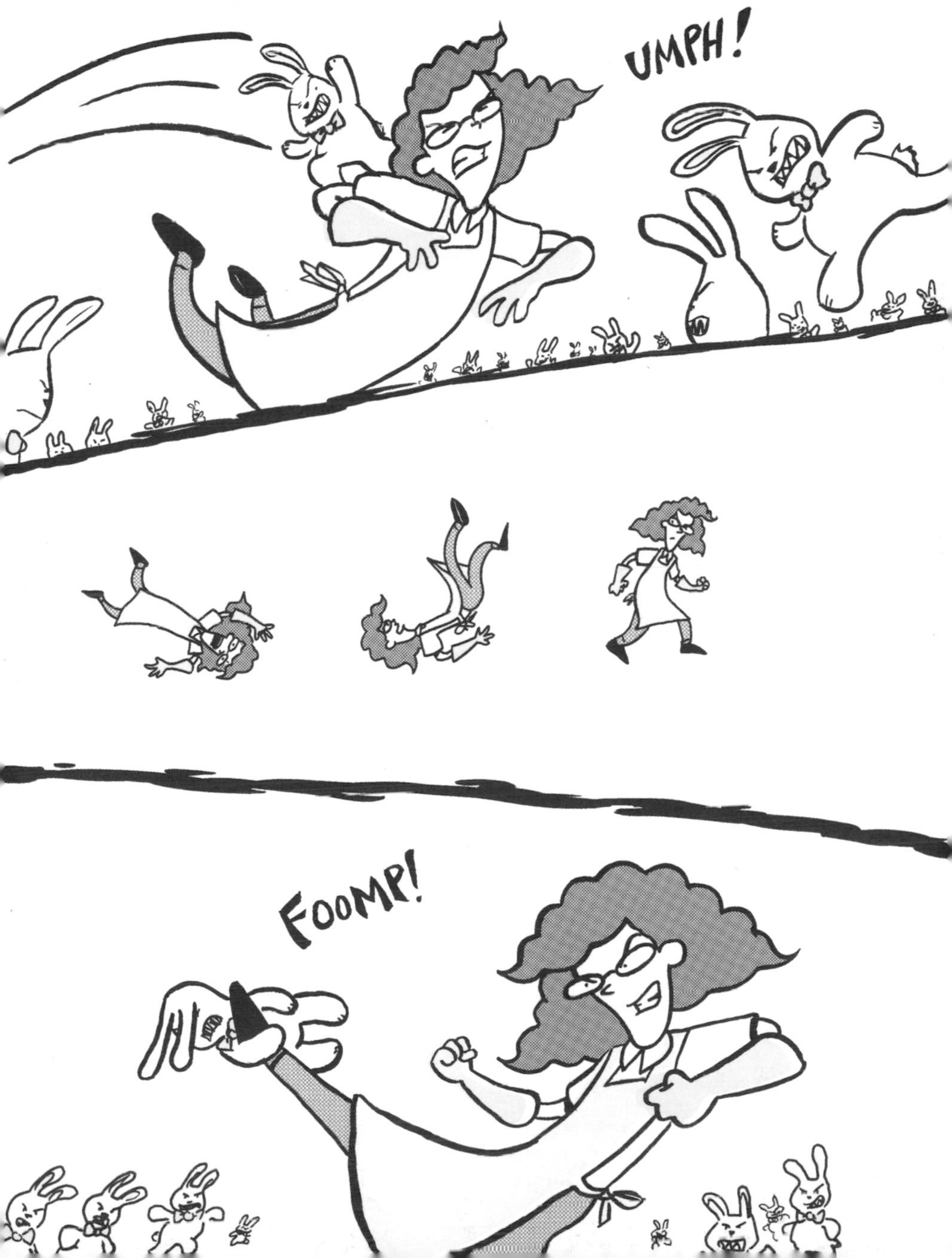
UMPH!
FOOMP!

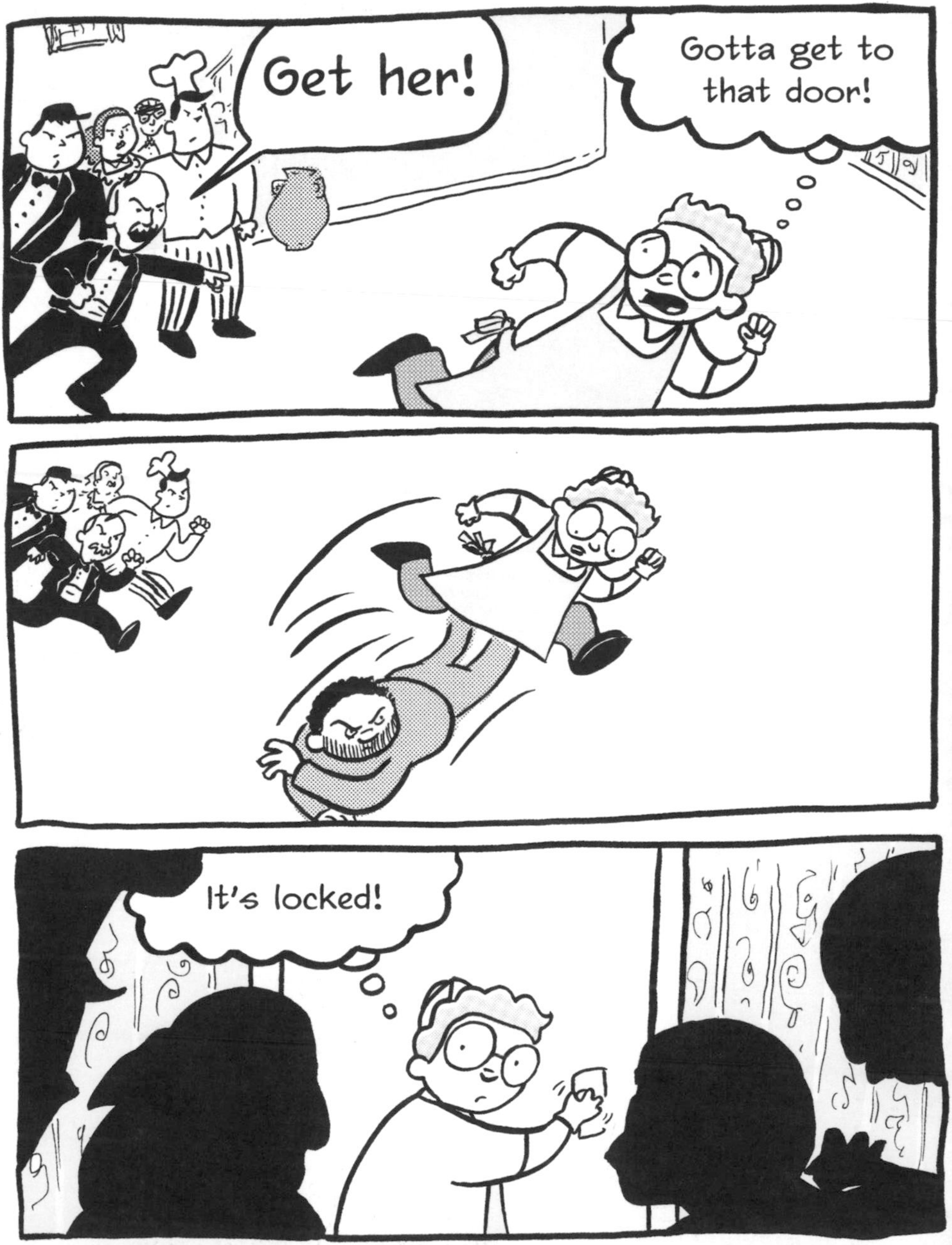
Get her!
Gotta get to that door!
It's locked!

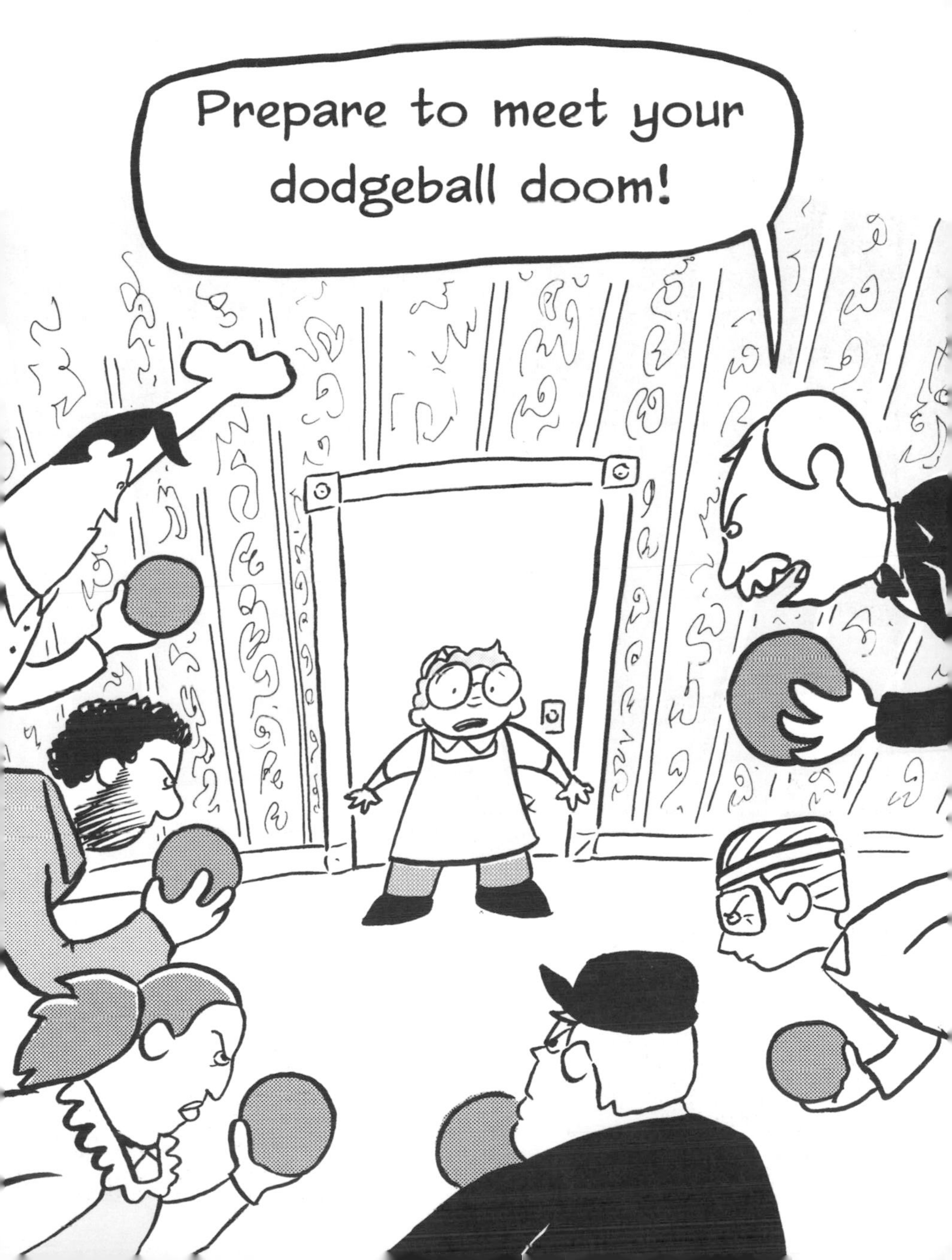
Prepare to meet your dodgeball doom!

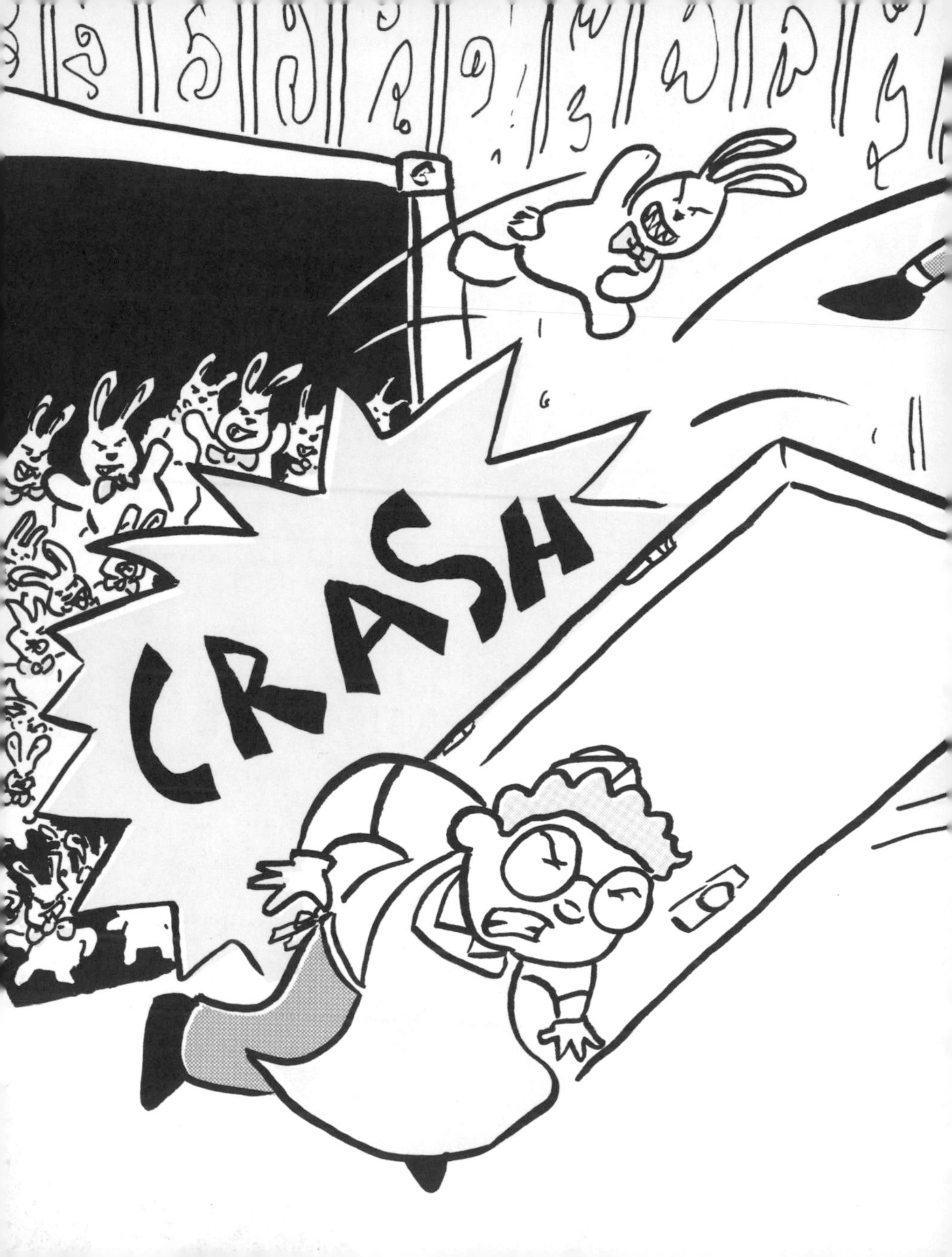
CRASH

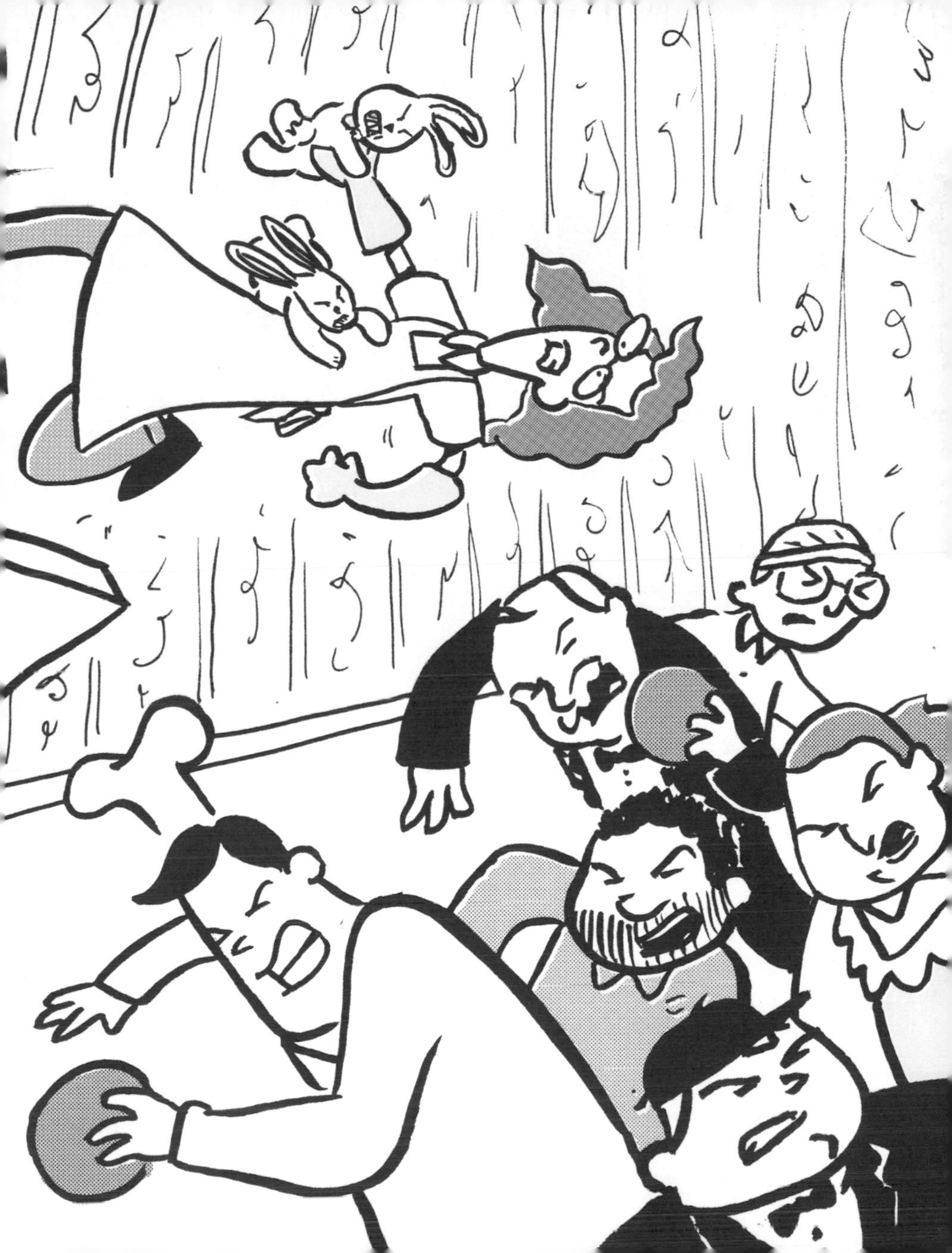

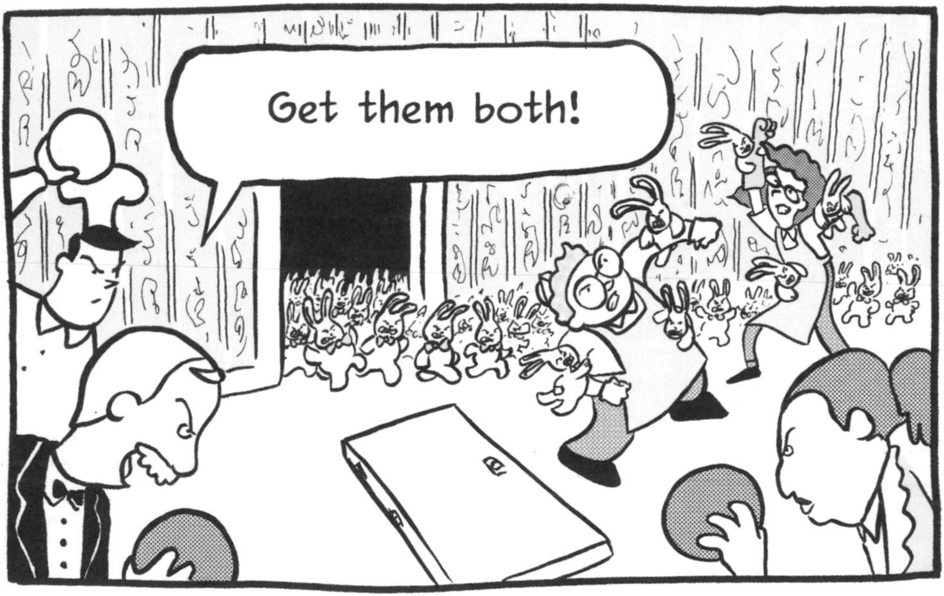
Get them both!

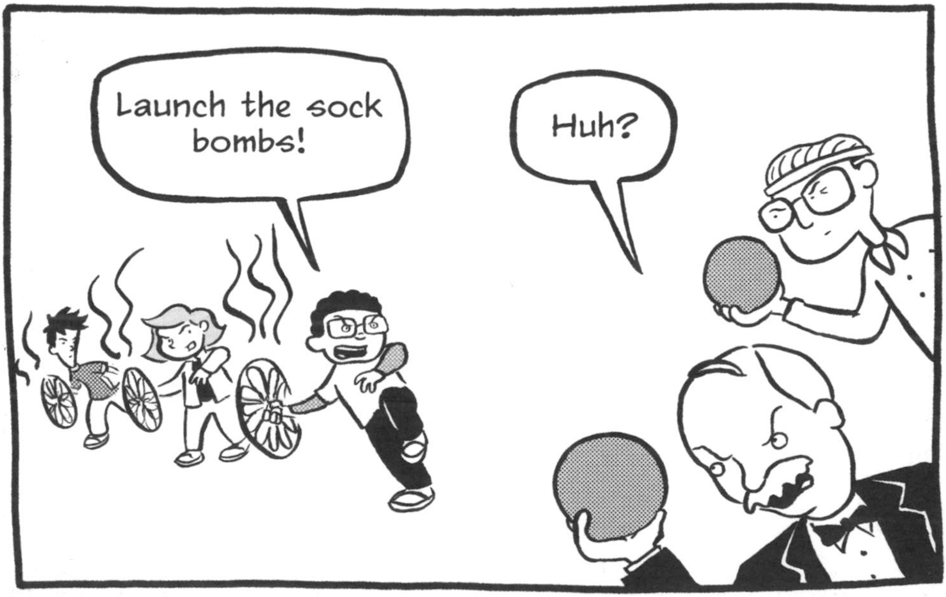
Launch the sock bombs!
Huh?

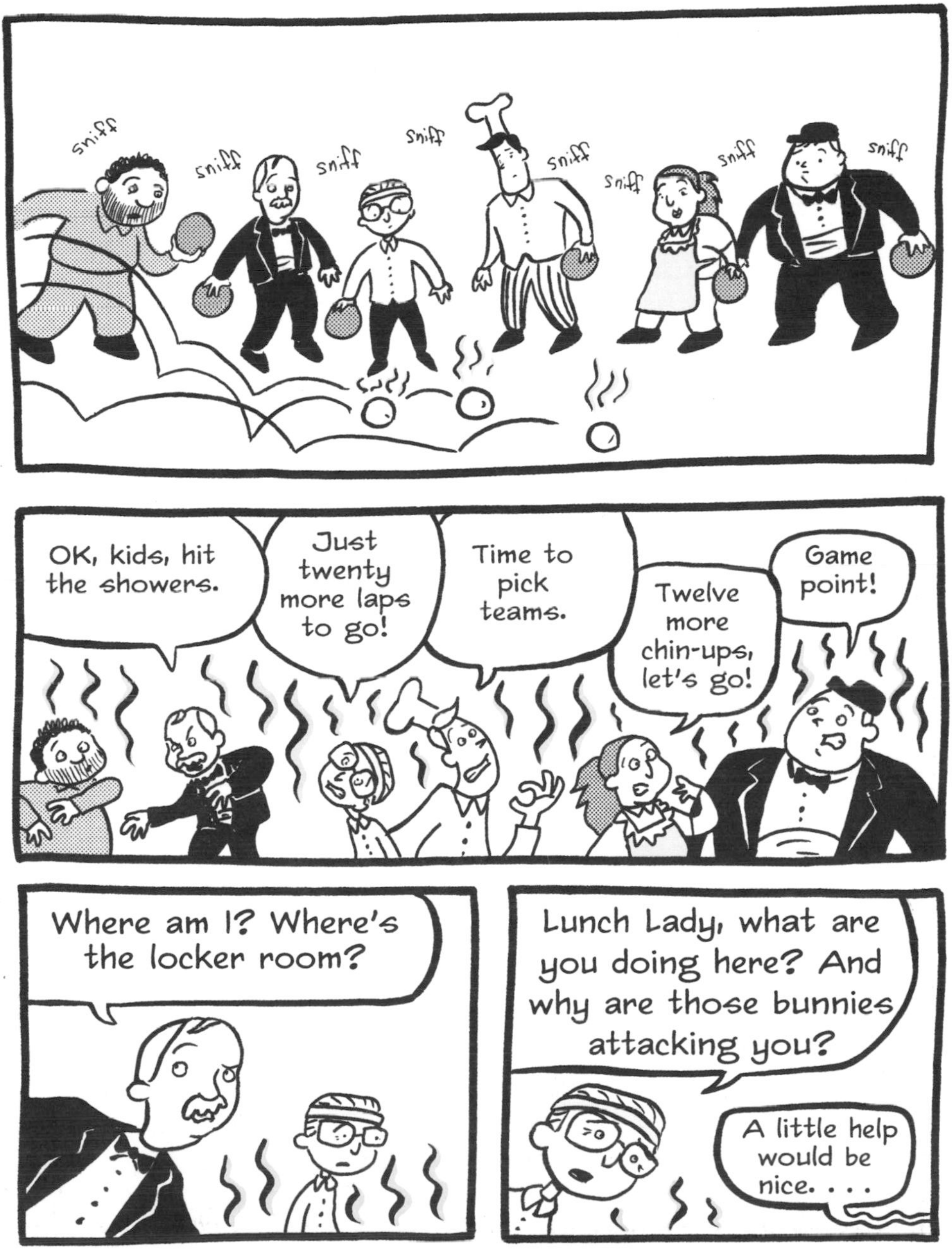
sniff
sniff
sniff
sniff
sniff
sniff
sniff
sniff
OK, kids, hit the showers.
Just twenty more laps to go!
Time to pick teams.
Twelve more chin-ups, let's go!
Game point!
Where am I? Where's the locker room?
Lunch Lady, what are you doing here? And why are those bunnies attacking you?
A little help would be nice. . . .

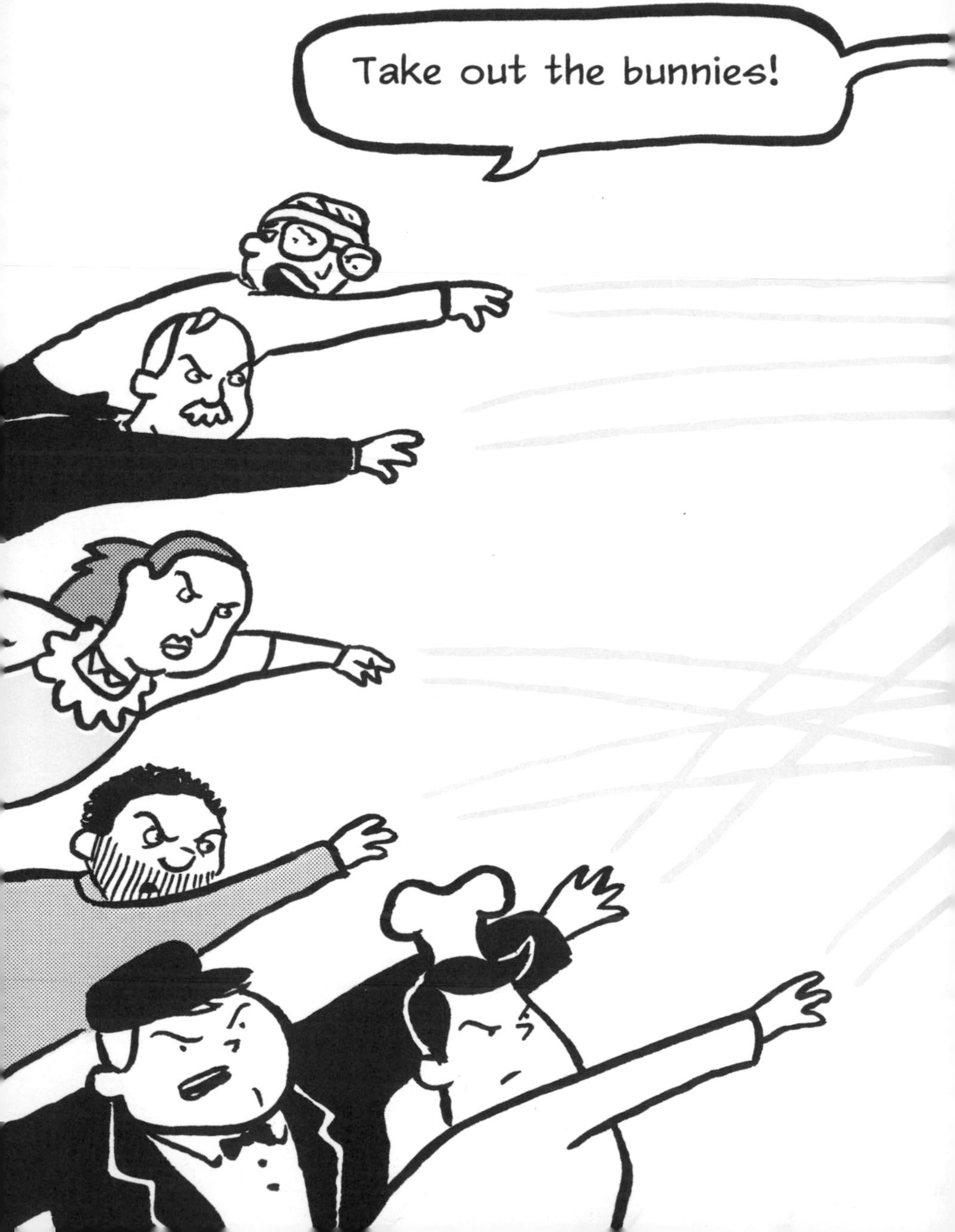
Take out the bunnies!

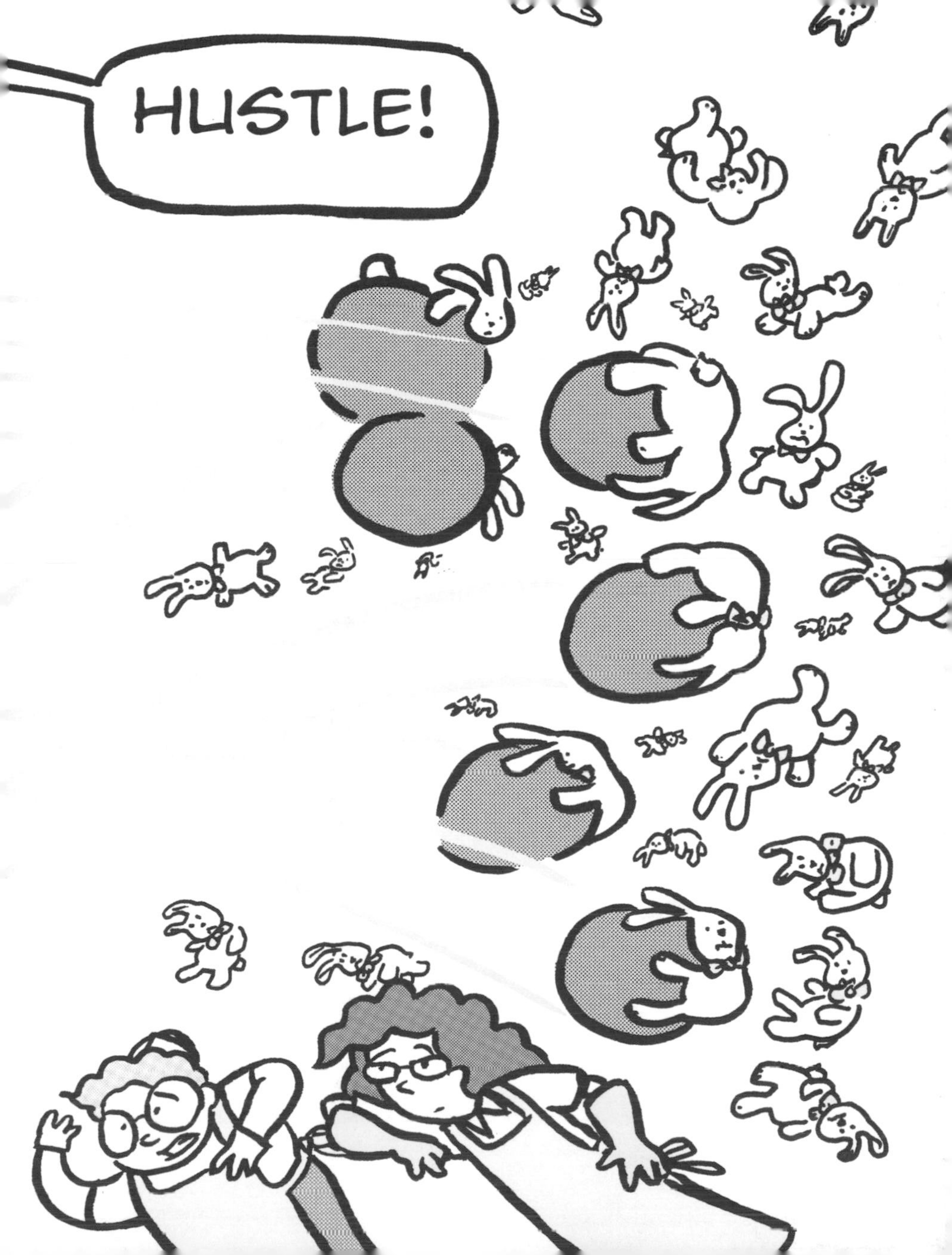
HUSTLE!

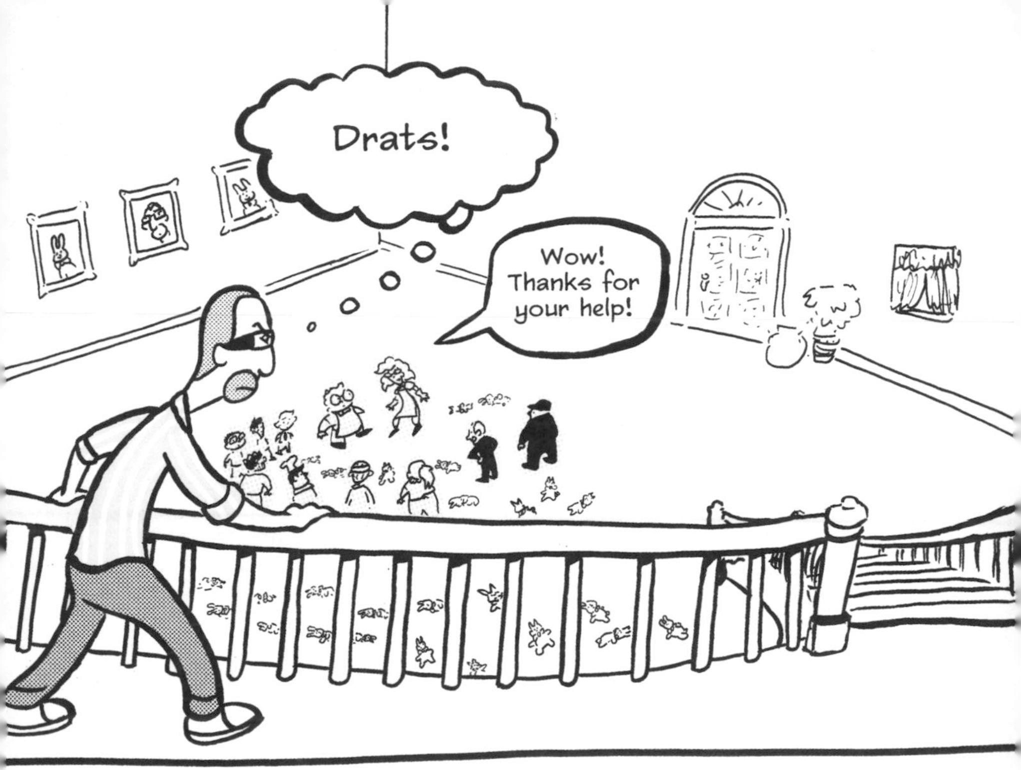
Drats!
Wow! Thanks for your help!

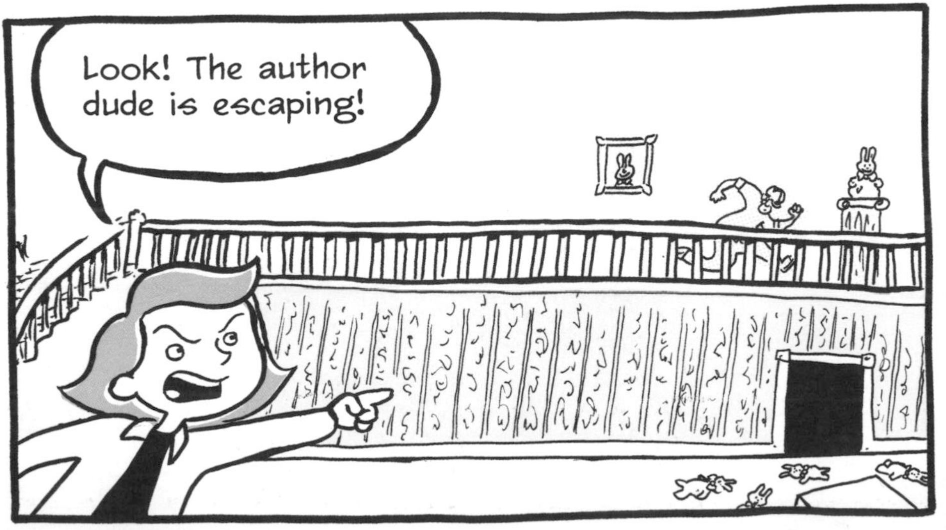
Look! The author dude is escaping!

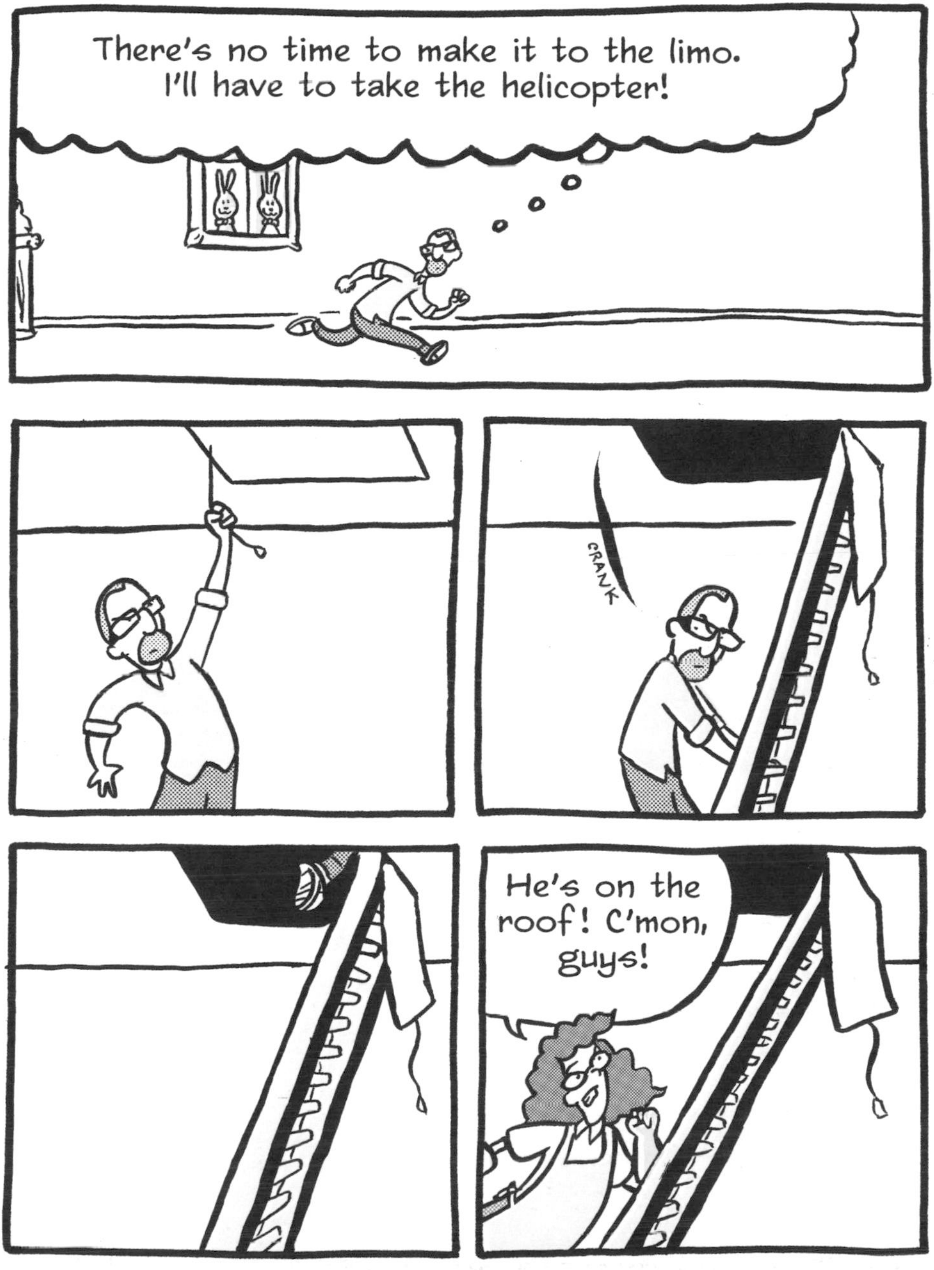
There's no time to make it to the limo. I'll have to take the helicopter!
CRANK
He's on the roof! C'mon, guys!

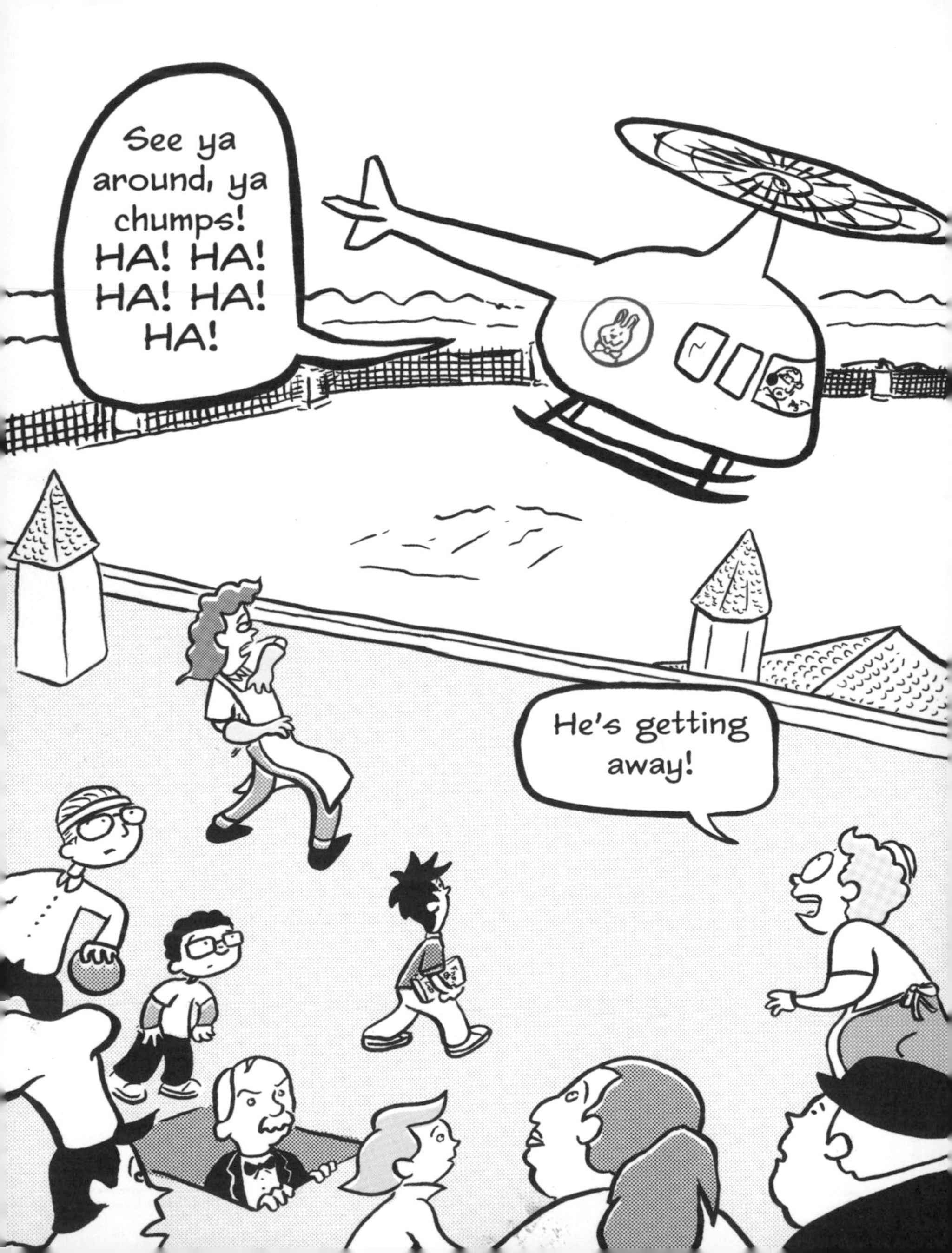
See ya around, ya chumps! HA! HA! HA! HA! HA!
He's getting away!

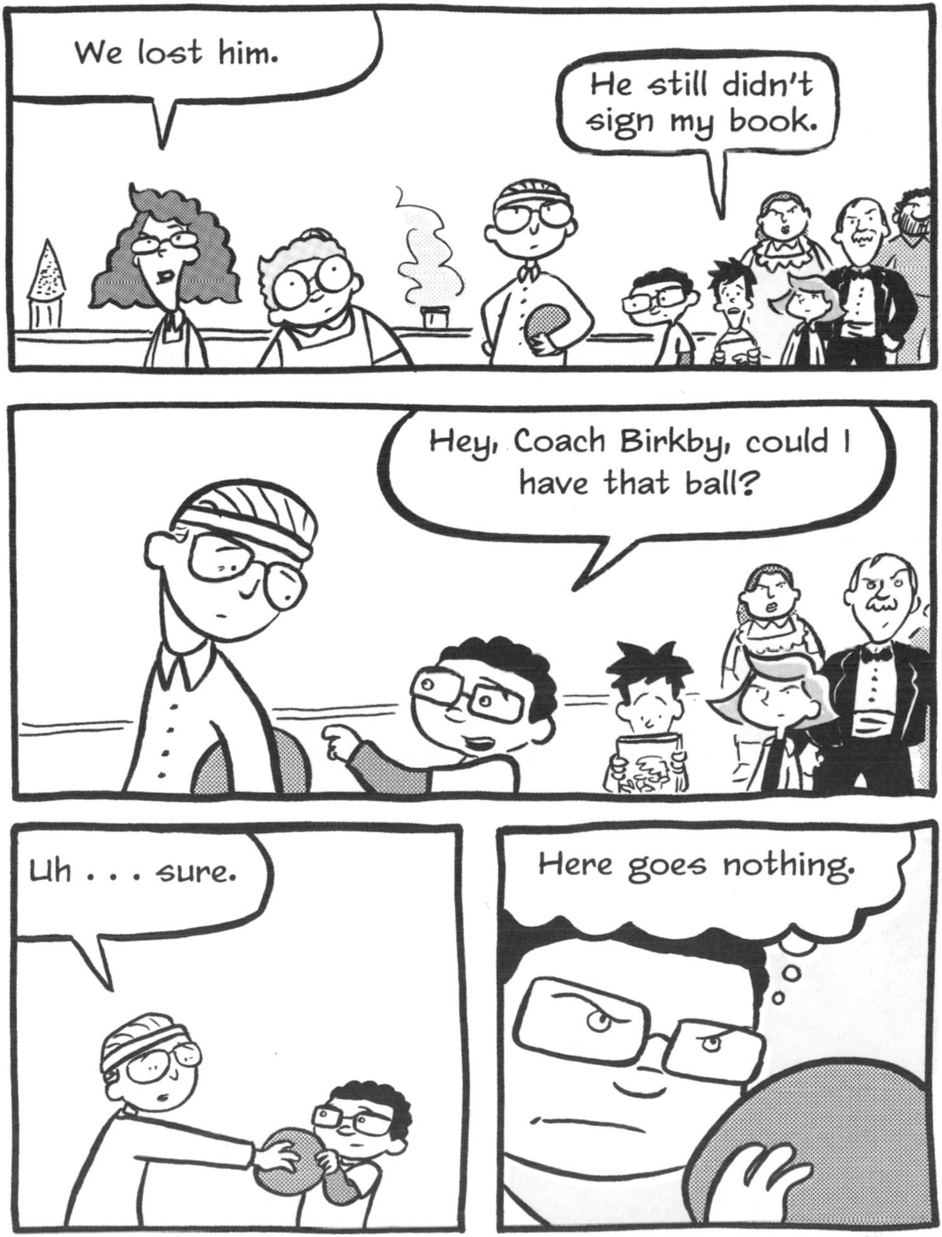
We lost him.
He still didn't sign my book.
Hey, Coach Birkby, could I have that ball?
Uh . . . sure.
Here goes nothing.

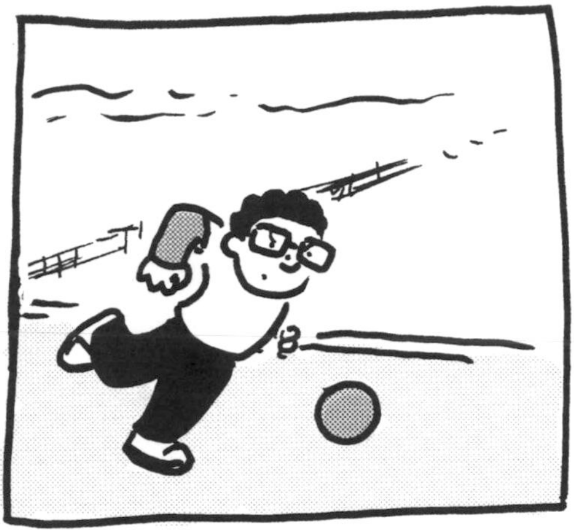

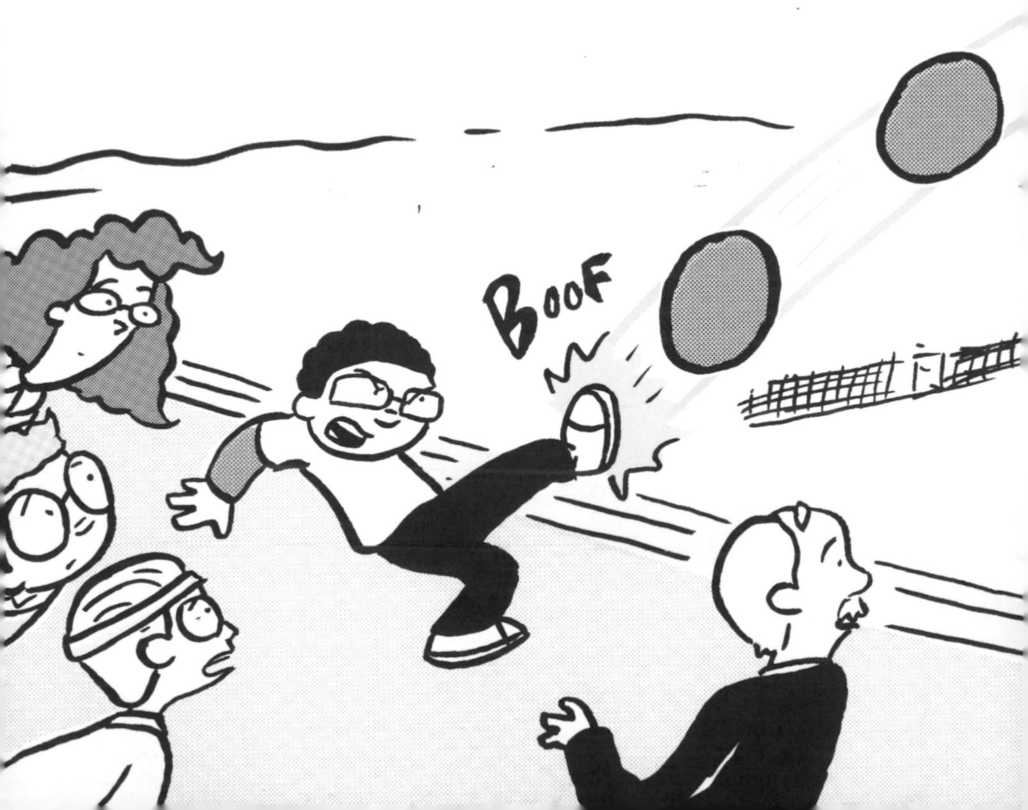
BOOF

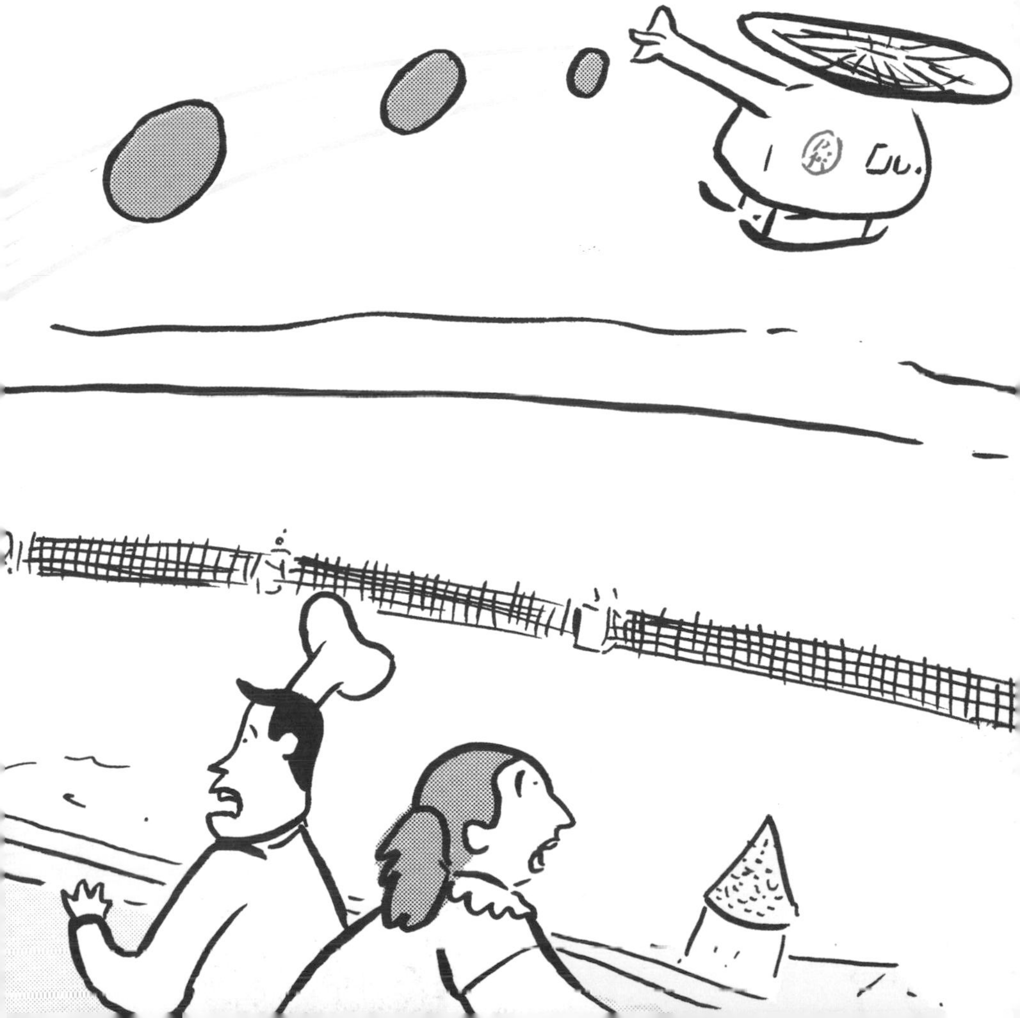

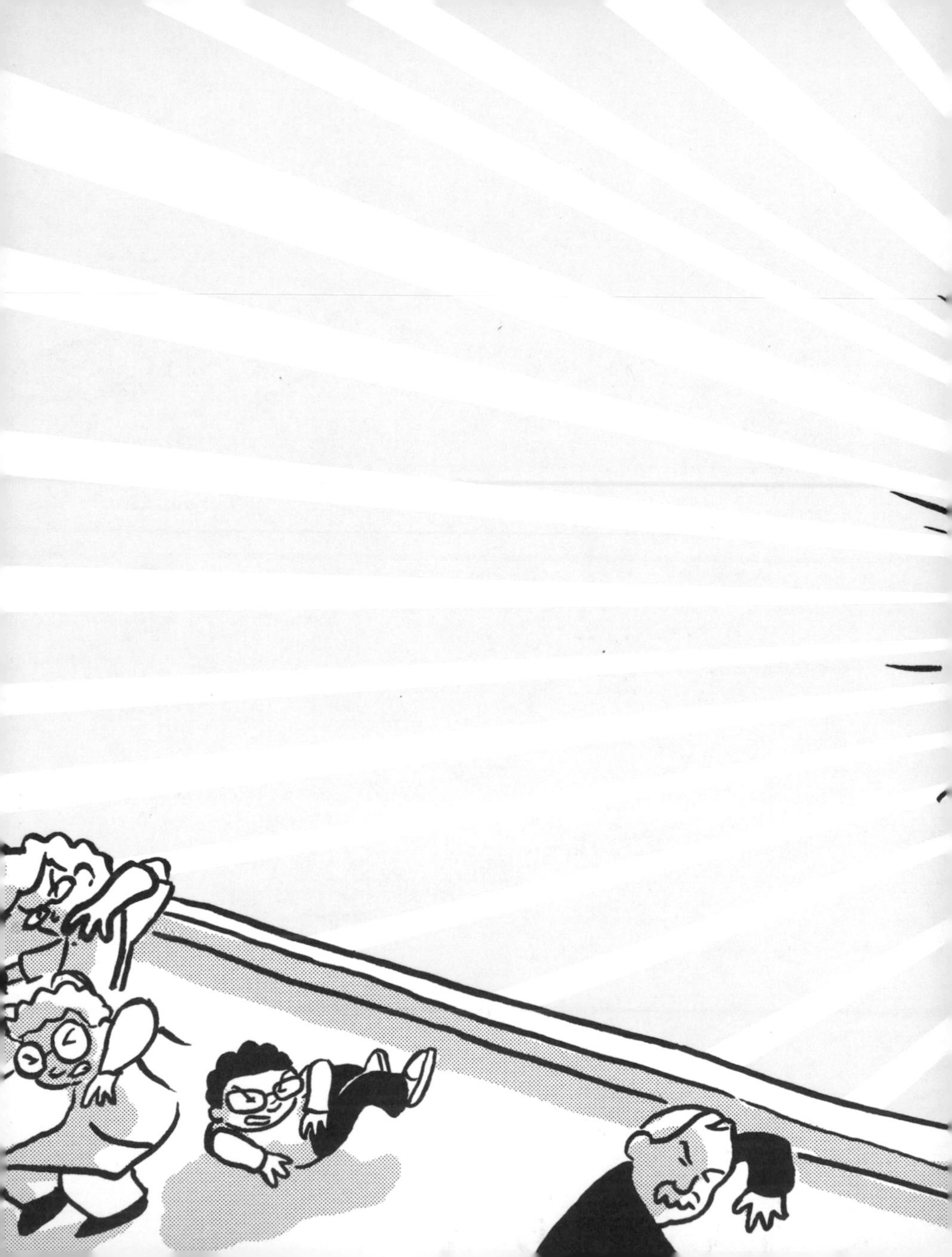

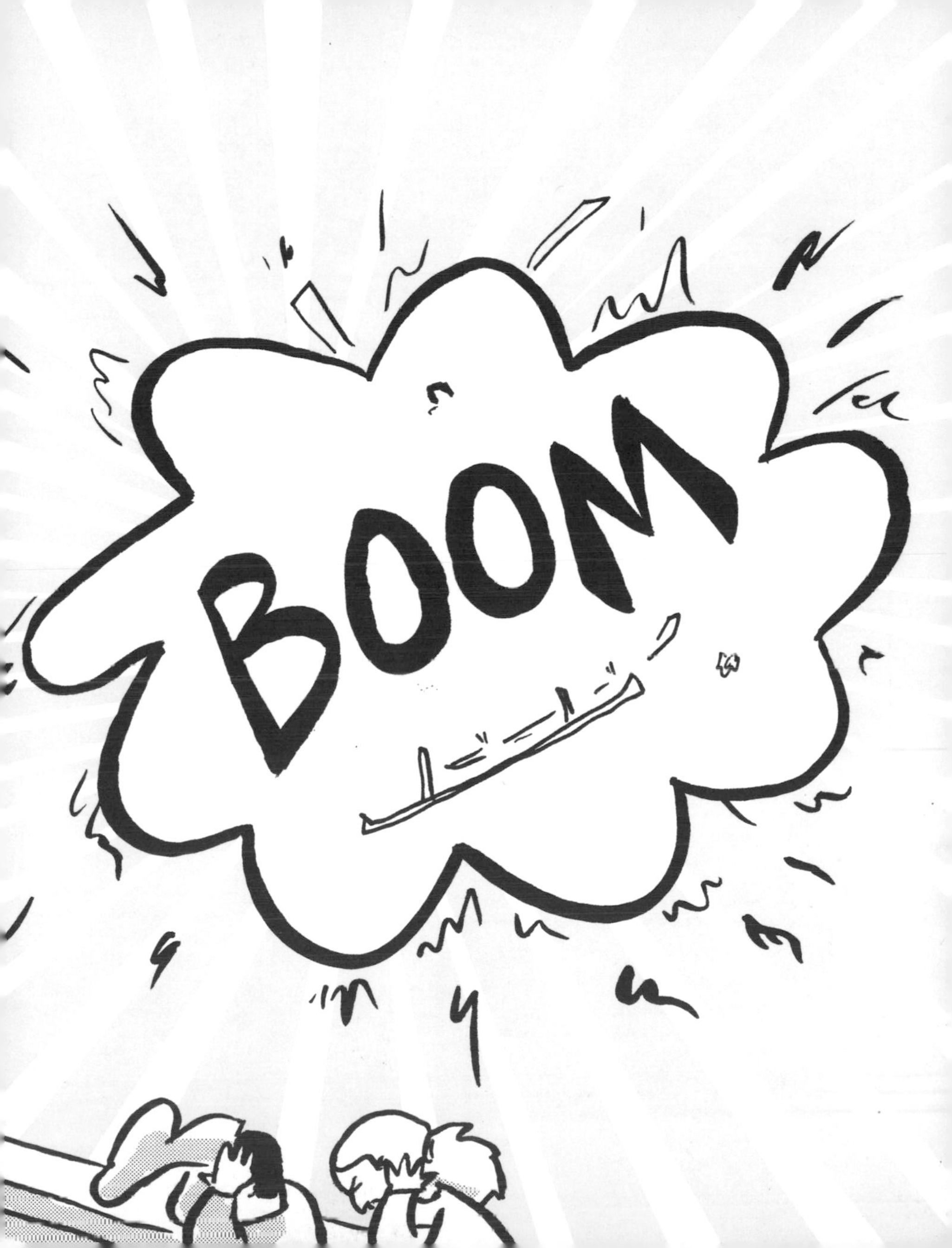
BOOM

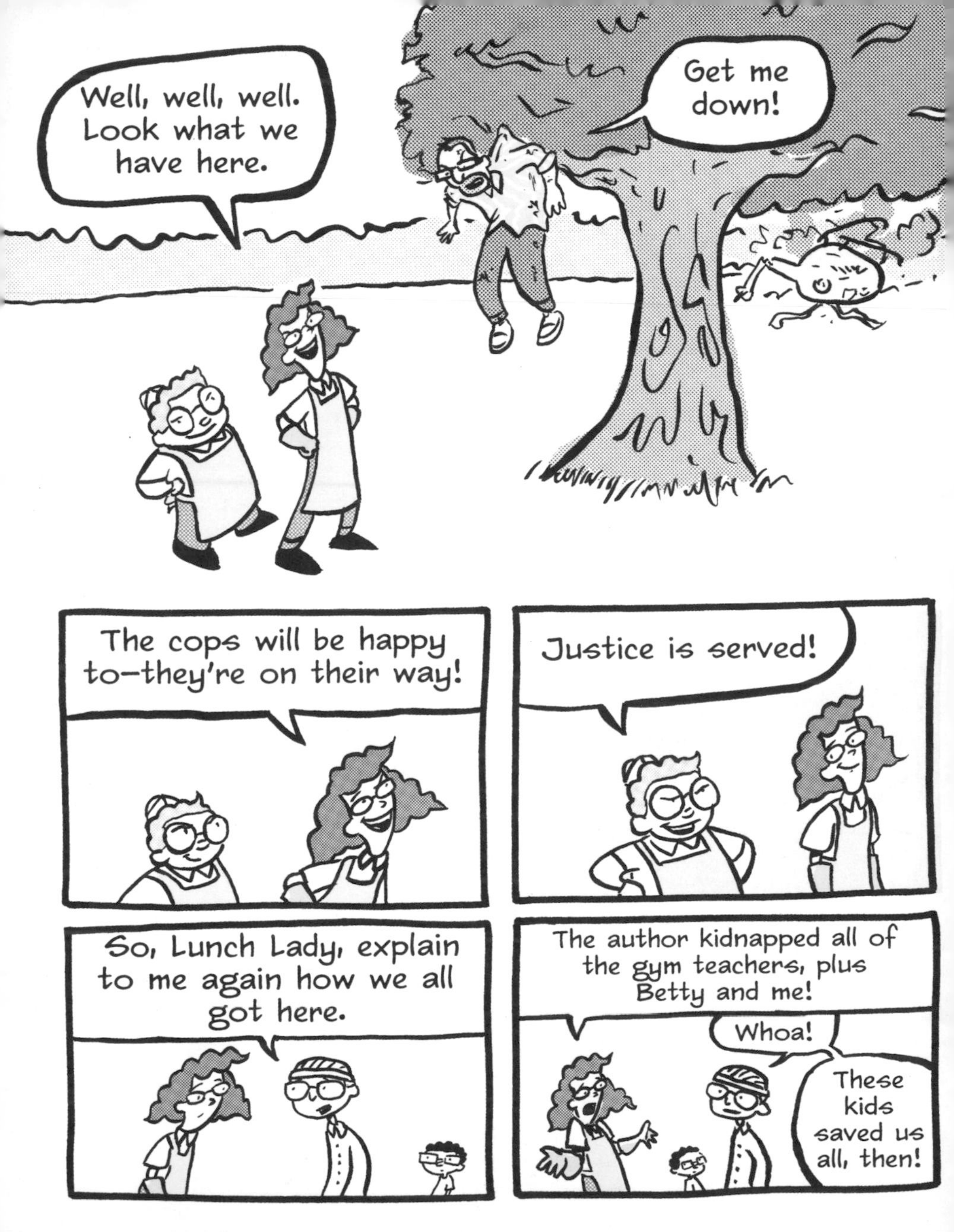
Well, well, well. Look what we have here.
Get me down!
The cops will be happy to—they're on their way!
Justice is served!
So, Lunch Lady, explain to me again how we all got here.
The author kidnapped all of the gym teachers, plus Betty and me!
Whoa!
These kids saved us all, then!

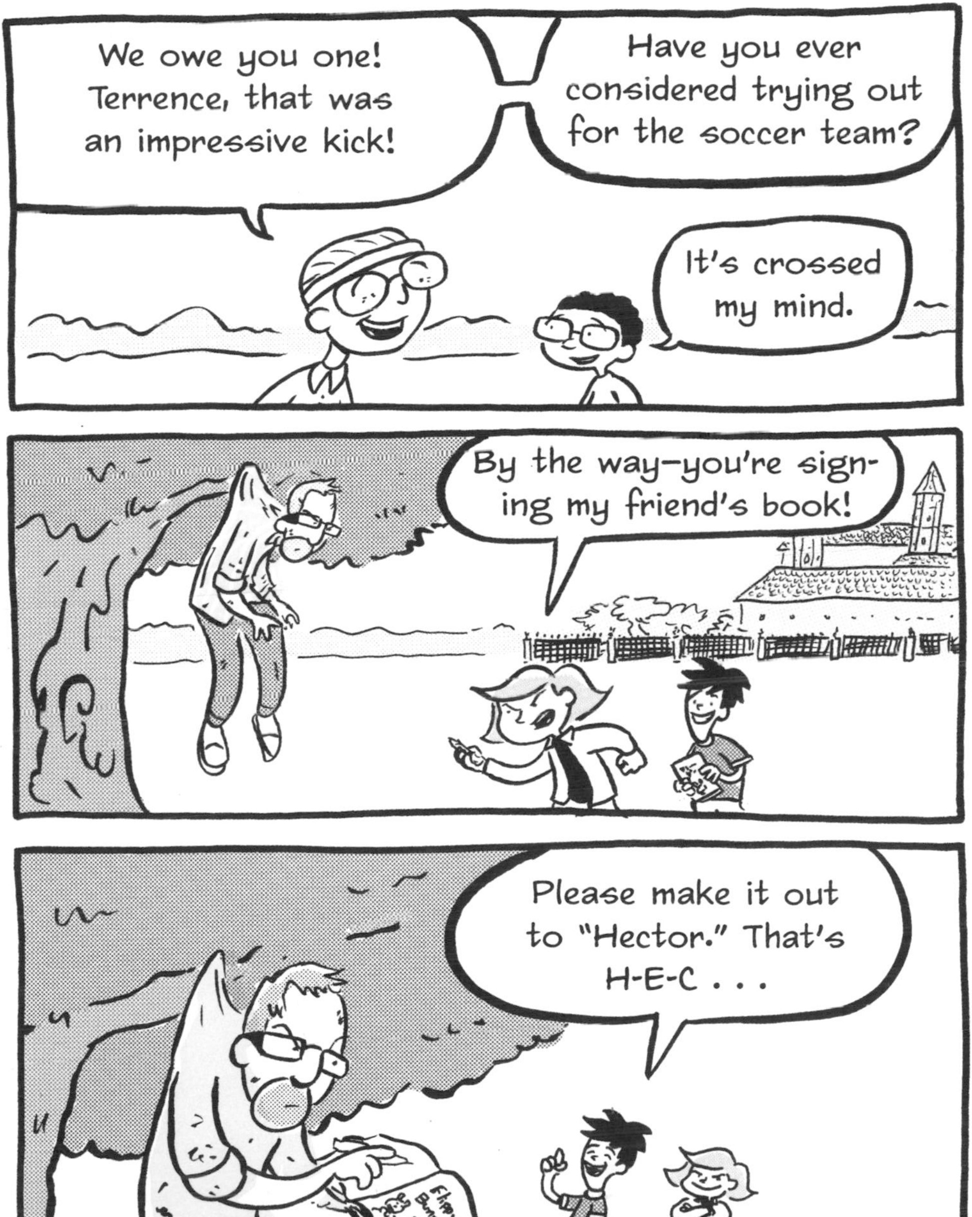
We owe you one! Terrence, that was an impressive kick!
Have you ever considered trying out for the soccer team?
It's crossed my mind.
By the way—you're sign-ing my friend's book!
Please make it out to "Hector." That's H-E-C . . .

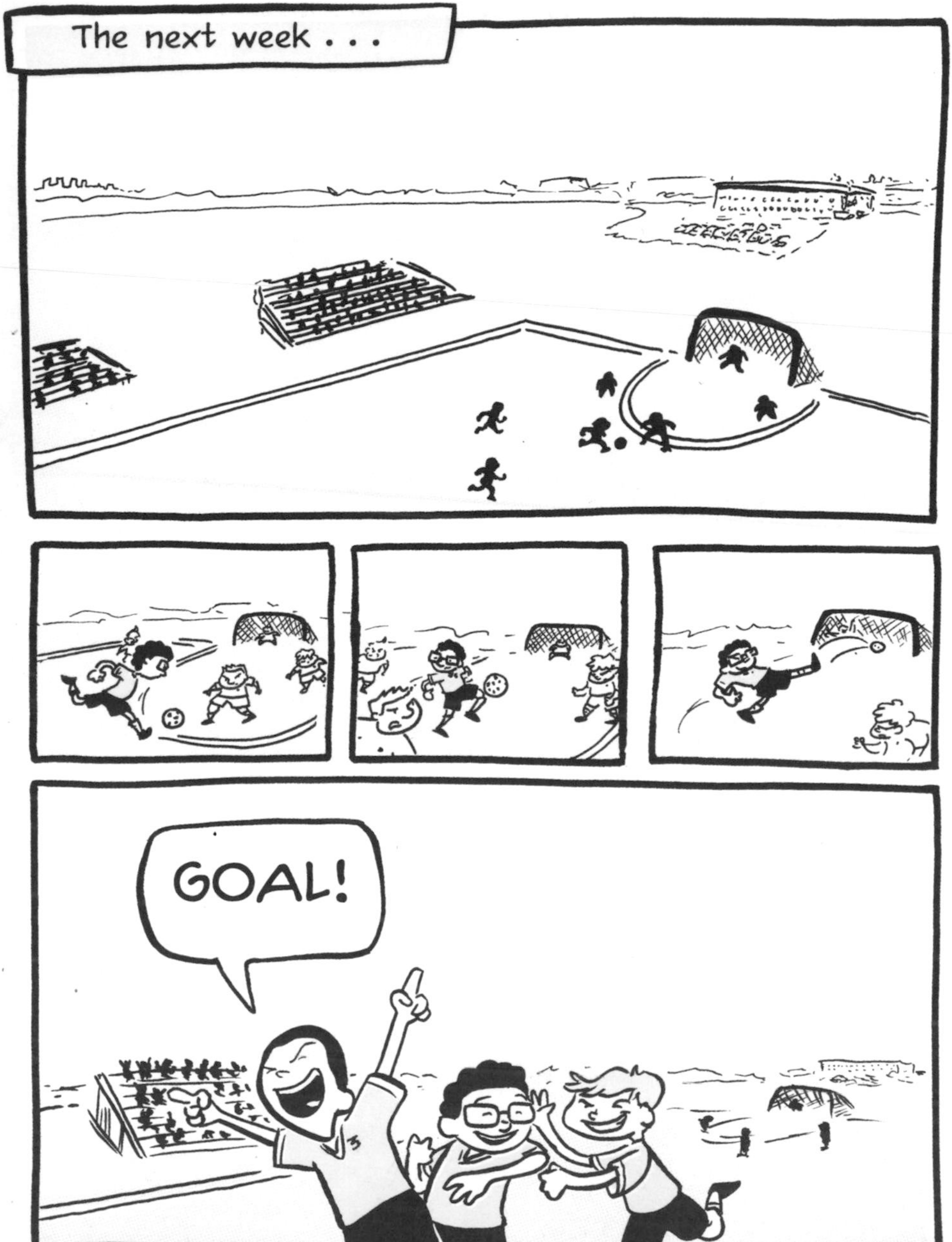
The next week . . .
GOAL!

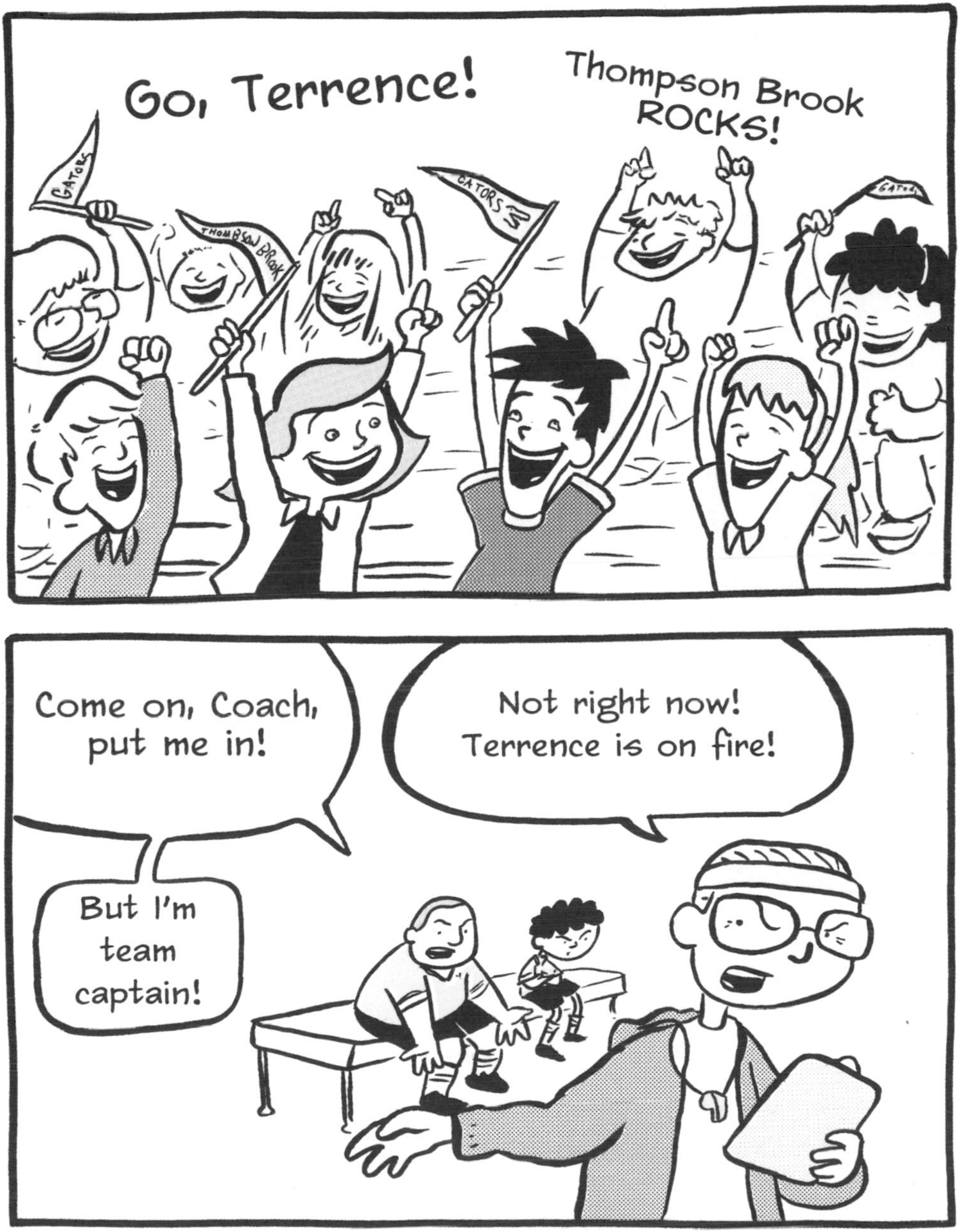
Go, Terrence!
Thompson Brook ROCKS!
Come on, Coach, put me in!
But I'm team captain!
Not right now! Terrence is on fire!

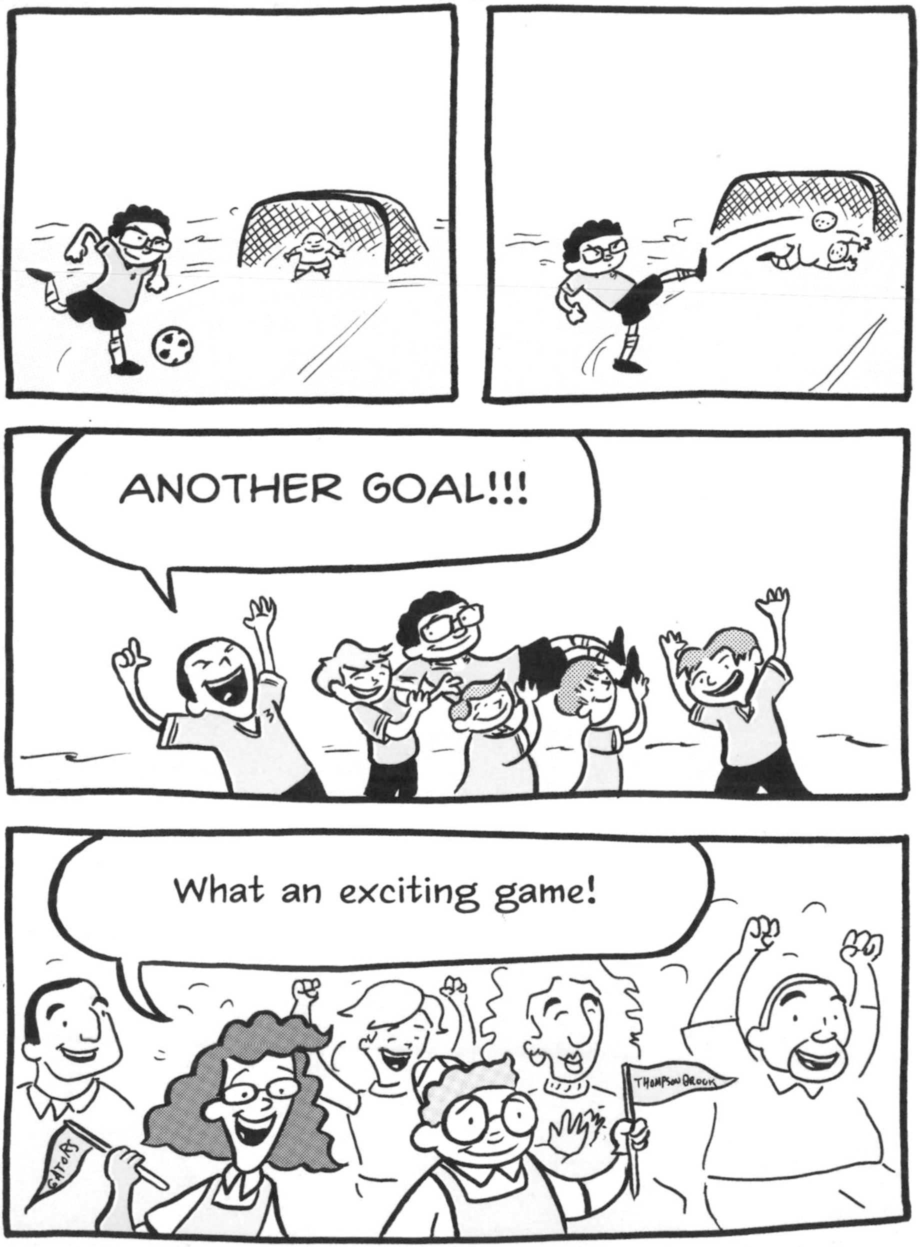
ANOTHER GOAL!!!
What an exciting game!
GATORS
THOMPSON BROOK

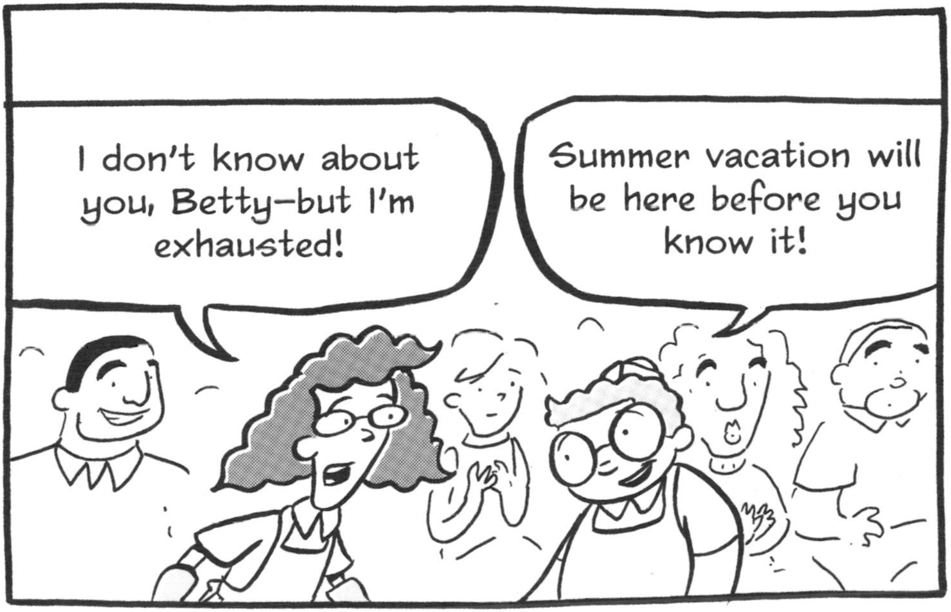
I don't know about you, Betty—but I'm exhausted!
Summer vacation will be here before you know it!

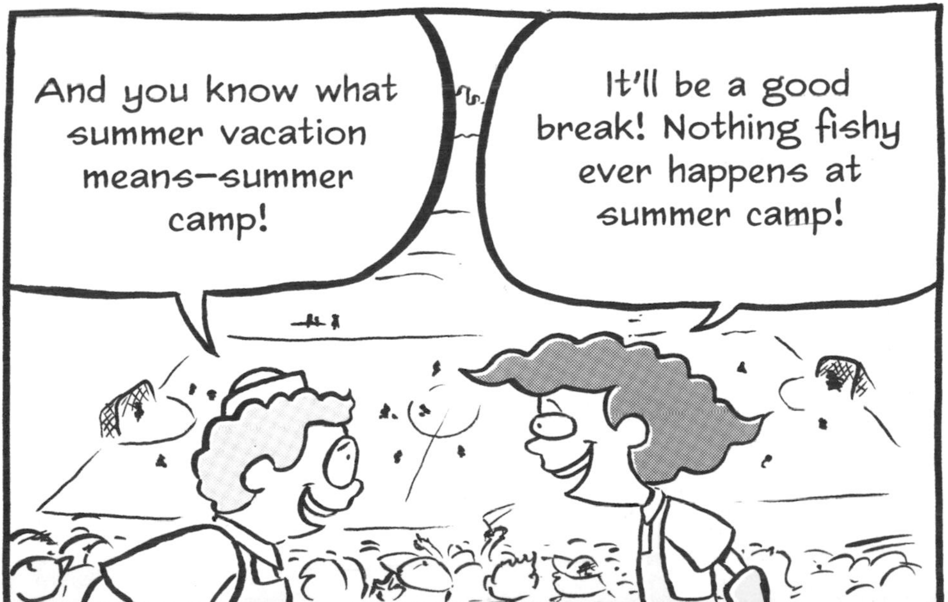
And you know what summer vacation means—summer camp!
It'll be a good break! Nothing fishy ever happens at summer camp!

FOR MELISSA AND STEVE
-J.J.K.

THIS IS A BORZOI BOOK PUBLISHED BY ALFRED A. KNOPF

Visit us on the Web! www.randomhouse.com/kids

Educators and librarians, for a variety of teaching tools,
visit us at www.randomhouse.com/teachers

Library of Congress Cataloging-in-Publication Data
Krosoczka, Jarrett.
Lunch Lady and the author visit vendetta / Jarrett J. Krosoczka. — 1st ed.
p. cm.
Summary: The school lunch lady, a secret crime fighter, investigates a suspicious author after he visits the school and the gym teacher goes missing.
ISBN 978-0-375-86094-2 (trade pbk.) — ISBN 978-0-375-96094-9 (lib. bdg.)
1. Graphic novels. [1. Graphic novels. 2. School lunchrooms, cafeterias, etc.—Fiction.
3. Missing persons—Fiction. 4. Teachers—Fiction. 5. Schools—Fiction.] I. Title.
PZ7.7.K76Lt 2009   [Fic]—dc22
2009014886

The text of this book is set in Hedge Backwards.
The illustrations in this book were created using ink on paper and digital coloring.

MANUFACTURED IN MALAYSIA
December 2009
10

First Edition